DISEMBARK

STORIES

JEN CURRIN

Published in Canada in 2024 and the USA in 2024 by House of Anansi Press Inc.
houseofanansi.com

House of Anansi Press is committed to protecting our natural environment.
This book is made of material from well-managed FSC®-certified forests,
recycled materials, and other controlled sources.

House of Anansi Press is a Global Certified Accessible™ (GCA by Benetech) publisher.
The ebook version of this book meets stringent accessibility standards
and is available to readers with print disabilities.

28 27 26 25 24   2 3 4 5 6

Library and Archives Canada Cataloguing in Publication

Title: Disembark : stories / Jen Currin.
Names: Currin, Jen, author.
Identifiers: Canadiana (print) 20230580793 | Canadiana (ebook) 20230580807 | ISBN 9781487011895
(softcover) | ISBN 9781487011901 (EPUB)
Subjects: LCGFT: Short stories.
Classification: LCC PS8605.U77 D58 2024 | DDC C813/.6—dc23

Cover design: Sharon Kish
Cover image: netsign on Adobe Stock

*House of Anansi Press is grateful for the privilege to work on and create from the Traditional Territory of many
Nations, including the Anishinabeg, the Wendat, and the Haudenosaunee, as well as the Treaty Lands of the
Mississaugas of the Credit.*

With the participation of the Government of Canada
Avec la participation du gouvernement du Canada | Canadä

We acknowledge for their financial support of our publishing program the Canada Council for the Arts, the Ontario
Arts Council, and the Government of Canada.

Printed and bound in Canada

DISEMBARK

For all of my families

CONTENTS

THE GOLDEN TRIANGLE

DEL WAS LEAVING the city, the state. To New York, she said, where everyone wore nice black leather jackets and smoked American Spirit cigarettes, where the living wasn't easy, but she hoped the girls might be, where she was sure she could snag a café job, a nanny gig, and somehow cobble together enough rent money for some loft in Queens shared with a bunch of other queers. Who needed luxuries like sleep? There was adrenalin. There was caffeine. There were women she hadn't slept with yet, a huge, seemingly endless pool—an ocean really.

She had always loved the Statue of Liberty, her strong bare arm rising up to the sky as if she was leading a Pride parade, her torch a huge lit joint. She had always wanted to get the fuck out of Denver, just as at seventeen she had run from St. Louis. She had decided that Denver was for losers, small shakes, the city Midwestern kids fled to with their snowboards and trust funds, their daddy and mommy issues. These rich kids took up residence in apartments on Capitol Hill and tried to live the cool life, wearing flannel shirts and torn jeans, buying second-hand skateboards and falling off of them. But they weren't cool, Del said emphatically, pointing at me as she said it. This was a point we often bonded on, the essential uncoolness of fake poor kids. Del and I had both scratched our way out of our shitty hometowns with no help from our parents or anyone else, and we considered ourselves survivors.

We were sipping slushy strawberry margaritas at Pepe's when Del told me all this, picking at the remains of her burrito. Her dinners were always left unfinished—she didn't like food all that much, preferring cigarettes, coffee, and pot. Her nutritional method was to stuff as many bites as possible into her mouth within the first few minutes after the plate arrived, before she realized what she was doing. For a few minutes, her hunger would overcome her disgust, and she could eat.

Del wanted me to know that she wasn't leaving me alone in the Mile High Sewer—her nickname for Denver because of its often noxious smell. She was leaving me her bike. In New York, she said, she'd be taking the subway, walking through the leafiest neighbourhoods in Brooklyn, the seediest blocks of the East Village, and she wouldn't need it. It was too dangerous, she said, trying to manoeuvre through the crowded streets. They weren't like Denver's wide boulevards with just a few tumbleweed cars. Traffic was always thick, she wanted me to know. Biking, she could easily get killed by a taxi. Besides, she concluded, the bike would probably get stolen within days anyway.

I didn't need her bike. I already had one. But it was still a consolation, a little piece of her to hold on to. I had never been to New York and I didn't know that I'd ever be able to go. But it would be nice to take Del's bike out for a ride now and again—it was more stylish than mine, a retro red Schwinn in good condition, no rust, with a basket on the front for her backpack and a six pack.

"I know you don't need it but you could use it to take rides with, you know, a nice girl." Del winked as she said this. She was always making little jokes about the fact that I was date-less.

I HAD FIRST gotten to know Del on a bike ride a couple of years earlier. I had recently moved to the city and within days found myself employed at the bagel shop where Del worked. After one of our Sunday shifts, she invited me to take a ride down the Platte River bikeway. We shared a joint out back by the dumpsters and rode far out through neighbourhoods I'd never seen before, where cherry trees were starting to pop out their blossoms and brassy new condos stretched up toward the sun. Tall grasses waved in the wind running up the creek and there was a smell of hot dryness—no sickening wafts that day from the Purina factory just outside the city. We pedalled lazily through the late afternoon, dazed, the light glinting on the short hairs on our arms, the glaring sun softened by the high.

We had only worked a few shifts together, but I had been harbouring a crush on Del since my first day at the shop. I hoped that the bike ride was a date, and when Del looked over at me at one point and gave a big smile, I thought it might be. But when we stopped to sit on some rocks and drink sodas we'd stolen from the shop, it became clear that it wasn't as Del rolled another joint while unrolling a meandering tale about her girlfriend Lupe and her lover Anna. I was later to learn that she often had two women on the go. Del's girlfriend Lupe was a single mother who still lived with the father of her young child in a mostly platonic arrangement. Anna was basically a straight girl, Del said, Irish Catholic to the bone, a virgin until she hooked up with Lupe and Del one ecstasy-soaked evening. "And she still considers herself a virgin," Del griped. "As if that wasn't real sex." She slipped the joint between her lips and lit it, sucking back a huge toke before she passed it to me.

I took a careful puff, trying to figure out from Del's tone which of the two women she was more in love with. Anna? She sounded angrier about her, so maybe. But Lupe's beauty, and the beauty of her child, were dwelled on for longer. So maybe Lupe?

I could tell by the way Del spoke that she had already slotted me in the friend category. She was giving me too much information, for one thing. With new dates, or possible dates, people usually don't talk extensively about their other lovers. Not that I had dated much—this was just what I had surmised from listening to friends talk.

I wondered what Anna looked like. Inexperienced, Del had said, with a bit of an edge. I felt a pang—I had only had sex with one of my friends in high school, also a straight girl, essentially. She started dating the editor of the school paper, a macho-nerd guy, after our six months of hooking up. She was never my girlfriend—we never talked about things like that. When she started dating the boy, she

4

acted like I was supposed to be happy for her, and I had pretended to be. But I never dated any boys. I couldn't take the ruse that far.

After we quit sleeping together, I cut my brown hair into a short spiky do and had a friend put in some purple streaks—that was all it took for a gang of jocks to take it upon themselves to single me out, yelling every time I set foot in the cafeteria for my lunchtime bread roll and little carton of skim milk. "Dyke! Dyke! Dyke!" they'd chant across the rows of tables. "Dyke! Dyke! Dyke!"

AFTER THAT FIRST bike ride, Del and I started hanging out a lot, smoking weed after work, going out dancing to Denver's only lesbian club, The Elle. Del had an old fake ID she gave me—I was only twenty, a couple of years younger than her—and even though the photograph looked nothing like me, the bouncer always let me in. I got the sense they didn't look too closely at the photos as long as the person had something with an acceptable date on it.

Del's lover Anna would usually pick us up in her shiny white Beetle—she was the only one of us with a car—and we'd cram in, me, Del, Lupe, another friend or two. Anna would be playing Ani DiFranco or Erykah Badu, and everyone would sing along, blowing weed smoke out the windows, gossiping, making jokes. Del liked to sit up front where she could keep her hand on Anna's thigh and give directions. "Go bravely forward!" she'd demand. It was one of their favourite quips—they never wanted to say "go straight."

Lupe, Anna, and Del seemed very comfortable together—they were always laughing, touching each other's arms or faces, sharing food when we all went out. They just seemed like friends—sexy friends. This was a revelation to me. I hadn't known any out gay people in Grand Junction, only my closeted high school friends and one very friendly guy who worked at the post office and who everyone in town talked shit about, saying he frequented a certain park on Saturday nights. I had no precedent for Del, Lupe, and Anna's relationship. Most of the adults in my hometown were married; my own parents didn't like each other very much but seemed determined to see the thing through until one or both of them died. The young people only dated one person at a time, although of course there was lots of cheating, lots of drama and histrionic jealousies. Yet what Del, Lupe, and Anna had seemed easy. It seemed to work.

It took me a while to notice some of the tensions, like Lupe withdrawing when she felt she wasn't getting enough attention. Her favourite way to do this was to decide suddenly that she was going home early—even if we'd just arrived at the club. Her face, open and happy just a moment before, would suddenly harden, and she'd look off to the corner of the room, avoiding Del's eyes. Del would plead with her to stay, she'd wrap her arms around her and kiss her neck, she'd try to drag Lupe to the dance floor or ply her with a gin and tonic, but Lupe wouldn't have it. She'd call a cab and be off in a blast of exhaust before Anna or any of the other friends could take notice.

Anna didn't seem jealous of Lupe or seem to mind Del's near-constant flirtation with any attractive woman who happened to be in the vicinity. But I noticed that she didn't like Del to touch her in public. When a favourite song would come on, Anna would shimmy to the dance floor and Del would be one step behind her, her hands on Anna's hips, her feet matching Anna's beat, but more than once I'd seen Anna lift Del's hands off her hips and drop them at her sides, continuing to dance as if this was just another one of her moves. I could never see Del's face in these moments, but I felt bad for her. Anna cultivated a cheerful non-possessiveness, an I'm-just-the-side-girl charm. This made her all the more alluring to Del—even though Del "had" her, she didn't really *have* her. Something in Anna remained untouchable, remote.

Back then, many of us believed more forcefully in certain categories—or at least we pretended to. We regularly dismissed certain girls as "straight" or referred to them as "weekend dykes" or "girls who were just experimenting." We were sarcastic even about the word "bisexual." Although Del never minded being any pretty girl's experiment, and in fact, these girls were more often *her* experiments. She could always meet new women, wherever she went, even just at the grocery store or some taco shop. She could get a date just by asking for a light on a street corner in Lodo on a Tuesday afternoon. And she went through dates like no one I'd ever met, bedding them and dropping them in a matter of days. Some of the straight girls Del turned out and then summarily dumped ended up becoming "real lesbians," as we called them back then, and after a week or two of teary phone calls begging Del to reconsider, they'd go silent, then suddenly pop up at the club a month later, smiling in the arms of some handsome hockey player or slinky punk.

Others of them never fully "turned," and some of these girls incurred our scorn, especially if they tried to bring their boyfriends to The Elle. Men weren't actually barred from the place, and some of us brought our fag friends or trans dates with us, but when men we assumed were cis or straight showed up, we tried to banish them with venomous side-eyes and rude remarks.

Anna would not say if she was a lesbian or not; she liked the word "queer," but didn't use it to directly reference herself. She made a joke sometimes about living life, not vicariously, but "bicuriously." This joke always made Del furious, although she tried to cover it with a smile.

DEL WASN'T SHY. It wasn't a word you'd ever think of to describe her. She was like a lit sparkler at the centre of the room, giving off sparks. She took me to a lot of parties where I'd hide in the kitchen, pouring drinks for strangers and making small talk with other introverts while she blazed in the living room. People often said that "she brought the party," and it was true that the dancing would usually begin within minutes of her arrival.

But she was also shy in particular ways. Certain butch women made her shy with their confidence. She wouldn't approach them because she thought they had more courage than she did, and this made her own courage falter. She dated mostly feminine women because they were easy for her to talk to. And they in turn found Del unthreatening—she was not "mannish" in a way that scared them—she was small and pretty, with a bleached-blond pixie cut and an open smile. Her own style was what we used to call androgynous—she was most often in jeans and a tight T-shirt. She seemed just like this nice gay friend any straight girl would love to have as a sidekick—but then they ended up being Del's sidekick, and lover for a while, until she got bored of them.

LATE ONE NIGHT after the club, on a night in which Anna hadn't come along and Lupe had gone home early with a headache, Del and I rode our bikes to her place—she owed me twenty bucks and said she'd just run in to get it. But I had to pee, and so locked my bike and went in with her, and somehow we ended up making out and then rolling around on the futon on the floor of her studio apartment. We did a few things, some of which I'd never done before, finally falling asleep around dawn. I woke up to the smell of weed—Del sitting at the kitchen table in her underwear lighting her morning joint, looking at me warily or maybe just tiredly. She made us coffee and we sat at the table and had the conversation. We were just friends, we agreed. Just friends, we reiterated. The night before had been a mistake. We were just friends, and it would stay that way.

THE NEIGHBOURHOOD I'D moved to in Denver was called the Golden Triangle—a name I liked but felt weird saying out loud because it always made me think of a golden triangle of pubic hair, although I was too shy to ever tell anyone this. The neighbourhood had historically been mostly industrial but was starting to change; there were a few art galleries in old garages and talk of condo projects starting up. I'd found my place listed in the classifieds in the free weekly—one of the few studios in my price range. When the landlord, a plainspoken man with an Eastern European accent who also owned the autobody shop downstairs, showed me around, he didn't talk about the light or the up-and-coming neighbourhood or in any way try to sing the apartment's praises. He wasn't that kind of guy. He told me the rent better be on time, and that I could paint it any colour I wanted but that I'd have to paint it white again when I moved out. He admitted there had been a cockroach problem with the last tenant, but swore he'd banished them—he even moved the stove to show me a trap and said there was another one under the bathroom sink. There were big windows facing south, facing an alley lined with dumpsters and the brick backside of an old tannery. I had never lived on my own before. It was five hundred dollars a month and I took it.

At night I'd lie in bed listening to the sirens and sometimes hearing rats or dogs squabble in the alley. I was fascinated by the rats—how they could climb up the dumpsters with their little claws, how quickly they skittered out of sight when I came out the back door. Back in Grand Junction I'd only seen rats once or twice in a local park—rural rats, barely the size of house mice. But these were urban rats, big as the ones I'd seen in movies, big as London or New York rats, I was sure.

I lay in bed at night catching whiffs of brake fluid and gasoline from the autobody shop downstairs and fantasizing about the girls I wished I could bring home, girls I'd seen at the club who I was never brave enough to talk to. Sometimes my mind tried to veer to Del, to the night we'd spent together, her soft skin, the way her tongue had felt in my mouth—but I quickly shut these thoughts out before they could go too far. I wanted every kind of woman from the club—the tall one who'd been a high school basketball star and now worked as a stripper on Colfax, the stocky one with faint acne scars who'd been in the navy, the rapper-poet with dyed red braids—I wanted them all. I didn't have any one type, I told myself, but this wasn't really true. I liked the flashy ones. I was always drawn to the loud ones, the ones who strode confidently across the dance floor to put their elbows up on the bar and glance around with a big grin like they owned the place.

BEFORE DEL LEFT for New York, she invited me on a bike ride. "Our final bike ride," I kept calling it, although she kept telling me not to.

"Don't be so dramatic," she said. "We'll ride bikes again. In New York!"

"You won't have a bike in New York," I said. "Remember?"

She laughed. "You can bring me mine on the plane."

It was another sunny Sunday afternoon, and we met up at Del's place after my shift at the bagel shop—Del had worked her final shift the day before. We sat on her front stoop for a while talking and smoking pot. When we were sufficiently high, we got on our bikes and rode out past Federal Boulevard to a bike path I'd only ever gone on once. It wound out of the city alongside a little stream I didn't know the name of, bordered by cottonwoods and tall grasses and blackberry bushes. It was June, and the cottonwoods were blooming, blowing big puffs of cotton everywhere like a snowstorm. The fluffs stuck to our clothes as we biked, rolling around in clumps like tumbleweed and piling up on the sides of the path in drifts. Every once in a while a big wind would blow down the stream bed, shaking the trees, releasing more snowy gusts. As the fluffs drifted by I tried to examine them—were they cells, were they tissue-paper ghosts?

Del was just normal, as she smoked chronically, but I was very high. There was a heavy buzzing sound I couldn't locate, cicadas maybe, but I wasn't sure it was the time of year for them. The crunching of gravel under my tires had never been so loud, each pebble distinct in its turning. There were so many kinds of birdsong, more birdsong than birds it seemed, lilting and rising. A little twitter, a rush of wings in leaves. I recognized a robin's call, nothing else.

There was no one on the path that day, so we could go as slowly as we pleased. Del meandered ahead of me, looking up at the trees. I wanted to feel calm, to just be present and take it all in, but I started to feel panicky. I'd smoked too much. My mouth was dry and my legs felt inexplicably tired. If I focused on my heartbeat, it seemed weird, too jumpy, so I tried not to think about it.

I called to Del that I wanted to stop for water, and she slowly braked, turning to smile back at me. We climbed a tree and sat on a wide branch curving out toward the path. Del pulled out another joint and held it up with a quizzical expression, and I told her no fucking way. "Do you have any idea how stoned I am right now? I seriously thought the trees were talking to me. I need to chill."

"You always exaggerate," Del said, as she lit the joint and took a big toke. "You're quiet a lot, but when you do talk, you're an exaggerator." She smiled at me. Her legs swung below her as she blew smoke into the leaves. Her tone was easy and affectionate, and I felt a weird little twist in my stomach, something welling up in me, sorrow, anger at her for leaving, and something else, some murkier feeling. I leaned forward and put my lips on her mouth.

She didn't seem startled—she kissed me back for a minute, still holding the joint, and then pulled back to tamp it out on the tree trunk. She blew the bits of ash away and slid the half-finished joint carefully into the front pocket of her jeans, then turned back toward me and leaned in, continuing the kiss. I put one arm around her back and pulled her closer, my tongue exploring each part of her mouth, her little teeth, the gap between one of her molars and the tooth next to it. I sucked on her lips, the thin top one and the plumper bottom one. She tasted like smoke and peppermint lip balm and a sweetish taste that was distinctly hers. The texture of the inside of her cheeks reminded me of the one time I had gone down on her, and I lingered there, starting to lose myself in the feeling. But then Del abruptly stopped responding and sat back.

"Whoa. Getting all sexy on me now, are we?" She pinched my knee playfully through my jeans.

I stared at her, holding on to the branch below me.

"Time to ride!" Before I could say anything, she shimmied over the branch and climbed down the tree, standing beside her bike as she fiddled with her backpack in the front basket.

My legs felt like heavy weights hanging down off the tree. The wind blew a gust of fluff in my face, and I closed my eyes, trying to gather myself together. I was a little less stoned after the kiss. The leaves of the trees still made their shushing noise, and the buzzing of insects or the vibration of the atmosphere, if that's what it was, could still be heard, but it was muted, less overwhelming and intense.

Below me, Del had pulled the half-joint out of her pocket and re-lit it. She studied the little river as she smoked, looking uncharacteristically serious. I wondered if she regretted kissing me back, if she regretted inviting me on one last bike ride. She probably didn't think it would get so weird—I was sure that she never expected me to make a move on her. Staring down at her, I couldn't really believe that I had. Since the one night we spent together, I had been mostly successful at keeping erotic thoughts of Del at bay. When they tried to creep in, I swapped in another woman's face and let the fantasy unroll with a stranger or any person who wasn't Del. What had I been hoping to get from the kiss? It seemed the wrong gesture somehow. It must have been the drugs, I told myself, although this didn't really explain it. Pot didn't usually make me bold.

I clambered down the tree and stood beside her, looking at the cotton fluffs swirling around our feet. The river was narrow but energetic—it tumbled over the rocks as if it had somewhere to be. A bird trilled behind us. Del wasn't meeting my eyes but she didn't seem upset.

"Something to remember me by, I guess," I cracked.

She didn't laugh at my joke and she finally looked at me then, still serious. "I'm not going to forget you, Max, if that's what you're afraid of."

I shrugged. "Everyone always forgets. It's the human way."

She looked annoyed and took another toke, staring at the river. "Stop being that way. You don't have to do that."

"What way?"

"I don't know. Fake, or something. I know you're sad I'm leaving. I'm sad too."

I felt my heart start jumping again. I wasn't sure if maybe my stone was coming back or if it was the flutter of some other anxiety. I looked over at her face. This was the most real she'd ever been with me.

She handed me the joint and I accepted it without thinking, taking a big hit and releasing it to the trees.

AFTER DEL LEFT for New York, I didn't go out much. After my shifts at the bagel shop, I'd usually take a bike ride, then head home. I'd started riding Del's red Schwinn because both of my tires had been punctured by the huge goathead thorns that littered Denver's streets in the early fall and I had been too lazy to fix them.

There was an arts supply store a few blocks from me, and after work one day I bought a pad of thick white paper and some good pencils. I got coloured pencils too, just because I liked the way they looked in the package, the bright solid rainbow, even though I never used them once I had them. I'd draw anything—faces, empty bottles on the curb, a bus stop bench. I wasn't very good but I kept at it because it was something to do. My loneliness was just starting to settle in when I got a call from Lupe one evening, checking up on me.

"We're worried about you. We haven't seen you at the club or anywhere." I wasn't sure who the "we" was—Lupe and Anna? Or Lupe's new girlfriend? She had started dating a stoical but cute firefighter soon after Del left town.

"Sorry—just, you know. Keeping quiet. Haven't really been out." My window was open for the breeze, and I could hear some neighbours arguing in the alley. The sun was starting to set, slanting its fat rays across the tannery's brick wall. I often sat on my couch just looking out my window at the shifting light. Denver was full of light, all kinds of light—on snow, on brick, on the tops of trees. There was so much variety—the intense hot light of July, the surprising beams streaking through clouds after an October thunderstorm. I often asked myself how I could be so lonely with all that light.

"There's a party on Saturday and we want you to come. Cute girls. Nice people. Come with us." It wasn't a question, but Lupe had such a sweet way of demanding that most people usually agreed, and I found myself saying I'd be at her place for pre-drinks around seven. Before we hung up she told me she wasn't living with the father of her child anymore; she'd already moved in with the firefighter.

THE PARTY WAS a pretty typical Capitol Hill affair—hipsters and queers yelling their conversations, bottles of cheap wine lined up on the kitchen counter, a keg on the balcony. There were a few people dancing in a circle in the living room who seemed to be on E, a certain energy coming off them, half-closed eyes and drifty movements. A couple of them would stop dancing every few minutes to sway together and make out.

Lupe held on to my arm and steered me into the kitchen. We'd been drinking gin and tonics at her place and planned to continue in that vein.

When we rounded the corner, I saw Anna immediately. She was standing by the fridge, arms crossed, holding a glass of red wine and examining the fliers and photos held to the fridge with magnets. She'd cut her straight blond hair; it grazed the back of her nape. She was wearing a very short black skirt that showed off her long legs and some black heeled sandals. I hadn't seen her in months, since before Del had left town, and I felt suddenly shy at the sight of her.

Lupe dropped my arm and swiftly stepped over to Anna, wrapping her arms around her before she knew what was happening. Anna's wine was jostled but she managed to keep it upright, not spilling even a lick as she turned to embrace Lupe. Her eyes met mine over Lupe's shoulder and her smile deepened.

Just then a tall guy with slicked-back brown hair and a button-up shirt, a professional type who looked out of place at this sort of party, stepped into the kitchen from the balcony and put his hand on Anna's shoulder as she was still hugging Lupe. "Hey." He looked from Lupe to me. "Your friends?"

Anna smiled and introduced us. His name was Andres and they worked together. When he headed off to the bathroom, Lupe stage-whispered, "Who *is* that guy?"

Anna laughed at her tone. "He's my date, I guess."

"You guess?"

Anna shrugged. "We've been hooking up."

Lupe raised her eyebrows. "And how's that going?"

"Okay. I'm just trying it out, you know. We'll see how it goes." Her cheeks were slightly flushed but it might have been from the wine.

LATER THAT NIGHT I stood in the corner of the living room nursing my gin and tonic and watching the dancers. The room was large, white walls, a few posters—sad Italians sipping espresso, Belle and Sebastian, Jane's Addiction. A cloth batiked with a large red and turquoise turtle covered the front window. It looked like many Denver living rooms I'd spent time in.

Electronic music pulsed on the speakers and I saw Andres coming down the hall. As he entered the living room, he slid into dancing, gliding across the hardwood floor. The ecstasy kids made space for him, letting him weave in and out of their circle.

I didn't expect it from his office worker attire, but I had to hand it to him—Andres could dance. He seemed totally present in his body, happy and free.

Anna watched from the doorway of the kitchen. Andres beckoned her with both hands as he swivelled his hips, but she shook her head, giving a small smile as she sipped her wine. He seemed unbothered by this and kept grooving. Lupe came into the room and hopped onto the dance floor, whipping her black faux-hawk around like a mane. Back in the kitchen she had decided to make Andres an ally, bro-joking with him in Spanish and fake punching his arm. Now she ground against Andres's butt, looking over at Anna and me with a lascivious grin. The ecstasy kids were laughing, swirling around like dervishes. One of them took the batiked cloth off of the window and draped it over their shoulders like a cape as they swooped through the room. Someone had lit sticks of nag champa in one of the bedrooms and the heavy sweet smell drifted down the hall, mixing with weed smoke.

Just then Bowie's "Let's Dance" started playing, and a cheer rose up from the dancers. Andres looked ecstatic as he shuffled his feet, grabbing Lupe's hands. He had unbuttoned the top buttons of his shirt and rolled up his sleeves. Strands of dark hair fell in his face and I wondered if he'd take off his shirt at some point—he really seemed to be cutting loose. I wondered if he was wearing one of those tank top undershirts that everyone called wife-beaters, and if I would get to see how hairy he was. It must have been weird for Anna to run her hands through all that chest hair after the smoothness of Del's skin.

Andres had a very laid-back vibe; he seemed to know he was just the date, no big deal, and he appeared prepared to enjoy this role to the fullest. He had a wide smile, lots of white teeth, and he kept flashing it. When we had talked in the kitchen, he had patted my back several times as if encouraging me for something. I didn't want to, but I liked him.

I looked over at Anna. She was watching Lupe and Andres with a bemused expression. Then she downed her wine and walked over to me, grabbing my wrist. Her face bent close to mine, mascara'd lashes, a slight jasmine scent, and she was talking into my ear, laughter in her voice, "Wallflowers unite. Let's dance."

I drained my glass and set it on the floor. We stepped to the dancers.

OCCASIONALLY I'D GET postcards from Del, cheesy touristic ones with pictures of the Brooklyn Bridge or Grand Central lit up at night. "How's my bike?" they'd always begin, followed by a few jokey sentences. She always told me she was working a lot and loving the city. Occasionally she'd mention some girl she was dating, a different name each time. The messages always ended with "Miss you" and at least three exclamation marks. I kept the postcards up on my fridge, my own little map of New York's biggest attractions. Someday I would visit, if I ever managed to save any money.

THE FIRST TIME I undressed Anna we were sitting on her couch after an afternoon spent wandering the art museum. I was afraid that my hands might shake, that I'd ruin the moment, but her eyes were so accepting, so warm, that I relaxed. I put my face in her neck as I unhooked her bra, smelling that light jasmine scent mixed with sweat. Her breasts were perfect, each just the right weight for my hand. And her bush was as I'd imagined—a slim triangle of golden hair, wet underneath, ready for my fingers, my mouth.

She made soft sounds and I listened for the changes in her breathing to tell me what she liked, what she wanted me to do next. The lights were off but it wasn't dusk yet. Sunlight came in through the white curtains, landing on her hair, her face and chest. She wasn't afraid to meet my eyes, to take my hand and pull it into her cunt, riding my fingers as her hips ground against the couch cushion. We hadn't put down a towel and I asked her if we should and she laughed and groaned and said yes, we should, but then it was too late, we were too far along, completely in the rhythm, she was sucking me in and I was following her and I wasn't going to pull out.

After she came she pulled my hand out and held it on her mound, her own hand curled over mine. Her warmth pulsed against my fingers like a heartbeat, and I had the sense of something, some energy flowing from her into me. Her eyes were closed, her whole body relaxed, and she seemed about to fall asleep, but then she opened her eyes and looked at me. "Thank you," she said. "That was really good." She smiled, a little shy but also impish, playful and dirty. She grabbed my hand and brought it to her lips. "And now you. Let's do you now."

During it all I thought just once of Del—her face flashed in my mind, followed by a twinge of guilt that I quickly dismissed. She wouldn't care, I told myself. It had been so many months. There had been so many girls. She wouldn't care.

I WAS WOKEN up one Saturday morning a few weeks later by the phone ringing and I groggily stumbled to answer it, thinking it was Anna or my landlord, who had recently told me that he'd sold the building to condo developers and that I had to move out within three months.

I lifted the receiver to my ear, stretching the cord as far as it could go as I went into the kitchen to make coffee.

Del's voice blasted through the wires. "I had to hear it from Lupe? Seriously? You couldn't even be bothered to tell me yourself?"

I'd never heard her so pissed off. It was a little frightening. I rubbed my eyes, feeling anxiety starting to tighten my neck. "I was going to tell you. I'd been meaning to."

"Meaning to? Pick up the fucking phone. It's really not that hard."

"I'm sorry, Del. I'm really sorry."

"What for? What are you sorry for?"

This stumped me. I wasn't sure, was the truth. I definitely didn't regret starting things up with Anna, but I also didn't want to hurt Del. I went to the fridge and pulled out a bag of coffee, spooning it into the French press, trying to wake up, to get my mind to start working.

Del continued. "You barely waited for me to leave town. Were you after her all that time, greebing, waiting for your chance, and you just didn't tell me?"

I filled the kettle, trying to think of what to say. I had been avoiding this conversation for weeks and now here it was, enveloping me like a wave.

"Why didn't you tell me?"

A sinking feeling dropped through my stomach. I was balancing the receiver between my ear and shoulder as I tried to turn the burner on and it slipped, bouncing across the floor. I chased after and grabbed it. "Sorry. Sorry about that. Listen, Del. It just happened. We ran into each other at a party. I'm so sorry I didn't tell you."

She was silent then, having run out of steam.

"I'm sorry."

There was a heavy sigh on her end, then shuffling noises, like she was opening a CD case. I heard music start up, a song by Massive Attack, I thought, followed by the sound of Del sniffling and then the click of a lighter. The pull of her inhale and full breath of her exhale were so distinct that I felt like she was in the room with me. I wished I could see her face.

"I just miss you guys. I miss you guys so fucking much," she said.

THERE'S ALWAYS SOME compromise. Mine was the cat, our longest argument—it lasted two weeks. Finally I buckled and Felix joined our household, a sassy calico from the rescue centre who likes to sleep on Anna's feet and shred the arms of the couch. I've never gotten used to his hair everywhere, but over the years I have started to find the fact that he watches us all the time less creepy. I've come to appreciate his presence quietly sliding through the apartment, pouncing on balls of dust, or laying shamelessly on his back with his legs open and his belly spread out, purring, waiting for one of us to pet him.

There were other disagreements before Felix, of course—the blue-shaded 70s lamp Anna thought hideous and wanted me to toss; Medusa, the enormous spider plant she loved and I hated, its numerous shoots—she called them "the babies"—trailing down to the floor. She likes to leave dishes in the sink; I want everything cleaned up right away. She likes to get up early on the weekends and go to the gym; I like to sleep with a pillow over my head until afternoon creaks through the blinds.

On rare rainy evenings, we read on the couch, Anna's feet in my lap, Felix purring underneath the spine of her book. Anna is usually wearing toenail polish, sea green or sparkling silver, her toes arching up as if they're riding a little wave, like the first time she pointed her toes at me that night at the house party, after she took off her shoes and started faking ballerina moves. Her feet were too hot, she had said, and the shoes were hurting. She had stopped the dance, bending down to unbuckle the heeled sandals and then doing something unexpected—tossing them to the corner of the room, where they narrowly missed one of the spaced-out dancers. It was the first time I saw her feet, long and slender, the nails painted coral, and when I looked at them I could already feel my tongue circling each big toe, could imagine pulling it slowly into my mouth.

Our fridge hosts a selection of our favourite postcards from Del, the greetings gradually changing from "How's my bike?" to "How are my girls?" My favourite is the one of the Statue of Liberty with Del's embellishments: a tank top drawn over Liberty's chest with the words "Dyke March 2002, Fuck Yeah!," her torch transformed into a smoking joint. Anna's favourite is a picture of the Botanical Garden with maples in every shade of orange and red, a big heart drawn on it in black Sharpie.

Del hasn't visited in a couple of years. The last time she came it was summer and the three of us picnicked with Lupe and her boyfriend and Lupe's daughter Bianca, already a teenager with her own girlfriend. We sat on a large blanket next to the fountain in Cheesman Park, wolfing down Anna's fruit salad and tamales Lupe had made the night before. Lupe told a funny story about the time she and Del dropped acid one summer solstice at this very fountain and how Del took off all her clothes and climbed into the pool, splashing water and reciting sonnets.

When we got home the three of us drank the rest of the rosé and smoked a little weed and fell into bed together. The sex was slow, at turns silly and tender. Del got out the paddle and tried spanking us but was too tired to do it convincingly and we all collapsed on each other laughing. We laughed about it again in the morning, tripping around in the kitchen's sunlight as Anna mimicked Del's half-hearted swipes. Del looking like a magician's assistant in Anna's green silk robe, the hem dragging on the floor as she made coffee, me in old cut-offs and a black bra and Anna— Anna in nothing at all, stalking across the room, reaching up to the top cupboard to get the big bowl to make pancakes, her long back, her strong legs.

Del keeps talking about how she's going to move back to Denver but at this point we don't believe her. Even though she complains about the city all the time, she's become a New Yorker—maybe complaining about New York is part of what makes her a New Yorker. She's always tired, always with dark bags under her eyes, always broke and working too many jobs, but she loves it. She loves the smelly subways, the constant rush of people, the blaring cars and speeding taxis, the bars open until all hours. She even loves the unbearable humidity of August, the heat rising off the gum-stuck pavement, bodies sweating so close together. She doesn't love being a small fish but she loves the size of the pond, all the women, new ones streaming in every day from the West Coast, from the South and the Midwest—sometimes even from Asia or Europe. There's usually one or two who want to date her, sometimes more, and she hasn't aged out of it yet.

Over the years her postcards have gotten more honest—sometimes she admits to being lonely, or tells us that she's depressed, that she's been trying and failing yet again to quit smoking pot. Every card always ends with hugs and kisses, *xxx*s and *ooo*s, so many of them filling the bottom of the card until it runs out. And she always says that she misses us. She misses us so fucking much.

JOEY, WHEN SHE KNEW HIM

A COLD DAY in January, in the middle of a snowstorm—the store bell tinkled, Sid looked up and there was Joey, shivering, big flakes clumped on his wispy long blond hair, starting to melt down his face. There was something endearing about his bedraggledness, his shy smile—she could tell right away he was family. He pulled the application out of his coat where he had been keeping it pressed flat against his chest and presented it like it was a birthday present. His fingers were icy, the paper damp at the edges.

Sid looked it over, noting he lived only a few blocks away, not far from her own apartment. Then she cleared her throat and, trying to sound authoritative, asked, "You have much experience in this line of work?"

Joey was earnestly giving the life story of each family pet and explaining his expertise in pet-sitting when Olivier, the actual Pets 'R Us manager, came out of the back office. He shot Sid an exasperated look. "Go clean the parakeet cages, Sidney."

At the time, Joey was attending the Traditional Chinese Medicine college out in New West. He'd ride the train there most days, rushing back to the West End to make it to his late afternoon shifts at the store or to catch an evening yoga class. Sometimes Sid would cover weekends for him so that he could do his hours at the student clinic, practising acupuncture on the poor volunteers. One slow Saturday at the shop he suggested that Sid come to the next week's clinic.

"Needles? No thank you." She was arranging the plastic toys by colour and size on a hanging rack and squeaked one at him. "Do I look like someone who would enjoy having needles stuck in their arm?"

"It's not painful. And, anyway, how would I know what kind of pain you're into?" He gave her a sultry look and licked his lips. They had taken to flirting with each other to pass the time.

"Can you say butt plug?" She held up a particularly suggestive toy and made a humping motion. Just then Olivier come out of the back office and she quickly put her head down and started hanging up the toys.

But Olivier wasn't there to reprimand them—turned out he just wanted to chat. "You guys are both gay, right?" he asked, and then launched into his spiel before either of them could answer. "My sister—she's, I guess, 'coming out'—I mean, she's still married, happily married, until recently, I guess, and now she has this 'girlfriend,' she says … my mom isn't happy. Really isn't happy." He looked from Sid to Joey. "What should I do? My mom and my sister are trying to get me to take sides."

In his early forties, Olivier already seemed ancient, though he had an air of sophistication that Sid and Joey admired—savvy fashion sense, a French accent. Even though he rarely joked and could be an outright asshole at times, they felt sorry for him. Being the manager of a pet store did not seem the appropriate vocation for a man who had such long dark eyelashes, who wore such nice shoes and often greeted people with a soft "Bonjour." He had never talked to them so informally before, and this breaching of the unspoken code of conduct between manager and employee was too much for either Joey or Sid to make sense of. They stared at him silently.

After an awkward pause in which Sid and Joey pretended to busy themselves with the plastic toys, Olivier said, "I guess I'll figure it out." He looked embarrassed and shrugged defensively as he headed back to his office.

Joey looked after him and licked his lips. "I *wish*."

"Really? Come on. He's way too old."

"He's hot."

"You think anything with two legs and a penis is hot."

Recently Joey had been cultivating a new persona, acting like he was at all times sexually voracious, constantly on the make, like every man was a potential fuck-mate. It was an act common to young gay men his age, but it didn't really fit Joey. Sid had only recently started to notice it, and still found it a bit jarring. Where had he picked it up? His roommates?

Joey tossed his hair dramatically and went behind the counter to get a box of fish food, which he started to unpack, lining the small canisters up on the shelf. "Want to come to the club with me tonight?"

"The club? You never go out."

"I know. I haven't been dancing in forever. I really want to dance."

AT EIGHT JOEY was standing on Sid's doorstep with a backpack full of clothes and a bottle of vodka. They tried on four or five outfits each as they sipped on tumblers of a drink that, at twenty, they still considered a cocktail: Sprite, vodka, a big slice of lemon, and a big slice of lime. They hairsprayed each other's hair, curled their eyelashes, painted their nails white. Later Joey would grind on boys, Sid would grind on boys and any girls who happened to be around. They would drink more, they would wait in long bathroom lines or go into the alley to piss, they would flirt, they would squeal and laugh. But before all that they were with only each other. Joey squeezed into a gold lamé half-shirt, Sid in an oversized men's button-up and black tie, in front of the big bathroom mirror, catching each other's eyes as they put on black eyeliner.

Sid still calls him Joey, even though it's not his name anymore and his husband Ian doesn't like it. Joey goes by Richard now— his middle name, the name of his grandfather, who was once rich (lawyer-turned-real-estate-investor) but lost the family fortune through incautious investments, and so Joey had to put himself through college by working at the pet store. The whole family was bitter about the lost money ever after and rarely visited the old man in his stuffy retirement home as he slid slowly toward his death.

Ian doesn't have to work—his grandfather made a killing investing in steel and coal during the Second World War (something the family tries to keep hush-hush) and all of his descendants have been living off of the proceeds ever since. But Ian is prideful and, unlike the rest of his family (to hear him tell it), has a decent work ethic, so after trying law school and dropping out and trying med school and failing out, he became a successful interior designer.

It is a cliché for a gay man, the career, but in this case, it is apt. Ian has the eye; he knows how to make a room look elegant, bright and airy or cozy and full of dark wood, depending on the client's wishes. He knows the best shops, the nicest fabrics, has an impeccable sense of colour. He once counselled Joey to buy Sid a pair of navy-and-red striped throw pillows, silk, for her couch—that was ten years ago, and she still gets compliments on them.

And Joey? After dropping out of college, he quit the pet store and started working at an upscale pet daycare. Later, he opened his own doggy spa (backed by Ian's family money) just a few blocks from their condo in the West End.

EVERY AUGUST, IAN and Joey throw a big party after the Pride parade. Their building has a pool on the roof, and they commandeer it from early evening until three or four in the morning—people dancing, drinking, smoking weed and doing lines until they finally have enough and stumble home. Sid is always there—sometimes with a date but more often between girlfriends and in search of effervescent cocktails, fresh cantaloupe slices, hors d'oeuvres featuring expensive goat cheese from Salt Spring Island.

Sid is excited to be at the party this year, to be out of the house. Finally back in school for her master's, she spends most of her days studying.

This year they've hired go-go dancers. Two boys gyrate around the pool in silver shorts, a glazed look in their eyes. One is beautiful—a round, shiny belly and lots of dark curly hair everywhere. Sid tries to talk to him when she first arrives but he only drops a few words her way before turning to his wiggling partner and imitating his movements. She watches as he pulls a joint from his tiny shorts to share with the other dancer—they barely slow down to light the thing. What was the deal Ian struck with them? Dance, dance as if your life depends on it, and don't stop for anything or you won't get your hundred dollars? (Ian, like most rich people, has a cheap streak.)

There's something mesmerizing about watching the boys twirl around each other, bathed in the turquoise glow from the pool lights, like two seals circling each other in a luminescent sea. They are covered in silver glitter and they are young—a decade or two younger than most people at the party. Although their movements are smooth, they look tired, and Sid wonders if Ian has hired them for the entire night, or just for a few hours. She sips her margarita, looking around for faces she recognizes. Everyone is beautiful but also a little grimy from the day's festivities, fake eyelashes askew, lipstick smudged, smelling of chlorine and sunscreen and sweat. She looks back at the dancers; they're grinding on each other but neither looks very into it. She hopes Ian is paying them decently, at least.

The prettier one with the belly reminds her of Michael, her best friend in high school, her "boyfriend" for a semester—they were each other's beards in grade 11 until they both came out spectacularly—in drag, no less—during an open mic night in the cafeteria. She still remembers some of the lines from Michael's spoken word piece—she's pretty sure he rhymed "trust" with "lust."

Michael's birth name is Miguel, and his Peruvian mother was pretty pissed when he changed it in grade 9. He and Sid worked at Dairy Queen together for two years. They'd clown with the hot dogs, make weird sculptures out of the tasty freeze and share makeup. Their manager, a worn woman who smoked two packs a day, had feathered greying hair and a tough edge that made them think she was a closeted dyke, loved them, loved (they thought) their eager adolescent gayness. She laughed when they camped it up, gave them the best shifts and free cigarettes to smoke on their breaks.

The last Sid heard, Michael had changed his name back to Miguel and was in Toronto, working in a café in the gay village. She takes a sip of her margarita. The bartender—a friend of Joey's—poured her a double, and she's starting to feel it. She closes her eyes, leaning into the sensation. But then a hand touches her shoulder—it's Ian, proffering a joint.

She takes a big drag and blows out a question with the smoke. "Where did you find these guys?" She motions at the dancers. "They're gems."

"At Rodeo," Ian says. "They dance there on Sundays. I asked them if they ever did private parties. They said maybe."

"Are they brothers?" This question makes no sense; the two look nothing alike. The other dancer is skinny and blond. But something about the way they move together reminds her of siblings practising a carefully choreographed dance in their living room.

Ian looks at her like she's stupid.

She takes another drag and hands the joint back to him. The weed is super skunky and she starts to cough, trying to explain, "One of them reminds me of a friend from high school—from Dairy Queen. You ever work fast food?" This question makes even less sense.

"Uh … no." Ian stretches out the "no" in what seems a parody of bitchy TV show queenness, except she's not sure it's a parody. But then he looks at Sid with affection. "Are you high already, girl?"

She fashions her face into what she hopes is a charming expression. "I certainly hope so." Around the pool deck, people are dancing and chatting, waving at people they know, clutching champagne flutes half-full of sparkling pink, weaving through the crowd to get another drink. Ian's friend DJ Lulu is on decks, set up in the corner by the bar. She's one of only a few women at the party, and one of maybe three other lesbians. Sternly handsome, she's wearing a black ball cap with LULU in silver letters pulled down low over her dark face. She concentrates on the music, head down, bobbing slightly to the beat.

The song makes the air throb and there's a feeling of heaviness, as if there might be a storm later, and suddenly Sid feels sexy, feels like dancing, but she doesn't have anyone to dance with. She sways a bit, holding her drink up so it doesn't slosh. Everything is wavy, subterranean. And where is Joey, her beloved Joey?

There he is—across the pool, ridiculous and retro-stylish in a tangerine caftan, laughing and vamping it up with his well-dressed friends. Even though the sun has dropped, he's wearing black cat-eyed sunglasses with rhinestones circling the frames.

Sunglasses at night, like that dumb 80s song Michael and Sid used to sing to each other as they mopped the floors with bleach water after close—using the mops as microphones, whipping their wash rags in the air like feathered boas. Michael in Sid's garish makeup— blue eye shadow, orange lipstick—and Sid's hair slicked back with his astringent-smelling gel, blobby like the bacteria that lives in dirty aquariums, the colour of mouthwash and slimy to the touch.

Was it one of those nights that they kissed? What a mess. Tongues mashed against each other's teeth, neither of them having any idea what they were doing, saliva dribbling down their chins—they gave up pretty quickly.

Pulling away, Michael had made a weird face.

Hurt, Sid quickly said, "Let's just be friends."

"Agreed," he had said, patting her cheek tenderly. "We're definitely friend material."

IAN WAVES OVER some friends, a group of guys Sid has met at their parties over the years. She remembers a few names—Sergio, Cole, Leonard. They hug her and tell her she's looking fabulous, trim—both are lies. She's put on weight and as usual couldn't find a nice enough outfit for the party, so is in cut-offs and not-white-enough high tops. But right now she's high and doesn't care. She's drifting in and out of the conversation, watching the dancers, one eye on Joey's theatrics, one ear listening to Ian tell a story about his uncle who owns a beach-side villa in Mexico. "He says, 'The gays are okay, and the Jews, but not these goddamned Indians, and those Mexicans …'" Everyone laughs, even Sergio and Leonard, two brown men in a party of mostly whites. Is Sergio's smile strained? He lifts up his glass. "Those damned Mexicans, eh?" he says, using an exaggerated Mexican accent.

Everyone laughs. Leonard sniffs, "Wonder what he has to say about the blacks—oh wait, don't tell me, don't tell me—I really don't want to know." He takes a big sip of his drink and lifts his eyebrows at the other men.

Ian smiles. "Who knows what he says about the gays when I'm not around. But the man's so rich—everywhere he goes, he sees money, makes money. He says it's like there are these endless streams of money floating in the sky. All you have to do is scoop your dipper in, get a dipperful."

"Insane," Sergio says. "Truly bizarre. Only a super-rich dude could have such mystical ideas about money. The rest of us just have to hustle along with everyone else."

"Yeah, down here on the *ground*. No scooping from the heavens for this man," Leonard says.

"Yeah," Sid chimes in weakly.

Cole, a rainbow heart painted in watercolours on his pasty chest, twirls his glittering pride beads around his neck and flutters his fake eyelashes. Everyone laughs and clinks their glasses. Ian sparks up another lethal-smelling joint and passes it around. Sid refuses this time, wondering if they're all as high as she is—she can't tell if the conversation they've just had was intensely uncomfortable or whether she's just being paranoid. She decides to sneak away to refill her drink and to find Joey, who has disappeared in the crowd on the other side of the pool in the darkening dusk.

BACK IN THE pet shop days, when they called each other the Pet Shop Boys, she'd take her women's studies textbooks to work, try to study when the shop was slow. She'd read to Joey, paragraphs of Audre Lorde, Judith Butler. Back then, Joey would listen. Back then, he called himself a feminist. Sometimes, when she was feeling particularly tender, she'd call him "Joey Boy," "Joey Joy," or "My Joy." When she was feeling snarky, it was "Bitch" or "Whiny Bitch." He called her "Mr. Sidney" or "Repent Sinner." When the store was empty and Olivier wasn't around, they'd yell "God hates fags!" across the aisles at each other, mocking the preacher in the States who protested soldiers' funerals to say that God hates America because America loves gays. The preacher's convoluted logic always made Joey and Sid laugh. "America loves gays," Joey would scoff. "That's news to me."

The store had a particular atmosphere, as all pet stores do—humid, musky. The smell was also comforting, familiar—similar, Sid imagined, to what barn smell must be like for a kid who grew up on a farm. Whenever she opened the door, she breathed it in—cedar shavings in the bottom of cages, fish food flaky as Brewer's yeast, mouse and bird droppings, new carpet on the scratching posts, chemicals for the aquariums.

And the animals—she loved them all, but especially the hamsters, each of whom she had given a name. Pebbles. Mousy. My Girlfriend. And the prettiest one, who she called Joey.

IAN LOVES TO call Joey "Richard," caresses the name, stretches out the syllables. Sid often has to remind herself that Ian can be generous, kind even. He flew to California to be with his parents when his mom got sick. He helped pay his friend's art school tuition. He gives money to gay charities. And he often buys her dinner, fills her up with cocktails, gives her free weed. Yet she somehow still feels judged by him—she isn't sure why. Her weight? Her clothes? She dresses mostly from thrift stores, and even her shoes, which she buys new, never stay bright—even the whitest sneakers seem to dim the minute she walks out of Sport Chek.

Ian is very finicky about his clothing, but he is too rich to dress too nicely, so goes for casual—a pair of new sneakers in some surprising colour, like orange, and chinos or designer jeans. A puffy grey jacket in winter, a crisp jean jacket in spring.

Joey, on the other hand, always dresses to impress. Ironed shirt and skinny tie even if he's just meeting a friend for brunch, haircut so fresh you can see the skin above his ears, at the base of his neck. He must carry one of those drugstore quick shine kits in his bag because his shoes always gleam, and Sid has more than once seen him pull out a small mirror to check for bits of salad in his teeth.

Sid's friends will remind her, when she complains about Ian, that he turned Joey's life around.

And they are right. But—

WHEN IAN MET Joey, he was in a deep depression, struggling through school, questioning if he would make a good doctor, taking extra shifts at the pet shop to pay rent. He barely went to his beloved yoga anymore because he couldn't afford it, and he even had to give up the free chanting sessions at the studio because he had to work Friday nights. He started sleeping in instead of doing his homework, blowing off the weekend clinics to smoke dope with his flighty roommates. Sid tried to talk to him about it, but he shrugged off her concern, saying he just needed a release.

Sometimes he would call her late at night, when she was already asleep. He would ask her things like am I going to make it, am I going to be okay. Sometimes his breath would catch, he would say his chest hurt and he couldn't breathe, or he'd be on the verge of hyperventilating, in the grips of a panic attack, and she would talk him down, soothing him with phrases she'd read in self-help books, telling him she was with him even now, holding his hands. Sometimes he would list all the people he knew who loved him, his mom, his brother, his dead grandmother, his old guru. Sometimes he'd even list random people, people he didn't know very well, like Olivier or one of his yoga teachers. She would never interrupt, would just wait until the litany ended, nodding, saying softly yes, they do, they do, yes.

But more often Joey would sit on the ratty couch with his room-mates, doing bong hits and telling borrowed stories full of bitchy exaggerations, or go out dancing and drink until he threw up or passed out. It was on one of these high-as-a-kite nights when he was out at Ponyboy—the club of the hour—that he met Ian, who was on E, single and ready to mingle. They went home together that night and within a month they were exclusive. Exclusive but semi-open, Joey explained, which meant they could still have sex with guys they met online or at the club, as long as they were safe, discreet, didn't tell the other about it, and didn't boast to their friends.

JOEY USED TO tell her all the time that he loved her. He'd also call her "lover." "Don't worry, lover, I'll be there," he'd say, promising to stop by her place on his way home from school. Sid still misses those days before cellphones, when they'd make plans at work to meet up and actually would meet up a few days later, or when they'd just show up on each other's doorstep with a new CD or a tip about some cool-sounding party in the neighbourhood. Back then, it seemed like people bumped into each other more often. There are people she used to run into all the time, people who still live just a few blocks from her, who she sees now only once a year at Joey and Ian's big party.

Michael also used to tell her he loved her. "Love you, girl," he'd call over his shoulder, as he rode his bike away from Dairy Queen after a late-night shift. But he never called her "lover" and he stopped saying he loved her after the one time they slept together.

THERE WAS A PERSON who used to come through the Dairy Queen drive-through all the time in a banged-up blue truck. The person's name was Mitch, and Sid thought she was a woman; Michael thought he was a man. They vied over who would get to work the drive-through when Mitch came through, and the lucky one tried to prolong the interaction for as long as they could, bringing Mitch extra salt and ketchup packets, saying they were sorry the kitchen was slow again, asking how Mitch's day was going.

One night Mitch came through late, much later than their usual hour, and Michael happened to be on the headset. After Mitch roared away, Michael came beaming to where Sid was cleaning the milkshake machine.

"What?"

He pulled a little baggy out of the pocket of his brown work slacks and waved it in front of her face. "Want to come back to my place tonight? Mom's at her boyfriend's."

"For real?" She felt a nervous electric excitement start up in her legs.

"Mitch is going to come over."

"Oh my god. Really?"

Michael nodded. Although he was trying to play it cool, he couldn't stop smiling.

THIS MANY YEARS later, Sid remembers only a few things about that night. The lead-up is still fairly clear—asking Sherry to buy them peach coolers, going home to take a shower and change her clothes. Mitch came by, she remembers that. And they drank the coolers, and some whisky from Mitch's flask, and they popped the pills. And there were jokes, and kissing, and fumbling. After a while everyone was naked in Michael's mom's king-size bed. She remembers wishing she had a dick—she didn't yet own a strap-on—so that she could do something with it. She remembers putting her hand down the front of Mitch's jeans and her triumphant gasp when she encountered wetness. "I knew it," she said.

"Knew what?" Mitch had countered, and she had felt embarrassed, even through the fuzzy warm haze of the drug.

She remembers Michael kissing the back of her neck, and thinking it felt so soft, so good. And she has a clear image of the two of them fucking, Michael on Mitch's back, both of them groaning.

Then it was very late, almost morning, and Mitch drove away in their truck and Michael was tearing the sheets off of his mom's bed, saying he had to wash them before she got home, and that Sid better go too.

THEY HAD A shift together two days later but they didn't talk about it. A week passed and they still didn't talk about it. Mitch stopped coming through the drive-through, but one night after work Sid saw his truck idling in the parking lot as she unlocked her bike and she knew he was waiting for Michael. She biked home crying.

The next day as she and Michael were smoking in the parking lot after their shift she gathered up her courage. "I saw Mitch's truck last night."

"So?" Michael's voice was immediately defensive.

"I guess, I just … we never talked about it. I mean, are you dating?"

He sighed. "I don't know what we're doing. We're figuring it out. It's just—fun, okay?"

"It was fun for me too," she said quietly.

"Yeah, well, he likes me, okay? He chose me. I'm sorry. But he did."

Sid looked down at the cigarette burning away between her fingers. She realized she was holding her breath.

MICHAEL DISTANCED HIMSELF after that. He no longer joked with her, no longer invited her over for Friday movie nights or asked to borrow her makeup. After Dairy Queen closed, he would clean like a demon and hurry to get out of there as fast as he could, saying he had plans. A few weeks later he quit and started working at the McDonald's across the street. At school, he avoided her. She'd see him sometimes biking home after work, or she'd see Mitch's truck in the parking lot waiting for him, but they rarely spoke and they never hung out again.

WHEN SID FINALLY makes it through the crowd to Joey, she can see that he is half-lit and in full-on entertainer mode. She stops a couple of feet away, sipping on her refilled margarita, even stronger than the last pour, and watches him. He's laughing, tipping back his head to show off his long neck, gesturing extravagantly with a gold (real gold? It can't be) cigarette holder that holds an unlit cigarette. He doesn't notice her, he's telling one of his stories, lapping his tongue like a little dog as his friends lean in, smiling. One of them asks, "Your new puppy?"

"No." He takes a fake-drag of the unlit cigarette and pauses for dramatic effect. "Ian's mother."

The group breaks into peals of laughter. Sid notices that one of them sounds like a barking dog.

She has the sudden desire to slip away before she's noticed, but just then one of Joey's former roommates, a gorgeous old queen who used to host a popular drag night—Pringles, everyone calls him, for reasons she's never understood—sees her and waves her over. "Dear!"

A big hug from Pringles, a round of greetings and gropings, glasses clinking, and Joey has his arm around her, she can smell the gin on his breath. He pushes his sunglasses up on his head. "I've missed you," he whispers into her ear, but she can't feel there's any way this can be sincere. They haven't seen each other in months.

Their last hang-out was supposed to be just the two of them, but it turned into a dinner with Ian, some Italian-Japanese fusion place in what used to be Chinatown. As usual, they had suggested a restaurant she couldn't afford and she'd been too embarrassed to tell them that. She stared for a long time at the menu of small plates, things like homemade chickpea tofu with pesto for twenty-seven dollars, and finally ordered miso soup and the least expensive beer. Ian had spent the night complaining about how it wasn't fair that his parents had to pay extra taxes on their two empty investment condos, and Joey had spent the night complaining about the silk trousers he'd had hand-sewn for their wedding, how he had to take them back three times, how the tailor just couldn't get it right. He hadn't even asked her about school, just carried on about himself while he and Ian devoured small plates of roast duck, parsley meatballs, gnocchi wrapped in seaweed. She left early, rode her bike home in the rain, feeling alienated and alone.

"I've missed you too," she says, and as the words come out she realizes it's true. But the moment doesn't have a chance to land—Joey is already distracted, flirting with his friend Bernard, talking about the last time they went to Rodeo, all the hot bears in chaps, and who might be going to the club tonight when the party starts to die down. DJ Lulu has put on another dangerously sexy tune, an undulating stretched-out beat that makes Sid think of swimming underwater, of slow kissing, and it's as if everyone's popped a molly all of a sudden, pupils dilated, slithering and prancing around the pool. Maybe they have all popped a molly, come to think of it, maybe that's why Joey's entourage seems so spacey and touchy, although no one's offered her any. This brings up a wave of loneliness. Why does she keep coming to these things? She doesn't even have a girl-friend this year to hide behind. She should be home, alone with her books. She takes a big gulp of her drink and tries to look insouciant.

Around the pool people are using exaggerated gestures to tell each other stories, lifting their arms up to capture it all in another blurry selfie. Someone pushes one of the drag queens into the pool and she shrieks, reaching for her hair. A couple is slow dancing and making out—one misstep and they'll fall into the pool as well. The music throbs; the bar is buzzing.

And suddenly Ian is there beside them. Someone has slipped a lei around his neck; its bright colours are echoed in the flowers decorating his designer shirt. He holds Joey's elbow and says something in his ear. Joey leans in, sliding his arm around Ian's waist, and his usual slightly dissatisfied expression softens as he listens, slowly nodding his head. For a moment Sid remembers his gentleness, the way his mouth used to quiver when he was nervous or about to share something important, how open his eyes used to be. He kisses Ian's cheek tenderly. Then they both turn to the group and smile as if they are on their honeymoon, bare feet in white sand, waves rising behind them as they pose for a photo.

Ian raises his glass. "To Richard! Ten years!"

"Of sobriety?" cracks Pringles, and everyone laughs.

"Ten years of the spa! Still going strong!" Ian turns to Joey and kisses him on the mouth. "I'm so proud of you, lover."

Everyone clinks their glasses and calls out, "To Richard! Ten years! To Richard!"

And Sid joins in, "To Richard!" But she can barely hear her own voice in the choir of congratulations. Above her head are strings of lights and farther up, stars she can't see. She feels the crowd of bodies encircling the pool, the thrum of their energy, and beyond, the hum of the glittering city. Her greenish drink glows luminescent as she holds it up to the deepening blue night. "To Richard," she says again.

BANSHEE

IT WAS THE sound of humming that woke me, low and mournful. But when I came to full consciousness, I couldn't hear anything. It was very late or possibly very early and the room was dark, darker than usual, a sort of pulsating soft black-grey. A fog must have rolled in off the river, dimming the lights of the surrounding buildings. As my eyes grew accustomed I started to make out the outlines of the dresser and the chair next to it. A pile of dirty laundry in the corner had been growing for weeks and had reached the height of a five-year-old. As I looked at its bulky shape, it seemed to shift a little. And then the humming started again, deep and melodic, soothing almost, until it veered up into a higher register that gave it a plaintive quality, as if it was asking a question it already knew the answer to.

We lived in a neighbourhood bordering the river, next to an industrial district, and there were often sounds at night—random banging, whirring from huge machines—but this sound was different. It was too close, for one thing. Like it was in the room. I clicked on my bedside lamp, hoping it would wake Matilde. No luck. She had her purple sleep mask clamped down over her face and I could see her heavy-duty orange earplugs jammed in tight. She had been up late watching videos on her phone and probably planned to sleep in until eleven at least. I pushed her a little, gently at first. Her breathing changed and she gave a little huff and snort as she rolled over to her side and kept sleeping.

The humming had stopped again and in the silence I heard a train creaking down the tracks bordering the river, and closer, the fridge gurgling its strange watery language. It felt like it was near dawn, but I wasn't sure, so I leaned over Matilde to look at the clock on her bedside table. 5:15. Goddamn it. Another night of hopeless sleep.

The pile in the corner shuffled again, and I shook Matilde more violently this time. She awoke with a start, sitting up and tearing off her sleep mask in one motion.

What the fuck? Her voice was furious, creaky from sleep.

Sorry, honey. It's just. There's something in the corner. Under the laundry.

She looked at me uncomprehendingly, then pulled out her earplugs. What?

There's something in the corner.

She glanced at the pile of clothes. The laundry? You woke me up because of the fucking laundry? She shook her head and pulled the mask back over her eyes and laid back down. Seriously. Just go to sleep for once. Go to sleep. She rolled back over on her side.

And turn the lamp off, she said, and promptly fell back to sleep.

I obediently clicked the lamp off and strained in the darkness to hear whatever I could. But I couldn't hear anything. No shuffling, no humming. Nothing at all.

In the last few months I'd been up a lot in the night, thinking. Worrying, to be more precise. I wondered about things like how many old people would die alone in their sweltering apartments in the next heat wave, recalling details from the obituary page read in passing, some retired nurse who died in her third floor walk-up, too stultified by the heat to make it out of her bed. Sometimes I'd keep myself up half the night trying to recall what I knew about salmon or orcas, making lists of things I needed to research come daylight. I wondered if the sea stars would come back, tried to remember the last time I'd seen one, more than one, a dozen purple stars splayed over the rocks at Bellhouse Park six or seven years ago on Galiano Island. I thought about earthquakes, "the big one" that was due on our coast, and the size of the tidal wave that would follow. I remembered footage from Japan, people running up the stairs of a concrete parking garage as the river rose. I contemplated the ricketiness of our own six-storey wood frame, how near the river, how quickly it would go up in flames. I thought of people fleeing the fires in the interior, and down in Oregon and California, stuck on stretches of burning road, cooked to death in their own cars. Late at night I thought of all this and I couldn't sleep.

I had started to depend on melatonin, chasing a few pills down with a glass of water doctored with a dropperful of valerian tincture. Usually this slowed down my mind enough to bring on sleep, although sometimes even this didn't work. Lately I'd been experimenting with the CBD gummies that Matilde brought home from the pot shop down the block. They tasted like crap, the strong weedy flavour only partially masked by sickening fake strawberry, but I chewed them dutifully, desperate for a full night of sleep.

There was no point in taking any more drops or chewing any gummies now though. It was nearly morning. I was awake. And there was no reason to stay in bed—Matilde would shove me away if I tried to snuggle her, and in an hour or so the construction across the street would start up, the cement machine clanking and grinding, the workers yelling as they banged their hammers. Down by the river the pile driving for the new condo towers would begin, each heavy clang hammering into my brain, accentuating the headache I had woken up with, my mouth dry as if I had downed an entire bottle of red wine the night before.

I looked over at the pile of laundry. I couldn't see it very well in the dim light but I knew what it contained. Three weeks of dirty clothes, mostly black because that's what my wife wore, drapey dresses and skirts smelling faintly of patchouli and cedar. She used to wear tight mini-dresses, bustiers, and fishnets, but in the last couple of years, her style had changed.

I hoped that Matilde would actually get out of bed today and do a few loads. We had made a deal several months ago, when Matilde got laid off from work, that she'd do all of the housework except for cooking—a chore we'd share—and I would pay the bills. So far I had kept my part of the bargain, but Matilde hadn't. Instead of cleaning, she got in touch with her creative side. She'd start projects—crocheting, painting, felting wool—and leave the materials strewn all over the living room. When she baked, which was often these days, she didn't bother to mop up the flour and cocoa powder, preferring to leave a light dust over the counters and kitchen floor. The couch cracks held the crumbs of oatmeal cookies and double chocolate brownies. Some days the unrelenting mess filled me with deep resentment, a helpless rage. On other days, I accepted it as our new life together. Whatever sort of day it was, I tried not to complain too much because if I did Matilde would stop touching me for days.

A Drake song that Matilde had been playing a lot on her phone ran through my mind, something catchy about we'll see what's about to happen next, and I hummed it thoughtlessly as I climbed out of bed. I thought I heard another voice join mine, humming at a lower register. I turned to look at the other side of the bed. Matilde was still knocked out under her sleep mask, a grim set to her mouth as if even in sleep she was saying you'd better not fucking wake me up. I don't know why I looked at Matilde—I knew very well where the humming was coming from. Turning my head slowly toward the heap of clothes, I watched as the pile started to shudder, black shirts and dirty tights falling down to the floor. The humming grew louder. A head emerged, bald, with a face puckered up like a knot of ginger. It was hard to tell the colour of the eyes, but they were large, bulging, the kind of eyes that as a kid I used to call googly eyes. They were staring right at me, not unfriendly. Then the humming stopped.

A thousand gorse fires on the island, croaked a dry voice.

I stared at their ancient face, surprised I wasn't more afraid.

Evacuate the towns. Crouch in a ditch.

I looked over at Matilde, but she was still fast asleep.

The rain. The rain. The floods the floods the floods. The voice was little more than a scratchy murmur, the voice of someone who had just woken up or who hadn't spoken in a long time.

The person shrugged off the rest of the dirty laundry and stood up. They were only a little over five feet tall, a lumpy figure with large breasts in a black robe. Her face was arresting, the face of an aristocratic ancestor—a prominent nose, lots of wrinkles. Her head gleamed, more bald than a newborn's—from what I could see she didn't have even one hair.

The winds, she croaked. Close your eyes. The dust the dust the dust.

I knew no way to respond to this. She seemed to have appeared out of one of my bad dreams, but I found it hard to believe I had summoned her.

No salmon again this year. The old woman shook her head, repeating a *tsk* sound.

This gave me pause. Just the night before I had been reading about a trend that had been growing in the last twenty years—runs of sockeye committing suicide. And at the farmer's market on the weekend, the fish seller had posted a sign on her truck: "No local salmon because of poor runs." I purchased a couple of tins of smoked tuna instead. My friend Dru had been telling me for months that I should have already given up *all* seafood by now—they kept sending me links to documentaries that spelled it all out. The last time we met for coffee, they told me that most of the salmon had died in the summer's heat dome; the juveniles couldn't survive the temperature of the water. In October Dru had gone to see the salmon run on Bowen Island, a tradition of theirs for many years—but the run was nonexistent. They saw only one salmon, leaping pathetically as it tried to escape the steel contraption that had been built by the local fish and wildlife workers. Volunteers would catch the salmon and then transport them upstream so that at least a few made it to their traditional spawning grounds.

The old woman walked out of the bedroom and went to the couch, shifting one of Matilde's half-painted blue canvases—she was experimenting with sharks and seascapes—so that she could sit down. She resumed humming. At times the humming veered into chant, at other times into a low wail. She rocked back and forth. It was discomfiting to witness, but I didn't know how to make her stop, or if I should make her stop, so I went over to the breakfast nook and started making coffee, watching her out of the corner of my eye.

Outside the window the seagulls were having their usual morning scream fest, circling around each other, diving toward the roofs and back up again with seemingly endless energy. They might have been harassing a crow, or some bigger bird, a bald eagle after their nest of precious babies—although this was less likely. When we first moved in, I used to see the occasional bald eagle or heron gliding over the river, but I hadn't seen either in a couple of years. The gulls reeled past the window, crying their high-pitched cries.

The old woman turned to watch them, transfixed. She quietly mimicked their sounds, then tapped and scratched at the window as if she could communicate with them. But the seagulls paid her no mind.

I pulled a bag of coffee out of the fridge. I thought of warning her that I was going to grind the beans, that it would be loud for a minute, but something stopped me. She didn't exactly invite conversation. She acted like I wasn't even in the room.

At the sound of the coffee grinder Matilde started to stir in the bedroom. I heard a huge yawn that I knew was accompanied by an equally huge stretch, her limbs starfished across the bed, feet arching. I heard her roll over and was afraid she'd go back to sleep.

Babe, I called. Babe? I think you should come out here. Right now please.

Even from the other room I could hear her theatrical sigh. I knew what was coming next and sure enough a Drake song started up, the beats echoey and anemic as they drifted out of Matilde's phone. She padded out a couple of minutes later, her black silk robe gaping open as she scratched her breast. She gave a big yawn and smiled at me, then turned to the couch, stopping short when she saw the old woman.

The woman had gone back to her moaning and rocking. She was bent over, looking at the floorboards. At times the moans sounded like she was in pain; at other moments the sounds were almost exultant.

What the hell? You could have told me we have a fucking banshee in our house.

A banshee?

Clearly a banshee. Matilde made a sweeping gesture. Look at

her. All crone-like. Wailing. Pure banshee. She turned off the Drake song and set her phone on the kitchen counter.

I would call it moaning, I said.

Moaning, wailing, whatever. She's a banshee. You know what this means, don't you?

I started spooning coffee into the espresso maker. Not really.

It means one of us is going to die.

We're both going to die at some point.

You know what I mean. It means one of us is going to die, like, soon. That's what a banshee means.

She could be here for one of the neighbours.

But then why would she shack up with us? She'd stay at their place if it was one of them. Matilde's tone was breezy, as if it was neither here nor there if one or both of us died in the next day or two. She pulled a long brown curl in front of her face and started trying to untangle it.

As was often the case, Matilde's reaction was not what I expected. I thought she might be afraid of this witchy-looking woman, or perhaps blame me, claim that all the disasters I'd been reading about had somehow conjured her up—our own personal little piece of the larger looming chaos. But Matilde seemed mostly just calm, slightly curious. And she hadn't smoked up yet today, so I knew it wasn't that fake numbed-out calm she got from pot.

She picked up her phone and walked over to the old woman, moving a painting and leaning it next to the couch so she could sit next to her. The woman was still rocking back and forth, her arms wrapped around herself, humming and looking at the ground.

Hey, look here, Matilde said. Do you like dancing?

She opened a video on her phone, some silly thing with Drake in it that she'd already shown me. A catchy pop hip-hop song started up and she set the phone on the banshee's lap.

It's a dance-off. She chuckled. He's totally going to lose. But isn't he cute? Later he does this really bad snake dance thing. She shook her head. It's so funny.

The banshee looked up then and took the phone in both of her hands. She watched the video intently. After a while, she started to smile.

I knew it, said Matilde. She looked over at me. I knew she'd like the dances.

I watched the coffee burble up its little spout, hissing steam, and I felt annoyed. Here was Matilde, making fast friends with this strange creature, who might be an apparition, actually, now that I thought of it, but in recent months she wouldn't even pick up the phone and call a friend. During the first year of the pandemic she'd continued to reach out, booking Zoom cocktail dates and coffee walks, but in the last couple of years she acted like she couldn't be bothered, and when I asked her about it, she shrugged it off, saying she just didn't feel that connected to most of them anymore. It worried me.

When the coffee was done I brought them each a cup—a big latte for Matilde, who liked her coffee milky, and a single shot of espresso for the banshee, who perhaps didn't drink coffee at all.

His hair is looking really good, Matilde said. And his beard. So dreamy. Sweetie, she turned to me. I want you to give me a Drake haircut. This week, okay? Bring your clippers home.

I watched as the old woman gingerly lifted the little cup and sniffed the coffee. Her eyes were closed. Sure, honey, I said. Sure.

ON THE TRAIN home I was exhausted. It had been a shitty day at work: late clients, overly picky clients, dye jobs that took too long, a hurried cold lunch from the corner store. I hadn't wanted to leave Matilde with the banshee, but I couldn't cancel the day—we needed the money. And Matilde had insisted that I go to work, that she'd be fine alone with the banshee, that she'd figure it out. I'd hesitated, but after a moment agreed—for although the banshee was exceedingly odd in her appearance and behaviour, she seemed pretty tame overall. She wasn't aggressive, she didn't lunge at us or play with the kitchen knives. She did say a lot of creepy shit though. Although the things she said weren't any creepier than the news I doom-scrolled every morning.

I looked around the train. A few people were still wearing masks, although it had been months since the public health authority recommended it. It seemed like some people were never going to get over the pandemic. I noticed that someone had propped the windows open to keep some air circulating even though it was cold January. Hardly anyone ate or drank on the train anymore, and it was something I missed, which Matilde found hard to understand, as she said it was gross and smelly. And it's true that sometimes people chewed too loudly or left a mess behind, puddles of milk-shake or wrappers on the floor. But what I missed was a perhaps strange sense of identification, a sympathy for the eater. On the train we were all in a hurry, we were all rushing somewhere, and some of us didn't have time to eat—so we had to eat where we could, be it on a train or a platform or waiting under an awning for a late bus.

Matilde had recognized the old woman as a banshee right away. But how? A banshee could show up in many forms, from what I'd read in my quick search on the morning train ride. They usually appeared in a womanly form, sometimes combing long blond or black hair. This was why some superstitious people in Ireland never picked up a comb from the ground—the comb might have been left by a banshee trying to entrap them. A banshee might show up as a washerwoman who, upon closer inspection, turned out to be washing clothes not in water but in blood. They could be weasels, they could be birds, they could turn up as toads or eels or even goats. They could often be found near rivers, and we lived near a river. Maybe we'd already been visited by one and just didn't know it.

Last summer, a crow moved onto our balcony for an entire week and acted very strangely. We initially thought it was injured but came to realize that wasn't the case—it was just hanging out. It often sat with its wings fanned around it like a black feathered gown. It was another burning hot August, the skies hazy with the smoke from forest fires, the light a painful orange, somehow both glaring and muted, and the crow often appeared to be panting, its little beak open to catch the air. Each morning I would stumble out of the bedroom to make coffee and the crow would hop up and waddle over to the sliding glass door, staring at me and caw-caw-cawing as if its life depended on it. I was afraid of it and never wanted to open the door, but Matilde would leave it little bowls of water and crusts of bread. After many days, the crow was just gone one morning. We didn't even see it fly away.

Had that been a banshee? No one we knew had died around that time, although our next-door neighbours did move away the next week, and Matilde got laid off the week after.

BACK AT HOME Matilde met me at the door, a little frantic. She pulled me into the foyer and whispered in my ear, This is getting really strange.

I thought you liked strange, I said.

She shushed me, putting a finger dramatically to her lips. She's on the balcony, she said.

The apartment smelled pretty awful, like charred chocolate cake underlaid with something chemical, but it was cleaner than it had been in weeks. Matilde's canvases were stacked up in a corner in the living room and her painting supplies had been put away. Someone had swept the dirt out of the entryway and the kitchen counters were clean. A lumpy brown mess sat on a plate in the middle of the table—the burnt, unfrosted cake.

I hope she doesn't jump, I said. Although maybe if she does she'll turn into a crow and fly away. I heard they can do that.

You've got to stop reading Wikipedia. She tugged my arm, pulling me through the kitchen and toward the balcony door. And I promise you, whatever you read won't prepare you for this.

Lolling on the overpriced chaise longue Matilde had insisted we buy in the summer and then never used was the banshee, lit up by the bright patio lights. She was crammed into a pair of fishnets and a leopard print mini-dress that I thought Matilde had given away some time ago. Over this she wore a little black leather vest criss-crossed with thin silver chains. Her lips were painted a bright pink. Even though it was frigid out, she didn't seem bothered by the cold as she stretched up her arm and snapped a picture of herself on Matilde's phone. She was younger than she had been this morning; her skin was smooth and she had sprouted a soft cap of short black hair.

Why is she dressed like you? I asked. I mean, the old you.

Matilde gave me a look. It's still me, she said. It's still my clothes.

You haven't worn anything like that in months. Maybe years.

And you miss it, don't you? Matilde leaned in and kissed me. I kissed her back, holding her hips, remembering a tiny pair of black lace panties she used to slip on and how it made me wild just to see a slice of her silky pubic hair peeking out. There were handcuffs languishing at the bottom of our tickle trunk that hadn't seen the light of day in over a year. Our dildos were no doubt covered in dust. I felt like I barely knew how to kiss her anymore. This thought made me stop the kiss.

It's been a long time, I said.

I know. She snuggled into my arms. It felt nice, but I was also a bit wary. She didn't touch me very often anymore and in the last few months she didn't seem to want to talk to me much either. Whenever I'd try to tell her about the things I was reading, about an article or a video I'd found, something Dru had told me, she'd only listen for a sentence or two, and then she'd tell me she couldn't talk about it. It's too overwhelming, she'd say. You're stressing me out. I can feel my jaw getting tight. And then she'd go out on the balcony to smoke a bowl.

And an image would rise in my mind, the flaps of a cardboard box closing, closing, and I would turn away, wondering who I could talk to, who would hear me if she couldn't.

I looked out the sliding doors to where the banshee lay preening. She lifted up one leg and pointed her toes, admiring her skin poking through the fishnet.

I was hoping you might have made dinner, I said. I'm starving.

Matilde gave me a look, but stepped to the kitchen and opened the fridge. All we have is wilted kale, some potatoes, and an old hunk of tofu. She sighed. I'll make a stir-fry if you get rid of the banshee.

Get rid of her? How?

I don't know. Put her in the bathtub?

What are you saying? Drown her? I don't even know who I'm married to right now.

I didn't say drown her. Matilde was rifling around in the crisper, pulling out some old garlic that had grown long green shoots like fingernails and a couple of crushed-looking onions.

You implied it.

I thought maybe she'd just turn to water or something. I don't know.

You aren't making any sense, I said crossly. Did you smoke already?

I smoked all day. I gave the banshee some too.

You got the banshee high? Jesus Christ. I took a cutting board out of the cupboard and started pulling the skins off the onions.

She didn't really seem to get high. She didn't seem to like it. She choked and then waved her hand away when I tried to give her another toke.

Nice.

You don't need to be sarcastic. What did you expect me to do?

I don't know—not smoke for one day because we have a goddamned shape-shifter in our house? I opened a cupboard to take out a glass for water and shut it harder than was necessary. As the heat that always accompanied an argument started to rise in my body, I heard the balcony door slide open. The banshee clomped into the kitchen in a pair of Matilde's old heels, smiling. Unsurprisingly, she was playing a Drake song on the phone. She gyrated a bit, bumping the kitchen counter.

Good fucking god, I said.

What do you know? I've been dealing with this all day. You were barely out the door before she started tearing through our closets.

What's that chemical smell?

I don't know. I thought it was maybe some old perfume or something she found.

That's definitely not perfume. It smells toxic. Metallic, or something. Burning. I stepped closer to the banshee and took a whiff. Yeah. It's definitely coming from her.

Matilde had taken the onions and was chopping them on another cutting board, wiping her eyes with a shoulder as they started to water.

My own eyes were stinging from the chemical smell mixed with the onion fumes and I blinked the tears away. Honey, I know you've spent a lot of time alone the last few years. And I know that can make us lose touch with reality a bit, especially when we smoke a lot of weed.

"We" don't smoke a lot of weed. I do. And you can stop it with the fakey counselling voice.

I'm not trying to condescend, babe. I'm just trying to understand.

The banshee was looking back and forth at our faces as if watching a tennis match. She swayed from side to side with her whole body, clutching Matilde's phone. I noticed her fingernails were painted a rich burgundy, a colour Matilde used to put on when we went out dancing.

Hey, I said. She's not humming anymore. When did she stop?

I can't remember.

As if on cue, the banshee set down the phone and went to the couch, pulling Matilde's guitar case out from underneath it. Opening the case, she set the guitar on her lap and started strumming it like a harp, keening a hair-standing-on-edge little tune. She closed her googly eyes and swayed from side to side. Then she stopped singing and stared at us as if waiting for us to say or sing something in response.

The guitar was a sore spot. A year ago, in a spurt of creative ambition, Matilde had charged it to our credit card without telling me, and then proceeded to play it only twice before hiding it under the couch. It had cost a couple hundred bucks, a couple hundred we didn't have. But Matilde had gotten mad at me when I complained, saying she needed a creative outlet, she was depressed, and I needed to be more supportive.

I had wondered then, as I wondered now, what being supportive meant. How did we support each other? Could we continue to? Where would we each be when it all ended? And what did I mean by "when it all ended"? The apocalypse everyone was so fond of talking about, making movies about, writing novels about? Weren't we already living through it, the unravelling, which had seemed to start slowly, or many of us thought of it that way. "Warming" was the word used. Repeatedly used. Like you might warm up a slice of cake or a bowl of soup. But it was already warm, very warm. Who were we kidding. It was hot and getting hotter. Everything moving so fast. And where would Matilde and I go, where would our neighbours go, our friends, once every last icecap melted and the city was underwater? What would we eat, with the oceans acidified, the wheat fields waterlogged, so many cows drowning each year in the floods?

I remembered a video I'd watched a couple of weeks earlier when I couldn't sleep. A Wet'suwet'en Elder wrapped in a yellow and grey blanket, a bird design on her back, was singing and drumming in the snow when she was arrested. The officer conducted himself with unconvincing gentleness, attempting a pious expression as he took her arm to lead her away to the waiting suv. She stopped singing for a moment to tell him, You should be ashamed. What will you tell your children, your grandchildren? When there's no water to drink, no food to eat?

THAT NIGHT, as we made our bed, pulling up the red cotton sheets and smoothing the red duvet, the banshee took off Matilde's heels and curled up on the couch. I heard her snoring from the bedroom. When I went to drape a quilt over her, I saw that her face was even younger, the skin taut and fresh, and she was sucking her thumb, holding what appeared to be a doll she had made from the scraps of one of Matilde's sewing projects. The veins on her eyelids were the inkiest blue, the most delicate tracery, and I felt like gently kissing each one, but instead I just patted her head.

Back in bed, I turned to Matilde. She was looking at me sadly, clutching her sleep mask and ear plugs. I'm sorry I've been such an asshole lately, she said. I love you.

I love you too, I said. And I leaned over to kiss her, slowly, and she returned the kiss, also slowly, savouring it, it seemed. We stayed entangled for a few minutes, her arms around my back, my hands in her messy hair, smelling her earthy scent. Then I turned off the lamp and Matilde pulled on her sleep mask and we both laid down and tried to sleep.

THE KNIFE

THE FRONT OF the church was dark now, the volunteers had all departed in their minivans, taking the decorations and leftover orange-frosted cupcakes with them. The street was quiet and I was alone in the rain in my soggy black trench coat, standing under a streetlight so she could see me when she pulled up. It was the first time she had to pick me up because of a stupid drunken mistake and I wanted to shrink under the eaves of the gloomy church, to disappear, but I didn't have bus fare and didn't want to walk home in the rain.

It was my own fault for going to a party in a church basement. My best friend Majohn had gotten the tip from his sister, and we didn't have anywhere else to go and didn't want to stay home passing out candy like losers so I put on a pair of black cat ears borrowed from my sister Lucy's costume and Majohn got himself up in a thrift store fur suit that could have been meant to be any number of animals. We shoulder-tapped outside the liquor store until a helpful stranger who needed five dollars got us a fifth of vodka and we drank it on the walk to the church.

By the time we were halfway there we were half-lit and thought it was a good idea to start knocking on doors. The first waves of little ghosts, ghouls, and princesses had already gone to bed and many houses had already turned out their lights and extinguished the candles in their jack-o'-lanterns. But a few carved pumpkins still leered goldenly and a few porch lights still burned.

The door of a nicely kept house with stone pillars was opened by an older man with dyed blond hair and big teeth. The arms of a cream-coloured sweater were tied at his chest; he looked as if he hoped to be mistaken for a Lands' End catalogue model, but he wasn't quite handsome enough.

"Now what do we have here?" he boomed over the strains of classical music floating from big speakers in the room behind him. I could see tall fringed lamps that looked expensive and under one of them a bottle of wine sitting on a small antique table. In the man's hands was a large ceramic bowl of candy.

"We're comic book characters," said Majohn, always quicker at a comeback than I was. He held out his hands. "Candy?"

"Aren't you a little old to be trick-or-treating?" The man clutched the bowl to his chest like it was his baby.

"We look old for our age." Majohn flashed an innocent grin. "But we're still in middle school."

This wasn't quite true. We were in our first year of high school. But close enough.

The Land's End catalogue man looked at us quizzically, then grudgingly smiled. "Young enough, I guess." He dumped a bunch of peanut butter cups in Majohn's open hands and then into mine.

"Be safe, now," he said, before shutting the door.

A block away we broke into a run, whooping and laughing. I took a big chug of our vodka and chased it down with a peanut butter cup. Majohn followed suit.

"That yuppie motherfucker!" Majohn howled, chocolate gathered at the edges of his mouth. We had recently realized we were old enough to use the word *motherfucker* and sprinkled it liberally into any conversation.

"Let's hit this party," I said.

"Word, motherfucker." He slapped me on the back.

THE PARTY WAS even dumber and more embarrassing than we could have imagined. The large room was lit too brightly and nerdy teenagers in costume bumped around to music from the previous year's top 40. A person in a wolf mask jumped up and down, yelling along to Cyndi Lauper's "She Bop." Majohn and I pointed and nudged each other. We had only recently learned from a girl in our English class that this song was about masturbating, and we lorded this knowledge over others who were ignorant of the song's true meaning.

On the way in we'd dumped our vodka bottle in the one men's room toilet, and the sight of it bobbing there made us laugh, but also made us afraid we'd be caught by one of the adult chaperones, and we had scurried out of there the minute a tall vampire came through the door.

Majohn hopped up on one of the large windowsills in a somewhat dim back corner and pulled a pack of cloves out of his costume pocket. He cracked the window and lit up, passing the clove to me. As I took a drag of the spicy sweet smoke, he started choking and bent his head down to blow smoke out the window. Before I could exhale, he jumped off the windowsill and walked swiftly away.

I felt a hand clamp down on my shoulder and before I could speak the clove was yanked from my fingers and dropped into a cup of soda, where it hissed. "What do you think you're doing?" asked Majohn's aunt Ligaya, her voice tight with fury. She dragged me back to the harsh fluorescent light of the kitchen where a bunch of older ladies were making little salami sandwiches on white bread and brewing coffee. She pointed to a phone in the corner. "You're going to call your mother right now and tell her what you did." She crossed her arms and watched me.

"Majohn ..." I started.

"Majohn had nothing to do with this." She looked around at the other women as if asking them to bear witness. "Thank goodness."

I had more than once seen Ligaya do this thing where she'd pray for Majohn right in front of his face, staring off to the side and addressing God as if he were in the corner of the room and only he could understand how deeply frustrating her nephew was.

But now she just shook her head, turning away from me. "I told him not to get mixed up with you."

This was a dig, I knew, at my family. My mom hadn't remarried after my dad died and had dated a number of questionable characters, some who had spent time in jail, some who didn't have fixed addresses or regular jobs. Majohn's family was deeply Catholic, but that hadn't stopped his parents from being kind to me and feeding me when I came to their house. Ligaya had never liked me though.

I thought of ratting out Majohn. That motherfucker had stranded me here. But then, he would have been in a lot more trouble than I was if Ligaya had found him. His parents, although nice, were strict. It wasn't uncommon for them to ground Majohn for a month at a time. And Majohn knew my mom wouldn't really do anything. She wasn't big on discipline, meaning that she didn't care much what I did, as long as I helped keep the house clean and made dinner for Lucy and Sarah.

THE RAIN DRIZZLED down my face and into the collar of my trench coat, cooling my neck and nearly erasing any lingering feelings of drunkenness. Tipsy, it would be easier to deal with my mom's annoyance, but I was glad to be almost sober. The night had sucked. Sucked balls, Majohn would say.

Out of the wet dark a pair of headlights turned a corner and headed toward me. I tried to look contrite, slouching under the streetlamp. As the car got closer, I saw it wasn't my mom's beat-up green station wagon, but a sleek black sports car. It pulled up at the curb and I felt a shiver of fear as a silver-haired guy in the driver's seat smiled at me. I stepped back. This old pervert had another thing coming if he thought he was going to lure me into his car for some

Halloween jollies. I was preparing to run when the window rolled down and I heard my mother's voice. "Ryan, get in." She was leaning over the silver-haired man and she didn't look mad.

"Mom? Who is this guy?"

"Get in, honey. You're soaking wet. This is Reg."

I climbed into the backseat. Looking through the space between the two front seats, I could see that my mother had her hand on this guy's thigh and I noticed he was wearing nice brown slacks. Her boyfriends usually wore jeans. Soft jazzy music played from the speakers, the kind you'd hear in fancy department stores. I looked away and tuned out, watching the slippery streets slide by, the black eyes of burnt-out jack-o'-lanterns staring from strangers' porches. When I tuned back in, my mom was saying, "I've been wanting you to meet him for a long time, but I was waiting for the right time to introduce him."

"And the right time was Halloween?" I asked.

"I wasn't planning on it being tonight. I wasn't planning on picking you up tonight." Her tone sounded kind enough but my mother was a master at couching passive-aggressive comments in pleasant-seeming tones. "But here it is. Here he is. Your sisters have already met him."

"What? They have?"

"Don't freak out, honey. Just tonight. They met him tonight. When he came to pick me up, he just came in for a couple of minutes."

I leaned back into the plush seat. His car was unnervingly clean. I consoled myself with the fact that at least I was getting his seats wet and hopefully a bit dirty.

A meticulous man. An odd match for my mother, who never cleaned the house if she could help it and let encrusted dishes pile up in the kitchen for days and then threatened to rescind my allowance if I didn't wash them.

Up front I saw Reg take my mother's hand, holding it still on his thigh. He turned his head slightly back toward me. His perfectly trimmed grey moustache gleamed in the passing light. "How was the dance, Ryan?" he asked.

"Okay." We were passing the drugstore a few blocks from our house. "Pretty lame, actually. I mean, it was in a church." I laughed to show I knew that it was uncool to go to a party in a church.

"Not your scene, huh?" I could tell he was smiling from the way the side of his cheek lifted.

Was he making fun of me? I decided to play it cool. I shrugged and looked back out the window.

But he wouldn't let me ignore him. He pulled the car up in front of our house and cut the engine, turning around fully to look at me. "I don't like churches either," he said. He smiled and squeezed my mother's hand. "Religion is a bunch of bs."

His swearing surprised me. Usually my mom's dates tried to make a good impression and held off on using obscenities until at least our third or fourth meeting.

"Yeah, it's pretty fucked up," I said. I could see my mother's shoulders stiffen. She didn't like it when I cussed in public or in front of my sisters, although when we were alone she'd sometimes drop an f-bomb and allow me to do the same.

Reg turned to my mother and laughed. "Pretty wise little dude you have there," he said.

She laughed in response. "Wise-ass is more like it."

This was my chance to escape before Reg demanded a handshake. I quickly turned the handle and leapt from the car. "Thanks, man. Thanks, Mom. Later."

I ran up the stairs to the house and Reg drove off into the night with my mother at his side, back to his apartment, to do things I didn't want to think about.

AT SCHOOL ON Monday Majohn was all apologies and excuses. He bought me a chocolate milk and chicken sandwich at lunch and took me to stroll around the track to "check out the honeys." He had his eye on a new girl named Tamiko who sported a half-shaved head, bleached hair, and pierced cheeks and eyebrows. She was a sophomore, and I was pretty sure she didn't know we existed.

"I can get her, bitch," Majohn told me as he led me closer to the bleachers where Tamiko was lounging with her punk friends. "Bitch" was another term of endearment we had recently taken up. We thought it made us sound tough and worldly.

As we neared the bleachers I saw that Tamiko was done out in dark-blue lipstick and a long black skirt and combat boots. She looked cool and serene, smoking with her friends. Majohn waved at her as if they already knew each other, and she looked confused but raised her hand hesitantly in return, smiling half-heartedly.

Majohn turned his face to me and said under his breath, "That's what I'm talking about, bitch."

"She doesn't know who you are, man." I slurped my chocolate milk. I felt protected in my lack of desire for Tamiko and her crew. I knew they were out of my league.

"She does now," he said, puffing up his chest like a pigeon. He rolled up the sleeve of his shirt and felt his muscles, signalling me to do the same.

"Give me a break, motherfucker," I said. Majohn had recently started lifting weights and going for runs. I preferred to retire to my bedroom after school, playing video games until my mother yelled for me to start dinner. If I got a little chubby I just drank diet soda for a couple of days until my jeans fit again. I used to be fat in middle school, but a growth spurt in eighth grade had thinned me out. These days I didn't need to exercise, but even if I did, there was no way I was going to start hanging out at the gym with a bunch of meatheads.

The bell rang and we turned slowly back toward the school. As we passed Tamiko again, a tall boy in black with a red mohawk took off his earphones and slipped them over her ears. She bobbed her head slightly to the music. Majohn suddenly broke away and jogged over to the bleachers. I kept my cool and kept walking. After a few paces I snuck a peek back and saw Majohn pull a pack of cloves from his back pocket and offer them to Tamiko and her friends. Tamiko lifted off the headphones and said something and they all laughed. Majohn bent close, cupping his hand around Tamiko's clove to light it. It didn't look like they were planning to make fifth period. I guess

I could have joined them, choked on clove smoke and traded dumb stories about music shows we waited in line to see but couldn't get tickets for, but instead I hurried off to class. It was algebra, the only subject I was doing well in.

MAJOHN USUALLY CAME over on Friday nights to have dinner with us and then stayed up late with me watching MTV after my mom went to her boyfriend's and my sisters went to bed. Cable was one of my mother's extravagances—Majohn's parents didn't believe in wasting money on it. Majohn loved Tears for Fears and always hoped to see "Shout" or "Everybody Wants to Rule the World." He often sang the lyrics about giving your parents hell in return for the life they had given you when I recounted fights I had with my mom. I was stuck on anything by Duran Duran and Depeche Mode. I often implanted myself in scenes from the videos, imagining that I was playing the synthesizer or the guitar, crooning alone as I walked the beach, or singing along with the band as they sipped pink drinks in a sleek restaurant.

That Friday Majohn said he couldn't make it because his parents wanted him home, so I stayed up past midnight hoping to see my favourite, Duran Duran's "The Chauffeur." It was one Majohn and I had only seen a couple of times together, but when it came on I always wished I was alone. But that night I was alone, so when the video finally did come on, I crouched close to the TV to watch every action.

It was in black and white, which made it seem sophisticated rather than old-fashioned. The women were gorgeous and elegant, with dark lipstick and long eyelashes. Heat rose in my neck and face at the close-ups of their sheer black stockings and garters. I stared at the long black gloves, the broken piece of mirror one woman kissed as if it were her lover, the shots of the bridge as the black limousine drove across it.

The entire video mesmerized me. Watching it, I felt like I had fallen into a slow, shadowy dream, hypnotized by the refrain of the synthesized piano. Even though I had only seen it five or six times, I had each frame memorized. I watched the chauffeur dance in the shadowy light and felt myself getting hard. I wanted to keep watching but also wanted to go to my room where no one would discover me.

Alone in my room, I would return again and again to two scenes. In one, the woman in a garter belt and corset steps out of the back of her limousine into a dim parking garage where another woman waits in a belted trench coat. Under her coat, she is wearing a garter and stockings, black lace panties and bra. There is a close-up of her eyes as they widen with desire. No words are exchanged, just the pulsing melody of the piano as the woman from the limousine slinks over to the other woman and opens her coat.

In the other scene, the chauffeur, a handsome man, turns into a beautiful woman. She takes off her chauffeur's cap and jacket, revealing short bleached-blond hair and bare breasts above a black leather corset. Her breasts are small and taut, shining as she begins the angular moves of her seductive dance.

Under my blankets, I touched my chest, grazing my hands softly over my nipples as I imagined the women stroking me. I envisioned the two of them in black garter belts, holding their pieces of mirror, running them over each other's bodies. The chauffeur pulling a small knife from her corset, trailing it up the seam of her stockings, sliding it over her nipples. She watched the women kissing, hands inside each other's lace panties, bras pushed to the side as they licked each other's necks and breasts. She watched them and licked her knife. Her nails polished in black, her heavy eyelids dusted in black.

THE NEXT DAY was Saturday and Reg took us all to the falls. My family had been going to the falls for years, since before my dad died. It was a big provincial park a couple of hours from the city, with a stunning drop of white foaming water that fell from a rocky cliff and a grassy area to admire it from as you sat on your blanket and chewed your picnic foods. It was too cold really to picnic, but my mother insisted it would be fun, so I packed the hamper and we set off.

My sisters promptly devoured their sandwiches and apple slices, and then ran around, playing some screaming chasing game. I sat shivering with my mom and Reg on the blanket, our coats wrapped around us. We watched the falls and made small pieces of conversation. Reg started telling a story about his time in the military. It involved a conflict over a woman, and Reg was the victor, apparently because he had pulled a knife on the other guy.

"That mofo didn't know what to expect," Reg said. "Of course, I wasn't going to use it. But he didn't know that." He laughed. "Scared little bastard." Then he paused, looking contemplatively at the waterfall. "We dated for two years," he said.

"You and the guy?" I asked.

Reg mock-punched my arm. "No, buddy. The lady. Not that I have a problem with gays. You been around as long as I have and you meet a few. It's no skin off my nose."

This was a first. Usually my mother's boyfriends didn't like "fags," as they called them, although more than one had told me that it was "okay for girls" if it was "casual." Meaning they had once had or hoped at some point to have a three-way. I was impressed that Reg had gay acquaintances. He didn't really seem like the liberal type, but I guess I had read him wrong.

As if she heard my thoughts, my mom reached over and patted Reg's leg. "He's very open-minded," she said. I hated it when my mother tried to sell me on her boyfriends. Most of them were stupid, racists and creeps. One guy, Fred—but he made us call him "Freddy" even though he was over fifty—used to refer to Majohn as "little China boy." When I told him it wasn't cool, he said it was all in fun and hummed a few bars of Bowie's "China Girl." "It's just like that song you guys listen to," Freddy said. "And Majohn doesn't mind. He even laughs when I say it!" The truth of it was that Majohn had this thing about respecting adults, even assholes, so he pretended to be amused but seethed quietly and stopped coming to my house until Freddy was banished by my mother.

"Fuck Bowie, man," Majohn said after that.

A lot of people thought Majohn was Chinese because his name sounded like mahjong and he looked Asian. His name was unusual, I'll admit, and had caused him some trouble—from teachers' mispronunciations to mocking from classmates. His

Filipina mother Malaya and white New Jersey–born father John had thought it was an act of deep devotion, or perhaps just cute, to combine their two names to create this new one. Over time, Majohn became proud of his name, and it came to distinguish him as someone who wasn't afraid to stand out from the crowd. If kids in middle school tried to make cracks about mahjong or some other dumb smear, he threw it back in their faces, calling them ignorant losers and motherfucker hillbillies. After a while the bullies left Majohn alone.

I seemed like an easier target—chubby, shy, headphones always clamped over my ears, blaring Depeche Mode or some other "gay" music. A group of mean jocks took it upon themselves to single me out—they even gave me a special nickname: "Slug." I never knew what it meant. Did they think I was slow? Slimy? Or just fat? I was definitely smarter than any of them; in middle school I had actually made the effort, got good grades. And unlike most guys my age, I bathed a lot, made sure that my hair was never greasy. Still, the torture continued daily until I graduated.

"What about you?" Reg asked me, taking a bite of his ham sandwich, careful to wipe any mayonnaise from his moustache. "What do you think about the gays?"

Direct questions like this usually make me uncomfortable, and I froze.

My mother answered for me. "Oh, Ryan's very open-minded too. Very open." She waved her hand at my black nail polish and blond-at-the-roots shoulder-length black hair. "Look how in touch he is with his feminine side." She laughed. "And the bands he listens to—you can't even tell the boys from the girls! Not that I mind. They're all pretty. I like the makeup."

She turned to me. "And some of them might be gay. Who cares? There's lots of gay people in the world. I mean, I wouldn't be surprised if one of your friends was gay, you know."

"I only have one friend," I said.

"But you'd be okay with it if Majohn was gay." She looked to Reg while making this point. "You just take people for whoever they are."

"Majohn isn't gay, but whatever." I grabbed another half sandwich and stood up. "I'm going to check out the falls."

"Just one thing," said Reg, finishing his sandwich and wiping his mouth one more time. He looked up at me. "If anyone ever tries to give you shit for anything, you come to me, okay? I'll have a little talk with them."

"What are you saying?" I asked. "You'll beat them up?"

He laughed. "Beat them up? No. I said I'd have a little talk with them. A little walk perhaps. Straighten them out."

"Uh, okay. Thanks." I walked away quickly. Why did my mom always have to make things so awkward? She could never just leave it alone. And Reg too. What was with the questions? Did they think I was gay, was that it? Had they talked about it? I imagined the two of them in Reg's sparsely furnished studio apartment, sipping whisky on the rocks and calmly discussing my possible gayness. The thought filled me with rage. I could even imagine my mother asking Reg if he knew any suitable young men. And complimenting him on how liberal-minded he was, how unlike her other boyfriends. Fucking gross.

REG STARTED COMING over a lot, bringing sausages or hamburgers to grill or a bottle of the sweet white wine my mom liked. He'd cook for us while my mom sat on a chair in the kitchen nook, entertaining him with stories from her work. She was a secretary at an elementary school and loved to talk shit about the teachers and the principal.

After dinner one night, while my mom was upstairs reading my sisters a bedtime story, I made the mistake of settling in on the saggy brown couch to do homework instead of sneaking off to my room to play Mario Bros. on my Atari. Reg took the opportunity to plant himself down next to me.

"Need any help with that?" He gestured at the algebra textbook open in my lap.

"No thanks."

He laughed. "Just as well. You probably know more about it than I do anyway. I think I failed it in high school."

"I thought you dropped out of high school."

"I didn't drop out. I just didn't finish. Didn't need to once I joined the army." He picked at one of his front teeth with his pinky nail, then caught himself and dropped his hand.

I stared at the fractions. In the glossy lamplight they seemed to slide around on the page. "Can I ask you something?"

"Sure." He smiled.

"Can I see your knife?"

His smile disappeared. "My knife?"

"Yeah. The one you were talking about the other day. Do you still carry it?"

"I've been carrying it for thirty years, Rye." He looked around the living room slowly as if trying to make a decision, his eyes passing over the soot-smeared bricks by the fireplace, the peeling beige paint my mother kept saying she'd get to fixing some weekend. His gaze finally settled on the old wooden credenza, the plastic lid of the record player my parents had gotten in the 70s. He turned to me and pulled a small rectangular object out of his front pocket and pressed a button. A short blade sprung out.

"Cool," I said.

"Do you want to hold it?" He passed it to me gently, as if it was something old and valuable, as if it was made of glass. "Be careful."

I held the switchblade's handle and turned it this way and that. The blade gleamed in the lamplight. It looked slim and sleek, like something a rock star would carry in his boot. "I want one," I said. "Just like this."

Reg took the knife back, closing the blade and slipping it into his pocket in one swift motion. "I don't think your mother would like that," he said.

"She won't care."

"I'm not so sure about that." He looked like he regretted what he'd just done.

"I won't use it or anything. I just think they're cool."

"I think your mother will say you're too young. Maybe when you're eighteen. For your birthday."

His assumption irritated me. How did he know he'd even be around by then? Given the way my mother went through boyfriends, he could be gone in two months.

"Whatever," I said, returning to my algebra book.

My mom came back and poured Reg a glass of the sweet wine and they started snuggling on the couch so I hurried off to my room.

TO REG'S SURPRISE, and mine, my mom agreed to let Reg take me to a pawn shop. We went after school on a Wednesday while my sisters were in dance class and my mom was doing aerobics at the community centre.

The place was in an old brick building on Burnside and smelled of dust, oil, and old leather. A woman with large dark freckles and a Caribbean accent greeted us. She was sitting on the floor, organizing a pile of cassettes that had slid off their shelf. There were stacks and stacks of them in plywood bookcases, coils of cords in baskets, piles of old stereo equipment, a tall rotating case with watches that were all stopped at different times. On the walls hung electric guitars and a few rusty bikes leaned against the back wall. A classic rock station was playing and the woman hummed along to "Free Bird."

"How can I help you?" she asked.

"Do you have any knives?" Reg said. "Nothing big. Just looking for something for my nephew here." He patted me on the shoulder.

I gave him a look and mouthed, "Nephew?"

He winked.

"Those are locked behind the counter." The woman hoisted herself up and strode to the counter, where she pulled out a shallow wooden box with a glass cover. Inside were knives of various sizes, none much bigger than my hand. "They're mostly hunting and fishing knives," she said. "See anything you like?"

I pointed at a one with a wooden handle, its blade hidden in a black leather cover.

She unlocked the case and took it out, handing it to me. I pulled off the cover, examining the short blade. It curved sharply, which I hadn't expected, but I liked the way it looked—it made me think of medieval times for some reason, knights on horses, bandits in the woods, fishermen in fairy tales. It fit perfectly in my hand. There was even a little hole to slip my thumb through.

"That's so you can hold on to it while you're skinning a deer or whatever," the shop woman explained. "Better grip."

Reg nodded in agreement. "A good size, it looks like."

I nodded too. "I think this is the one," I said.

THERE WERE RULES. I couldn't take the knife to school. I couldn't show it to my sisters or tell them about it. I couldn't cut myself with it (my mom had recently had a training at her work and learned that cutting was a phenomenon among disturbed young people). I couldn't give it to Majohn or take it to his house. I had to hide it in my bedroom and I wasn't allowed to bring it anywhere else in the house. I agreed to every rule. I still didn't know exactly why I wanted a knife and I was still surprised that my mother had let me get one. Was she getting more lax since dating Reg? Was she just supremely confident that I wouldn't hurt anyone else or myself? Even I knew that a boy with a knife is a worrisome, possibly dangerous, thing.

But Reg must have worked some sort of magic on her, because my mother seemed unperturbed by my new acquisition.

IT WAS ONLY a week before I took the knife to school to show to Majohn. We were walking around the track as usual, chugging chocolate milk and telling dumb jokes. Majohn was still trying to get closer to Tamiko. They had actually spoken on the phone a few times, but they still weren't going out. Majohn was working on a plan to take her to the movies and to McDonald's for lunch. I told him McDonald's was lame and he should take her to the Black Cat, a cool coffee shop downtown. He countered that it was cheap not to take his date out for lunch. "Then take her somewhere *nice*," I said.

"I can't afford anywhere nice." He kicked a tuft of grass at the side of the track with his sneaker. "I need to get a job."

Majohn and I were just at the age where we could start working, and both of our parents had been dropping hints that we should.

"Maybe you can get a job at McDonald's and treat her to lunch on your break," I cracked.

Majohn gave me a dirty look. "I'm serious," he said. "I have to show her I can bring it. That I'm, like, for real."

I glanced at the bleachers. Tamiko and her crew weren't hanging out there today. They'd probably decided to skip their afternoon classes and head downtown. Maybe that's why Majohn was so testy—they hadn't invited him along.

"Want to see what my mom's boyfriend got me?" I asked.

Majohn shrugged. "I guess."

I pulled the knife out of my pocket with a flourish and whipped off the leather sleeve.

"What?" He looked shocked.

"I know. Cool, right?"

Majohn looked around furtively, but there was no one nearby, just the track smelling of rain and old tires, the drooping wet grass. "What are you doing, man? You don't bring that shit to school." He shook his head. "You could get expelled. Put it away."

"I thought you'd think it was cool."

"It's not cool. It's scary. Seriously, man. Put it away."

He didn't call me "bitch" or "motherfucker," which meant he was upset. I hastily slipped the sleeve back on and shoved the knife down deep in my pocket. "Sorry. I didn't mean to freak you out."

He looked annoyed and started walking faster, toward the school. "We'd better get to class."

The bell hadn't even rung, but I hurried after him as if it had. "Look, I'm sorry, Majohn. It was stupid of me. I'm a stupid mother-fucker, you know." I tried to smile.

He shook his head and kept walking. "Sometimes I don't know about you. You won't even smoke a clove anymore, you won't even skip class, but now you have this knife. It's just weird."

"It doesn't mean anything. It's just something my mom's boyfriend got me. I'll leave it at home, I promise. I won't bring it again."

Majohn just shook his head angrily and rushed into the building. The bell blared and I followed after him, taking the stairs two at a time.

BACK HOME I slammed all of the doors on the way to my room, but it was a Wednesday and there was no one around to experience my wrath. I climbed into bed, pulling the covers over my head, and put my earphones on. I tried to think of a song that was sad enough to play, but none of them seemed good enough. I lay back in bed. What had I done? It was stupid, and now Majohn was mad at me. I thought of Majohn smoking on the bleachers with Tamiko and her friends. He was looking cool, saying all the right things. Tamiko was laughing. Tamiko. An image of her in a lacy black bra and panties flashed in my mind, and I got hard and felt ashamed in the same instant. But I couldn't stop myself—no one was home. I started unbuttoning my jeans. The Tamiko in my mind now had a riding crop and was hitting it against her hand as she sat with her legs suggestively open on the couch. My family was on vacation. She was saying her parents didn't expect her home, we had all the time in the world. I stroked myself faster. Tamiko was pulling off her panties, climbing on top of me. She was so wet, so warm. I came hard into my hand, panting into the blanket covering my face.

AFTER A FEW months Reg stopped coming around. My mom became depressed. She drank lots of weird herbal tea, mixes she got at the health food store that she said were for cleansing, and cried a lot on the couch, wrapped in a scraggly crocheted blanket. I tried to comfort her by playing sunny Beatles songs on the old stereo and cooking apple pancakes on the weekends. I picked my sisters up from their dance lessons and took them to the park on weekends, pushing them on the swings and the merry-go-round.

One Saturday night we all dressed up in my mom's old dresses, brightly coloured polyesters in paisleys and stripes, and wigs from her partying days—bouffants, Cleopatras, long blond curls. We put on a show for her, prancing around the living room, the dresses slipping off my sisters' shoulders as we lip-synced to "Come Together" and took pictures with her camera. She laughed for the first time in weeks and called us her cherubs. Watching me sashay across the living room, she said, "You know I don't care if you're gay, right? You know I'll still love you."

My sisters laughed and chanted, "We'll still love you too! We'll still love you!"

"Mom, shut up," I said. "Everyone, shut up."

She swiftly changed the subject. "What happened to Majohn? He hasn't come over in a while."

Of course I couldn't tell her the truth, so I made up a serviceable lie. "He got a girlfriend," I said. It was only after I said it out loud that I realized it probably wasn't a lie. He and Tamiko were probably dating by now. I followed it up with a truth. "He got too cool for me."

"Oh sweetie," my mom said, patting my wig.

I shrugged away. "It's cool. I was getting sort of sick of him anyway. Always showing off. Flexing his muscles and dumb shit like that."

My mother shot me a dirty look at the word *shit*. My sisters snickered.

"I mean *stuff*." I took off my Cleopatra wig and set it by the stereo. "And he smokes now. It's gross." My mom hated smoking.

"Oh honey, well. Maybe it's for the best."

"Yeah." I knew I didn't sound very convincing.

REG WAS ONLY gone for a few weeks. He returned one evening when we were all out on the front porch playing gin rummy. It was spring and the neighbourhood was full of droning lawnmowers, neighbours pruning rose bushes and planting gardens. Reg roared up on a shiny red motorcycle, and when he pulled off his helmet, I could see that his silver hair was shorter than ever—a crew cut—and his face was deeply tanned. He'd been on a road trip, he said. Texas. That's where he traded in his car for the motorcycle. He apologized for not sending us postcards.

He bent my mom over backward to kiss her and she shrieked happily. Or was she acting? Either way, it was back on, it appeared. Had he told her it was only a vacation, only temporary? I wasn't sure. My mom sometimes told me too much about her dating life but at other times she withheld her confidences. I could never figure out why certain things were shared and certain things weren't.

My sisters hugged Reg's legs but I kept my distance. "No postcards, huh? That's no way to treat a nephew." I glared.

He laughed and tried to grab me in a bear hug, but I squirmed away.

My mom looked back and forth at us, confused. "Nephew?"

"Private joke," I said sarcastically, giving Reg an exaggerated wink.

My mom looked at him questioningly.

"Not in front of the girls," he said, then mouthed the word *knife* at my mother.

My sisters were looking bored anyway, so my mom sent them back up to the porch to play cards.

After an awkward pause, Reg explained, "When we went shopping for the knife, I told them he was my nephew so it wouldn't seem strange."

"Oh … the knife." My mother sounded hesitant. Had she forgotten about it? I never brought it out while she was home. In fact, I hadn't even looked at it in weeks. It was tucked away in my bottom dresser drawer, under my socks and boxers. It only showed up in my imagination, when I thought of Tamiko. I imagined her taking it out of its sheath slowly and sliding it carefully across my arms, then down my stomach. I never went so far as to imagine her cutting me—the sight of blood made me nauseous—but I did imagine her pressing the blade into my skin, telling me to take my clothes off or she would slice me. She held it between her teeth, as I had once seen a brawny actor do in an action movie. She licked it and held it up to the light.

"Still got it, buddy?" Reg asked.

I shrugged. "I guess. I don't really take it out much."

He patted me on the back. "Well, it's there if you need it. If anyone at school starts giving you crap."

"He's not taking it to school." My mom's voice was indignant. "What are you saying?"

"Not *to* school. I mean … if bullies at school … he could meet them off the grounds …"

I had never seen Reg stumble like this before. He was trying to bring the pleased look back to my mother's face, but I had a feeling that wasn't going to happen—at least not tonight. And something about my mother's expression—lips clamped, eyebrows knitted together—told me that it wouldn't be long before she told Reg to take a hike. She'd already made it through the heartbreak, after all. She wasn't going to let him put her through that again.

"Well, I'd better hit the homework," I said. It was hard not to sound cheery. "Later, you guys." I took the stairs two at a time, patting my sisters' heads as I passed them.

MAJOHN HAD BEEN avoiding me for months, but toward the end of the school year he sought me out again as I was walking my new route in the field by the back fence. It had been a dry spring and the grass had a burnt look. The air smelled like dry hay and rubber. I was going over algebra equations in my head for the test I had that afternoon.

"Hey, Ryan!" Majohn jogged up to me.

I turned to him. "Hey, Majohn." He was wearing a new black New Order T-shirt and some grey Converses that he'd drawn anarchy symbols on in thick black marker.

"I go by MJ now, actually."

"Really?" I tried not to snicker.

"Yeah. Trying to keep it short, like simple, you know."

"Okay."

"Listen …" He looked around the field, then back at the school.

His friends were draped over the bleachers, smoking and laughing. I saw Tamiko leaning over her hands. It looked like she was painting her nails. What colour? I wondered. Probably black.

"I'm sorry about freaking out. You know, about the knife," Majohn said.

I shrugged. "That was a long time ago."

"I know, but I just wanted to say."

"Okay." I looked over at the track where a couple of preppy girls were jumping up and down, practising a dance or a cheerleading routine. I wasn't interested but I watched them as if I was.

Majohn seemed nervous; he kept running his fingers through his black bangs and pulling them back from his face. "It's sort of awkward to ask, but …" He looked away from me, back at the bleachers. "Do you still have it?"

I felt heat rise from my stomach and flood my face. Was he going to make me part of some practical joke? Humiliate me in front of his cool friends? I tried to make my voice stone. "No."

"Oh."

"Why do you ask?"

"No reason." He combed his bangs back again. He had grown them out over the last few months and they fell down to his cheekbones. His face looked thinner, and strangely, older, as if he'd been travelling in some rugged country for a few years and had just returned. Even his shoulders seemed broader. He looked at me closely. "I can still tell when you're lying, you know."

"Why do you care?"

"I was going to see if I could buy it off you."

I stared at him, not knowing what to say. Behind him the group on the bleachers were starting to gather their bags and cigarettes. Tamiko was waving her hands in the air to dry her nail polish. Today she looked tomboyish, in ripped black jeans and an oversized T-shirt that nearly came down to her knees. I quickly averted my gaze, feeling embarrassed. I had still never had an actual conversation with her, had never really looked her in the face.

"Not for me," Majohn said quickly. "It's for Tamiko. I want to get her one."

I still didn't say anything. The girls on the track were doing lunges, and then one crouched down and the other climbed onto her back. It looked like she was about to balance herself on the other girl's shoulders. Definitely cheerleaders.

"So she can feel safe, you know?" He tried to meet my eyes. "She's small. I want her to be able to protect herself."

"Well isn't that sweet." I had meant to be only lightly sarcastic, but a bitter edge crept into my voice.

Majohn looked at me, surprised.

I tried to even out my tone. "Does Tamiko even want a knife? I mean, have you asked her?"

He looked bashful. "I was going to surprise her."

"It might just freak her out."

Majohn shrugged and shifted uncomfortably. "I just want her to be safe."

"You want to be a hero, is what you want."

"Listen," Majohn said, "I know we don't hang out much anymore, but you don't have to be rude."

The bell rang. The cheerleaders sprinted past us, laughing. Maybe they were on the track team. I dully watched students stream toward the building, some dragging their feet, clutching greasy fast food bags; others gossiping in clusters or throwing a football back and forth as they ran, yelling. I stared down at the dry grass, wishing I knew what to say.

Majohn turned and jogged back toward the bleachers where his friends were huddled, waiting for him. Tamiko held out her arms as he ran closer.

I thought of the knife back home, nestled in the drawer with my socks and underwear. I imagined taking it back to the pawn shop, the woman with freckles putting bills in my palm. I imagined handing it back to Reg and telling him I didn't want it anymore.

I imagined Majohn giving it to Tamiko, the two of them lit in cozy lamplight, sitting on the floral couch at Majohn's house, the knife wrapped in some tacky paper patterned with gold hearts and roses. Would she smile and lean in to kiss him, or would she hold it limply like a dead fish and look at him with disgust?

I watched Majohn's gang trail toward the school doors. The tall mohawked kid looked like he was chuckling at something as he bent down to grind out his cigarette in the grass. Majohn had his arm around Tamiko's shoulders and was whispering in her ear. Beside me was the dusty field, the grass dead before summer had even begun. Behind me were blocks and blocks of drab houses and rundown apartments that lead to my own small house with its peeling paint and broken bottom step. In front of me was the school where I would have to spend the next three years. I hoped I wouldn't always be alone.

DARK AND RAINY

I STILL THINK of her. She's coming home from work or on her way to a date with a soon-to-be lover. She's wearing a blue dress, the kind that flares at the knees, that would twirl if it wasn't flattened by damp—I'm seeing it, an electric blue, and over it a dark wool coat, buttoned tightly. And she's hurrying in the rain so doesn't look up at the row of cherry and chestnut trees, the knobby trunks and bare reaching branches. She clutches the handle of her black umbrella and looks down at the cold rain driving through her tights, chilling her ankles, and wishes she was already there, at the restaurant looking over the menu, deciding perhaps on the salmon or the pilaf, or already at home, wrapped in a warm quilt on the couch, balancing her cup of tea as she reaches for the remote control.

And she doesn't see him. And he doesn't see her.

IN THE SHADOWY kitchen alcove there were always five or six two-litre jugs of Coca-Cola lined up next to the fridge. On my first visit, Karla gestured to them and said, "Those are for Berl. But help yourself—there's always one open in the fridge. He drinks the stuff like water." She shrugged and gave a slight smile. She took a large orange plastic cup out of the cupboard and showed it to me. Apparently it was reserved specifically for Berl's soda drinking, and although she didn't say it, the implication was that Berl wouldn't be happy if anyone else used it.

Berl was a large man, over six feet tall and built like a barrel, yet there was something gentle and child-like about him. He wore jean overalls with checkered flannel shirts underneath and steel-toed work boots, and he didn't talk very much. An electrician, he worked most weekdays, but he didn't drive, which is why Karla was always the one to pick me up and drop me off.

The children were from Berl's first marriage and had only recently moved in. They were sweet children, but they both had a slightly feral look about the face that kept me somewhat on guard. Karla told me that they had weekly court-mandated visits with their mother, a heavy drinker who ran around with sketchy men.

Both children wet the bed and one of my jobs was to go into their rooms after they'd been sleeping for a couple of hours and sniff at the air over their beds. If I smelled urine, I was to wake them up and change the sheets and their pyjamas. I usually pretended to forget this duty. I rationalized that it was better to let them sleep comfortably, even if it was in the warm beds of their own piss, then to put them through the shock of a sudden late-night awakening. I figured their parents could give them a bath in the morning.

The little girl, Ivy, was six and sucked her thumb obsessively. She often wanted to play "Baby," speaking in lispy toddler-talk and rolling about on the sofa with her arms and legs waving in the air. I indulged her, wrapping her in a blanket and patting her back, pretending to burp her, saying, "Good baby, good baby." But her tolerance for the game always exceeded mine, and after a time I'd have to tell her that was enough. She liked to cuddle up next to me on the couch while I read picture book after picture book meant for children half her age while she marvelled at the illustrations. She could read most of the books herself, but never wanted to while I was there, insisting instead that I recite them to her.

The boy Thomas was a couple of years older and only wanted to watch TV. He favoured action movies or cop shows, but he wasn't picky—he'd watch anything. After dinner, he'd ask for potato chips, and I'd give him a handful in a little bowl. He'd plop down on his stomach on the carpet in front of the TV and shovel the chips into his mouth, enraptured by whatever was on screen.

The second night I came to their house we all sat in the living room, a room every bit as dim as the kitchen, lit only by a couple of weak lamps. I was reading to Ivy on the couch when Thomas turned from the TV and said he wanted to go to his room to do homework.

"Homework?" I'd asked him. "You're only eight. What homework could you possibly have?"

He shrugged and glanced off to the corner of the room with a sneaky look. "Everything. Math. Stuff."

"Bring it here then." I patted the couch for him to sit next to me. "I'll help you."

An angry expression streaked across his face and he turned back to the TV.

I had been instructed to never let him stay alone in his room for more than a few minutes. Karla had explained the issue: Thomas had a masturbation problem. Once he started, he couldn't stop, and if left to his own devices would jerk off for hours at a time. It even interfered with his sleep, she told me.

Karla told me that she had been made aware of this one night soon after the kids moved in. She and Berl lay panting in the dark after having sex and they gradually became aware of a sound from the other side of the wall, a huffing and shuffling from Thomas's bed. He had been listening to them, she realized, and was at first so angry she told Berl they'd never have sex in the house again. But then she calmed down and made him go into Thomas's room to stop him.

After that she and Berl moved their bed to the other side of the room and the kids started counselling.

Both of the children had dark smudges under their eyes. Ivy's were so deep that they looked like bruises. Thomas's made him appear older than he was, a miniature middle-aged man who needed only a cigarette dangling from the corner of his mouth to complete the look. Karla told me sometimes Ivy awoke crying from nightmares and had to come sleep with her and Berl. Karla worried about this happening too often. She didn't want Thomas to feel left out.

THERE WAS A tired glamour about Karla, although she wasn't that old, only in her thirties. She was quite tall, as tall as Berl, and she always wore low heels in bold colours like turquoise or gold, even on weekends when she didn't have to go into the office. Over her dresses she wore a long camel-hued trench coat, belted at the waist, that gave her the mysterious air of a spy or sexy detective. But the most arresting thing about Karla was her hair. It was dark and thick and hung past her shoulders. Often when talking or thinking she'd unconsciously tuck several strands behind her ear even when they weren't falling in her face. Sometimes I wondered if I had a crush on her or if it was just her hair I was attracted to.

I WAS GLAD that Karla was the one to drive me. In my previous babysitting jobs it was usually the fathers, and some of them had been creeps. One time a pot-bellied guy with coffee breath tried to hug me as I was turning to get out of the car, and when I shrugged him away he mumbled some dumb excuse about being so grateful for the care I showed his kids. After that the rides home were pretty awkward. Inexplicably, he started to overpay me. Sometimes a wink accompanied the extra cash—I wasn't sure what he hoped I'd give him for the money but I never did give him anything, except my silence. I never told his wife and after a couple of months I quit the gig.

The babysitting jobs were only to fill the gap until I could get a real job at Arctic Circle, a fast food place where my best friend worked. The manager promised he'd hire me once I turned sixteen. I could legally work there at fourteen, but he preferred to hire "older girls" in at least their third year of high school because he claimed they were more mature.

I TRIED TO be a respectful babysitter. I wasn't the kind who ate all the cookies and chips in the cupboards or refused to do the dishes, or got on the phone and yammered with her friends all night, leaving the kids to tear around the house on their own. If there was a bowl of change on the entryway table or a jar of quarters in the parents' bedroom, I didn't help myself. I paid attention to the kids, I cleaned up after them and put them to bed on time. I did have one habit I wasn't proud of, though.

Karla and Berl's room was just down the hall, across from the bathroom. The door was usually closed but one night in their hurry to leave for their movie they left it ajar. As I tried to study on the couch, I kept thinking of that door beckoning from the end of the hallway, open as if in invitation.

I was always looking for something unexpected, something that would tell me a story, would reveal the parents in a different light. These were people who gave me complete access to their homes for a few hours every week, but I had no access to their inner lives—I barely knew them. I wanted to find dirty magazines, love letters, porn videos, sex toys, and lingerie—and sometimes I did.

On the top of one dresser there were a few perfume bottles and a wedding photo in a silver frame, beaming Karla and shiny-faced Berl. I opened the top drawer, sifting through the contents, mostly cotton panties similar to the ones I wore, bright colours and jazzy prints that came in packs of four. Like most women, Karla had a few flimsy lace items and I ran my hands over them. As I grasped the edge of a filigreed red bra and rubbed it between my fingers, a current pulsed through my hands and up my arms, and I felt my nipples tighten under my sweatshirt. My hand kept roving along the bottom of the drawer. I wondered if tonight I would find what one of my friends called "husband's little helper"—a vibrator, or a dildo. But why husband's helper, I had asked my friend. It's for the wife, right? Isn't she the one being helped? It helps him if he gets too tired, she said. If she wants more. If he can't keep it up. These were adult conversations, conversations my friend was comfortable with, having already slept with three boys and given several others blowjobs.

Something hard poked my hand, but it was just the roots of a little bundle of lavender, twisted together with purple ribbon. I lifted up a handful of panties and held them to my nose, breathing in. Some innocuous detergent, a trace of lavender on cotton and the polyester scent of cheap lace.

In the closet hung Karla's dresses, pastels and bold colours, some with lightning-bolt shapes or stripes, some with shoulder pads or big polka dots. A silky black number caught my eye and I pulled it from its hanger. It had high slits on both sides and an embroidered red dragon curled across the bodice. I held it to my chest and went to look in the mirror on the other side of the room. The dress was too long for me, but the torso looked like it might fit. I shimmied a little, imagining myself on some dance floor, the music swelling as I twirled in the arms of ... who?

Berl's side of the closet provided other intrigues—flannel shirts freshly laundered, a jean jacket smelling slightly of his signature musk, a touch of sweat, some mechanical oil. I slipped a checkered flannel off of its hanger and pulled it over my head, strutting to the mirror. I crossed my arms in front of me and affected a lounging posture, curling my lip in a sexy sneer. But the effect was not what I hoped. The shirt was comically large, and even as I tried to arrange it over my sweatshirt, it stubbornly refused to look cool. It resembled nothing but some hand-me-down of my father's that I'd wear to sleep on cold winter nights. It showed me only that I was not a stud.

ONE NIGHT AS Karla was driving me home she took an unexpected turn on a busy street a few blocks from my house. "Sorry." She pulled into the parking lot of a Rexall. "I just have to stop here for a minute." She rushed out of the car and into the store before I could say anything. I looked around. There were only a few other cars in the lot, one a few spots away in which it appeared two people were making out, a slow fog starting to climb up the windows. I thought of the urban legend from my mother's time that still circulated in the halls of my own high school—a couple getting it on in a car, a scratching at the window, some madman on the prowl. And the couple later finding his hook-hand attached to the door. The fear: what he would have done to them. Even as a teenager I recognized this story for what it was, sheer nonsense, an attempt to scare young women away from having sex. I recognized it, but the story still freaked me out, and it made me angry that it got to me at all.

I turned away and examined the uninspired drugstore displays—pink boxes of cosmetics stacked on top of each other, a large teddy bear with a red bow around its neck, a poster of a woman in a Santa hat smiling, her huge teeth shining in the garish light.

It was a cold night. I snuggled into my coat, wondering why Karla's errand couldn't wait until after she dropped me off. Just then she came hurrying out of the store, stuffing a small white bag into her purse. "Sorry," she said, as she got back into the car. "I just didn't know how late they'd be open."

We headed toward my street. It was a Tuesday night, not much traffic. Although it was only early December, a few over-eager holidayists had already strung up their Christmas lights. The colours glimmered and pulsed across the windshield as we drove by. "Some day you'll have to get one of these." Karla nodded at her purse sitting in the space between us. "And pray it's negative, in your case. At least while you're young, that is."

From the beginning, Karla had talked to me like an adult, which I appreciated, and a few times she had told me things that made me feel like her friend or confidant. But I was still surprised by this reveal. A pregnancy test? This was what she was stopping for so late at night?

We drifted under streetlights, over the glinting night-frost on the black streets. She held the steering wheel with both hands, her eyes on the road. "We've been trying for a couple years. Berl's anxious for another child."

This surprised me. It wasn't that Berl wasn't an engaged parent—he was very engaged. He asked the kids questions about their days at school, he assigned easy chores around the house to give them a sense of responsibility. He tried. He tried very hard. He'd wrestle with Thomas all over the living-room floor, or take him out to his truck and try to teach him how to use his electrician tools. He'd buy the kids presents, board games that were too advanced for them, plastic dolls in stiff ugly dresses that Ivy found too stupid to bother playing with, or toy fire engines for Thomas that fell apart in a week.

Sometimes I'd catch Berl standing in the doorway of the living room, hands hanging at his sides as he watched the children romp around on the carpet. The look on his face—as if he was trying to figure out what to do, if it was okay for him to join them or if he should just let them be.

"And I want one too, of course." Karla laughed. "By the time she was my age, my mother had four kids. As she likes to keep reminding me."

She pulled up in front of my house, a small one-storey painted dark green, no Christmas lights. Our next-door neighbour's house blared neon red and white, their path lined with huge lit-up candy canes and their front yard dominated by a blow-up Santa that was as tall as their balcony.

I wasn't sure what to say in response to her confidences, and when she turned to look at me, I blurted out, "I don't want kids."

She didn't look surprised. She tucked her hair behind her ear. "I don't blame you. They're a lot of work."

"I'm not going to change my mind," I said. "Everyone always says I'm going to. I'm not."

Karla smiled. "Well, just be careful with the boys then. Be sure to make them use protection. Or are you already on the pill?"

The pill? "No," I said, looking over at the huge Santa. It was drooping slightly forward and I hoped it would tumble onto the neighbour's lawn and short out all of their obnoxious lights. "I'm not."

She looked at me, waiting.

"I'm just not."

She nodded as if she understood but I doubted that she did.

SHE'S A TOMBOY—that's what they used to call girls like her. Tall, in corduroys, walking with her shoulders hunched forward in a jean jacket, black hoody pulled down low over her forehead. She's too cool for an umbrella even in this city of abundant rainstorms. Hands stiff from the cold, scrunched in her pockets—I think of those hands, what I would have liked them to do to me, a lonely fifteen-year-old who didn't yet know any girls like her. She's watching the toes of her sneakers fill up with water as she walks, the laces soaking up the rain like fat white worms. Her mind's on something. She's not totally aware. Or she's vigilant, looking over her shoulder, glancing up and down the dark street. She sees him coming through the sheets of rain, his headlights drawing shadows from the trees' long branches. She sees him coming and she thinks he will stop.

AFTER A FEW weeks Thomas got sick of television—all he wanted was to be as close to me as possible. He'd try to push Ivy off of my lap and climb on in her place. Or he'd snuggle at my side for as long as I'd allow, feigning interest in the toddler-level picture books as he pressed his thigh against mine. He kissed my arm. He kissed my cheek if he could reach it. I wasn't sure how to deal with this. Most of the kids I babysat were content to zone out in front of the TV for hours on end or play on their own. Most of them only wanted a little hug when I tucked them in; some of them didn't want me to touch them at all, preferring to cuddle with their stuffed animals.

I tried to set a limit for Thomas—just two hugs a night, one when I arrived, and one before he went to bed. But it didn't work—at the slightest provocation Thomas would cling to me as if he was drowning and I was the raft that would keep him alive. He'd run screeching from a fight with Ivy, faking some injury that I'd have to coddle. He'd pretend to be scared of stupid passages in the books we read just so he could jump into my arms. Ivy noticed and tried to sneak her way in as well, and inevitably the two of them would fight, pushing and shoving to get a better spot next to me.

I tried another strategy: a pillow on each side of me when I read to them on the couch. I decreed that they could not reach over the pillow and that they could not touch me or each other. But this didn't work either. Thomas would find a way to squish his leg under the pillow or Ivy would reach over and brazenly trail her fingers across the back of my neck.

So I gave up these boundaries and just tried to distract them. I brought a deck of cards from my parents' house and taught them rummy, but they struggled with the rules and soon lost interest. I fed them large bowls of mint chocolate chip, doling out extra scoops that I'd been instructed by Karla not to give. I figured anything that kept them out of their bedrooms and off of my lap was essentially okay.

FOR CHRISTMAS BERL hit the jackpot—he finally bought Ivy and Thomas a present they both adored: a huge Lego set. The kids would spend their evenings building elaborate cities and crafting intricate plots that occupied them for hours, right up until bedtime. It made my job a lot easier. I'd join in sometimes, playing some minor character, but often I'd just do homework on the couch with one ear cocked their way in case things got out of hand.

Ivy favoured a robot Lego person she called the Princess and wanted all of the stories to revolve around her. Thomas demanded that his hero, a ninja Lego, dominate the plot. Sometimes the two would battle but just as often they would work together against an outside antagonist—a "criminal" (I wasn't sure how they'd learned that word) who needed to be punished. The kids especially liked building jails and locking the criminal up—although sometimes he would escape and then would need to be beaten and locked up again. It was the one plot the two children could consistently agree upon and they seemed to never tire of playing it.

The games took a weirder turn when after a couple of weeks Ivy introduced the Monster, one of the stiff blond baby dolls Berl had given her. The Monster would essentially show up just to wreck the place—she'd stomp on whatever structures the kids had built and yell "Die die die!" "Give me my baby!" was another variation on the Monster's theme. The Princess was the Monster's baby, and the Monster had come to rescue her—from what, it was never clear.

Thomas didn't appreciate this new character and would try to fight back with his ninja, making it jump around the Monster's legs and up on its shoulders and head, yelling incomprehensible dialogue about spells and magic. But Ivy refused to back down and the game would degenerate into the two of them screaming at each other and hitting each other with the toys.

I banned Lego for a while after that and we returned to reading picture books on the couch.

One night I was reading to Thomas while Ivy was in the bathroom. We sat under the weak light of one of the living room lamps, turning the pages slowly as we discussed the pictures. I'd just warmed up heaping bowls of Berl's homemade spaghetti and meatballs, and the house still smelled of garlicky tomato sauce and fragrant beef. Underneath it was a musty wood smell from the damp seeping into the old window frames—it was raining again, a cold January rain that dashed against the windows, the sound like someone throwing handful after handful of tiny pebbles at the glass.

Thomas looked up from the book spread across our laps and asked, "Can I see your boobies?"

Perhaps I should have been prepared for a moment like this, but I wasn't. Still, the answer came quickly. "No. You can't."

"Why?"

"It's not appropriate. They're private. They're mine. Just like you have private parts of your body."

"I don't have any private parts." He flipped the edges of the pages with his thumb and looked at me out of the corner of his eyes.

"You do. Everyone does."

"I saw Karla's boobies."

I wasn't sure how to respond so I waited to see what else he'd say.

"When she was getting out of the shower. The door was open

so I looked. I saw her thing too. It had hair."

"Thomas, that's not okay." I made my voice stern. "You shouldn't be doing that. Even if the door is open, you don't look in when someone's in the bathroom. It's private. Don't do that again, okay?"

He looked back down at the book and played with the pages, an inscrutable look on his face.

"Okay?"

Ivy came back then, before I could get an answer out of him. She nestled in on the other side of me and we continued reading about Clifford the Big Red Dog and his galumphing adventures. The children laughed and made jokes and the tense moment passed.

LATER THAT NIGHT on the drive home Karla told me that Ivy was waking her and Berl up almost nightly and that now Thomas was having nightmares too. I had noticed in recent weeks that Karla looked even more tired than usual, the dark circles under her eyes deepening to match the children's. I didn't want to add another brick to her heavy exhaustion but I had to tell her about the incident with Thomas, and so I did.

She didn't react initially—she just kept driving slowly, staring straight ahead. She tucked her hair behind her ears a couple of times and kept her eyes on the road. Waves of rain rolled over the asphalt. I looked out the window at the large puddles drowning the curbs, sewer grates clogged with dead leaves. Entire sidewalks were eaten up by these rain-lakes. The streetlamps reflected in them, thin wavering moons.

When we pulled up in front of my house, Karla said, "I always lock the bathroom door. That story Thomas told you was a lie." She turned off the ignition and looked out the windshield. My house was dark except for the porch light—it could barely be seen through the sheeting rain. It was past eleven and so my parents were already asleep, the curtains drawn. "The counselling doesn't seem to be helping." Her voice was quiet.

She rested her forehead on the steering wheel. "I know it takes time. It takes time." A sigh came up from somewhere deep inside her body. "But sometimes I'm just so exhausted."

"Maybe Berl could help?" The question was out of my mouth before I knew what was happening. "I mean, I know he helps out but, maybe if he gets his licence again ..." I didn't know why I was suggesting this. I certainly didn't want Berl driving me home.

Karla lifted her head and looked over at me, her expression tinged with incredulity, as if she was just then registering how young I was, how little I actually understood. "No, Natalie. He can't help with driving. He'd still be in jail if he hadn't had such a good lawyer. He won't ever get his licence back."

She looked down at her lap, her face serious. I felt like I'd disappointed her and I wished I hadn't opened my stupid mouth.

I had understood that Berl had done something bad while driving and that it was probably related to alcohol, as there was never any of it in the house and Karla had made a point of telling me the first time I came over that they didn't drink. So he had been arrested for drunk driving, I assumed, but did that mean he could never drive again? I hadn't yet studied for the driving test and didn't know any of the rules of the road or any of the laws. My friends and I drank—a lot, often—but none of us owned cars and most of us couldn't drive. We were usually drunk in the back seats of the night bus or on the long sodden walks home from house parties. I guess I had always assumed that after a significant period of sobriety Berl would be able to get his licence again.

The rain washed over the windshield. Heavy drops drummed down on the roof of the car. I looked over at Karla, wishing I could do something. I thought of trying to lighten the mood by telling her about Ivy and Thomas's jokes, how earlier they'd been comparing the antics of Ivy's doll the Monster to those of Clifford the Big Red Dog. I wanted to make her smile. But I could tell that there was something desperate and inappropriate about this desire. I was just the babysitter, after all.

JANUARY DRIPPED AND sleeted to its close. In a month the early daffodils and pale crocuses would start to sprout and I would finally be able to begin my job at Arctic Circle. It paid a dollar more an hour than babysitting, and I would be able to get twenty hours a week, bringing in an unprecedented amount of money. What would I do with it all? I wanted to buy some black jeans, a new winter coat, and my parents kept telling me that I should start saving for college if I wanted to go because they wouldn't be able to help with that.

One drizzly February evening Karla picked me up as usual, and as we chatted on the ride to the house I kept thinking I should tell her it was my last night, but my courage kept slipping away from me.

As we entered the back door, I heard laughter in the living room, and something I hadn't heard before—a play-growl that could only belong to Berl, a truly comedic sound. Peering into the living room, I saw him on all fours, trying to avoid the Lego pieces scattered all over the rug as he lumber-crawled toward the children. "Bear is coming," he said between chuckling growls.

Ivy and Thomas were also on all fours, laughing as they scrambled away from him. "Oh no, it's a bear, he's going to get us!" Ivy screeched, her voice rising ecstatically with the melodrama of it all.

"Get her, Dad, get her!" yelled Thomas as he bounded up on the couch and put a pillow over his head that he peeked out from under. "Get her first! She's the bad guy!"

Berl stopped and reared up on his knees, flailing his hands in the air and roaring. The children screamed delightedly. I don't know that I'd ever seen them look so happy.

Karla came up and stood next to me, smiling and shaking her head. "Hey, Mr. Bear," she said. "I'm sorry to interrupt but we're going to be late for our reservation."

I would have imagined a bit of chagrin from Berl at being found in such a ridiculous position in front of the babysitter, but to his credit he didn't look embarrassed. He smiled at me as if I was part of the family. I thought I might see something abashed in his eyes—some shyness at my witnessing this helpless love, his almost desperate desire to please his children. But I didn't see it. He turned to the kids and stretched out his huge arms and they rushed toward him.

IT WAS NEARLY midnight and Karla was digging through her purse looking for her wallet. Exhausted from an evening of Lego theatrics, I leaned my head back against the seat and surreptitiously watched her, noticing the way her slightly smudged mauve eyeliner accentuated the dark shadows under her eyes. She already looked so tired—it didn't seem possible that she and Berl could be serious about having another child. But Karla had never told me the results of the test and for some reason I had assumed this meant it was positive.

Still digging through her purse, she said, "I wanted to tell you, in case you were wondering." She pulled out her wallet and took out a few bills, handing them to me. "I'm not pregnant after all." There was a slight pause and then she said, "Thank God."

I wasn't prepared for this response and said the first thing that came to mind. "But I thought you wanted a baby?"

"Berl wanted a baby." She rested her hands on the steering wheel. "I just want to take care of the two kids we already have."

I nodded. I knew it wasn't the best time to tell her, but I also knew there wasn't going to be a good time, so before I could think on it too much longer I quickly said, "I'll be sixteen next week."

Karla gave me a subdued smile. "Wow. Sixteen already. That's great. Happy birthday."

"And since I'll be sixteen, I'll be able to work at Arctic Circle. My friend got me a job. So I won't be able to babysit anymore. I'm sorry."

She nodded slowly as if agreeing with something but didn't look at me. Then she turned the keys in the ignition. The wipers started up, squeaking rhythmically as they scraped across the glass. This was my signal to quickly say my final goodbyes and open the door but as I turned to leave Karla put her hand on my arm and left it there. She had never touched me before and I was startled. My heart thrummed in my chest.

"Come visit the kids sometime, okay? They'll miss you," Karla said.

I'd never noticed before how deeply sad her eyes were.

I DON'T KNOW when I started thinking of her, if it was the year I finished grad school, the year my friend Julie spent the night in jail after the cops spotted her truck weaving across the road on the way home from that pool party. Maybe it was later, when I had moved from Denver back to the West Coast, when I started working for the publisher in Seattle and always stayed late, walking home alone in the rain, past dark storefronts and gardens of dripping hostas and ferns. I can't remember. She was just there one night, a misty apparition in the corner of my mind, taking shape as I walked uphill in the drizzling rain, noticing the way the bare branches held up their pearls of water as if for the streetlights' admiration.

In my imaginings she appeared in different guises, walking down different streets, but she was always young. I don't know how it was that I had decided she was young. Maybe I had heard something. Maybe Karla had told me that night in the car. I can't remember. The conversation had been so brief—Karla hadn't wanted to say much, I remember that. Her halting words. "He took a life." The way she phrased it was so distant, so unlike how she usually spoke.

"A woman's life." A young woman's life? This was years before Karla met him, before Ivy was born.

Sometimes I imagined Ivy and Thomas all grown up, living in a different neighbourhood or even a different city, somewhere bright like Phoenix or Las Vegas or L.A, somewhere where it rained less often. I thought of how they might look, what kinds of lives they might be living. Did Thomas become an electrician? Did Ivy? I kept seeing them as the children I had known, Ivy sucking her thumb, Thomas eating chips in front of the television in that dark house with its damp windowsills smelling of mould. I wondered when Berl finally told them what he had done, or if Karla had been the one to do it. Perhaps their mother blurted it out one drunken night and forgot by morning what she had said. But I bet the children never forgot. Did they keep seeing her after their court-ordered visits expired? I wondered if their mother ever stopped drinking, if Ivy or Thomas ever started.

I STILL DON'T understand, really, why I think of her. How sometimes, when I'm back in Portland and it's a dark night and I'm on my way to meet a friend for a drink on Hawthorne Street, she'll come to mind. I'll step off a curb just as it starts to rain, and I'll think of her. Later the rain might turn stormy, the wind might rear up, buckling my umbrella and tearing at my face and clothes. But it's just as the rain is starting that I think of her, the fat drops falling as she walks the green blocks of Southeast, lost in her thoughts. She adjusts her tights under her dress. Maybe her coat isn't warm enough and she pulls it close over her chest. She might be on her way to meet her lover, imagining the taste of her lips, the smell of her hair. She might be hungry, wishing the pasta was already steaming in front of her, the clams slightly open in the sauce.

Maybe I'm waiting for her at the bar, the band warming up onstage, guitars twanging as they are tuned, the sound of a tumbler being scooped in ice, the solid thump of it on the bar as the bartender lifts the bottle high for a double shot. It's not my drink—I'm waiting for her, and I'll order something when she arrives. I'll order something when she finally arrives.

NEW BEDS

AFTER READING THE short story, she was very emotional. She thought of past affairs, lovers lost—and the hot tears fell.

Later, making love with her lover, she cried more—during and after.

It had been two weeks since they had made love and two days since they had bathed. The smells were sweat, sweet armpit, salt, and musky hair—also fresh, earthy, like a pumpkin torn open.

FALL WAS, SHE concluded, sad. Early on, it seemed exuberant—the trees glimmering in so many shades of gold and orange. She'd halt her bike or pause her walk just to stare at the difference between a vermilion and a scarlet leaf stuck to the sidewalk.

But finally it was just sad. A few yellow leaves clinging to thin branches and the never-ending rain creating a slush-mush of rotten brown leaves that clogged the gutters.

THE DAY SHE read the short story, two lesbians—an acquaintance and her girlfriend—came to pick up a bed her lover had advertised on the Queer Exchange, an online buy and sell. Earlier that afternoon, she and her lover had bought a bed at a shop on Granville Street for a lot of money, the most money she'd ever spent on an object, although it was the cheapest bed in the shop.

Shopping for the bed had been enjoyable. Resting their heads on green cotton pillows, caressing oak and maple frames. Looking at all the floor models, examining the patterned fabrics of duvets they wouldn't buy and admiring stainless steel lamps curved over leather couches they couldn't afford.

After they had decided the floor model was comfortable enough and that it was okay to spend that much money, they were rung up by a chatty, queer-seeming clerk with slicked-back black hair and a button-up shirt. They started talking about excess, how North Americans have too much stuff, and about the book by the Japanese writer that was all the rage, getting everyone cleaning out their closets and feeling minimalist and righteous. The author recommended laying all of your clothes out on your bed and then picking items up one by one, holding each shirt, sweater, or pair of pants to gauge how you felt about it. She recommended emptying your handbag each day when you came home from work and thanking it before you hung it up on a hook that belonged only to it. The book made many assumptions. One was that every woman had at least one handbag. Another was that people would throw out their old belongings rather than give them to a thrift store.

The clerk had read this book and had gone through all his stuff, even getting rid of board games. Her lover had read it and had given half of her dresses to Goodwill—not Salvation Army because they were homophobes.

The clerk told them that the hardest thing to get rid of was his favourite T-shirt—an old one from high school with an indistinguishable logo, now a net of holes. In the end, he couldn't do it. "I cut it up into rags," he said. For some reason the image of this extremely well-groomed man cutting up an old stained T-shirt for rags was strangely comforting—it made the fact that they had just spent so much money on a bed more bearable somehow.

They went home and made love on the old bed before the younger lesbians came to pick it up. It was November, rainy, grey and grainy light in the light blue room and her lover's blue eyes were bright and tender, alive in the dim.

THE BED WAS new to them, these young lesbians, although old to her lover who was giving it away. One of the young lesbians had already lived with several lovers. This was a marvel to her. She thought that this hopefulness, this ongoing ability to begin again, must be the province of the young, although it was difficult to think of herself as ever having been this way, even when she was young.

As the young lesbians lifted the mattress up to the roof rack, they were laughing. The mattress almost slid into the muck of leaves and mud but they caught it just in time and hoisted it up. One tossed a coil of rope to the other and they began to tie it on.

She watched from the window. Her lover was already in the

kitchen making more coffee and singing snatches of an old blues tune.

The book of stories by the influential lesbian—dead now for decades—was there on the coffee table, waiting for her to pick it back up. The lamplight glinting on the gloss of the cover obscured the image of the writer's face, but in her mind's eye she could see her large glasses and slight smile, which she chose to imagine as wise.

THE CHARISMACIST

AT THE START of our second workshop, our teacher John walked into the room with a flowering Christmas cactus and set it in the middle of the table. "Take a gander at that," he said. "Feast your eyes." He pulled up a chair at the head of the table and looked around at each of us. "That's what your stories should be doing," he said. We waited for him to elaborate. He didn't. Finally, one of the students quipped, "Flowering?" And he cracked his bright white smile and pointed a finger at her emphatically. "Exactly," he said. "Exactly."

The next week he brought in warm blueberry muffins, baked by his wife, Marilyn. We already knew her name because he'd already mentioned her several times. He sat at the head of the table, and sitting next to him I could smell the tones of bergamot and cream as he sipped from his huge travel mug of Earl Grey. "A little nourishment," he had said as he set the plate of muffins on the table. "You are all looking a little peaked. It's hard work, this writing. Hard work. Not for the faint of heart." And he smiled his all-encompassing grin.

He was in his early fifties, still sexy, with dark wavy hair cut short, a few streaks of grey. He often told self-deprecating jokes and talked about taking his daughters to the playground or the difficulty of choosing the right gift for Marilyn's birthday. He told funny stories, like the one about reading a dinner table scene in a student's story, growing hungry, and getting up to make a salami sandwich. But when he returned to read, chomping away, the story turned bloody and gruesome and he couldn't finish his snack.

It was clear from the beginning that he favoured poets, which was surprising, as his own prize-winning stories were not very poetic. He had kindly let Keesha and I enroll in the workshop even though we were amateurs when it came to fiction. We weren't the only outsiders who wanted to work with him—John's workshops were highly praised by students throughout the program and filled up quickly. In fact, it was a playwright friend who had encouraged us to take the class. I had also enrolled because I had the sense I would like John—I had often passed him in the hall as he was striding to his office, a bundle of manuscripts under his arm, and he had always smiled at me, even though we'd never been introduced.

That semester, Keesha and I were the only two poets in the room. The rest were diehard narrativizers, and perhaps I was imagining it, but I felt that they resented us—although perhaps they only resented the attention John showered upon us, the congratulatory comments he lavished on our stories. In one class he said Keesha's description of a sunset was the best he'd ever read in a student story. That same class he'd pointed out one of my "perfect" sentences which described a femme fatale character. "The fingernails," he said. "It's all about the nail polish here."

He complimented our imagery because that's what there was to compliment—neither Keesha nor I understood plot at all. Keesha's endings were melodramatic, and my dialogue was forced at best. In our poetry class, Keesha was writing tight little half-rhymed couplets with echoes of Gwendolyn Brooks, and I was reading Olga Broumas and writing lyric after lyric about my ex-girlfriend. Our teacher in that class, a passive bearded man who favoured cardigans in pastel colours, didn't get us in the same way John did, he didn't read into our work with the same depth. When John talked about your story in workshop, it came alive—it took on a meaning larger even than what you had intended.

During our fourth workshop, John read an excerpt from Keesha's story to exemplify a point while discussing another classmate's story. I could see by the look on this classmate's face that she was not happy with the comparison. Her name was Samantha and she had dyed charcoal-black hair and wore severe white makeup and bright-red lipstick. I usually stared at the red imprint of her lips on the rim of her take-out coffee cup as I listened to her skewer our classmate's stories. The thing about Samantha was that she was really smart and so were her stories, and so her feedback—delivered with biting precision—was usually pretty spot-on, although it lacked anything so frivolous as compassion.

When it came time for my story to be workshopped, a short piece about a warehouse rave I'd attended a few years earlier, Samantha was the first to speak. "The protagonist is just so selfish, so ..." She bit the end of her pen contemplatively, smearing a bit of red lipstick on it. "Unlikable. And the scenes—I mean, on page five, we get a full page of description of the room. As a reader I'm thinking, 'Who cares? Give me the action already.'"

There were several nods around the table. John cleared his throat; his face bore a friendly attempt at a neutral expression. "The description may need a little work, it's true," he said, "but don't you think Benny is onto something important with this story? The relationship between the two sisters especially. I think it's very important. Very brave." He looked around the table and then lowered his voice a notch. "I mean, Benny seems like a nice girl, and then you read some of these scenes and—whoa! They surprise you, right? There's risk in them. They're a little risqué. The kissing in the bathroom ...?" He raised his eyebrows.

It was only the fourth week in, but I had already heard John use the adjective "brave" to describe three other stories. It was what he said when he wanted to encourage the writer but didn't know what else to say. And now he was bringing up the sex scene, which even I knew was awkwardly written. Feeling demoralized, I slumped in my chair and let him try to rescue me.

"I was bored," Samantha said flatly. She wasn't intimidated by of any of us, not even charming John.

"That is what it is, Sam," John said, taking a measured sip of his Earl Grey. I didn't think Samantha was the sort of woman who would appreciate this shortening of her name and I wondered if John also sensed this. "But I still think that Benny's story has merit, and with some work, this story will blow our socks off, I bet." He turned his pearly smile at me and winked. I was caught off guard by this and started to blush. I had seen John wink at a few other students, but it was the first time he'd winked at me and I wasn't sure what to feel. I stared down at my draft and drew little doodles in the margins.

"Maybe it will even be ready for you to read at the conference, Benny," he said, handing me back my story. I glimpsed a few exclamation points in his signature green ink.

We were all attending a large writing conference in Los Angeles in a few weeks' time, and John had been pumping it up since the beginning of the semester. He had organized a reading for us at one of the small bars near the convention centre with some of his former students who lived in L.A. Each time a student in our class wrote something he thought was good or had the potential to be, he'd suggest that we read it at the event. I didn't think my story would be ready and was considering scratching it all together and starting on a new one, but I smiled weakly at him as I took the draft to let him know I appreciated his confidence.

I thought I heard Samantha sniff huffily at John's suggestion, but I might have been imagining it. I do imagine things. My ex-girlfriend often pointed out to me that writers are always making up stories about others' actions and motivations, and though the writers think they are very insightful and that their interpretations are correct, they are often very wrong.

A FEW WEEKS later we arrived in sunny, smoggy, palm-treed Los Angeles. For many of us, it was our first conference, and we were excited, chugging large coffees as we diligently attended early morning panels, playing at being professionals. Within a couple of days, though, our excitement gave way to cynicism as, exhausted, we tromped through the huge convention centre without even noticing any of the literary stars and decided to skip the panels we'd circled in the hefty program guide the day before and instead drink midday cocktails at the hotel bar. The last afternoon, Keesha and I toasted each other in a booth by the window as the sunlight streamed over us and we shared the books we'd picked up for cheap at the book fair. I held up a Wayne Koestenbaum book I'd been meaning to read that I got for only ten bucks. "I think you're going to want to borrow this one."

Keesha pulled one from her stack and flipped to a poem she'd already read and wanted to share with me. As she started reading I looked behind her into the dim recesses of the room. Someone at one of the small tables lining the back wall caught my eye.

"Is that John?"

Keesha looked up at me, her finger holding her place on the page.

"Sorry to interrupt. But is that John?"

Keeping her place with her finger, Keesha gingerly turned her head. "Yeah."

We both stared. John was perched on the edge of his stool, talking animatedly as he leaned in toward a young-looking woman with long red hair and stylish glasses who sat across from him. They were both sipping beers. At one point, John reached over and touched her arm, leaving it there as he talked. She was smiling at him; it seemed she was hanging on to his every word.

"I wonder what's going on there," I said.

Keesha shrugged and looked back down at her book. "Probably a former student. You know how they all love him."

It was true. At the reading the night before, dozens of his former students had crowded the small dark bar. I had spilled my gin and tonic trying to squeeze through the packed bodies, and my hands shook while I read—I hadn't anticipated such a big audience and it made sharing my work even more nerve-wracking. To my surprise, John's fans were not just young women, but included men and a couple of people who looked genderqueer. There were several people of colour, which Keesha said was a relief, and several older people—students who had taken a break from their careers to do their master's. And all of them seemed to love John. They patted him on the back or touched his arm, they bought him beers, they reminisced over amusing things he had said in workshop or the first time they had gotten published thanks to his help. A few even hugged him. It was all very warm, although it did feel a bit like a fan club meeting.

"They do love him," I agreed, looking away from John's table and focusing on Keesha's face. I decided to pretend I hadn't even seen them. "Will you keep reading? I'm sorry I interrupted."

She started reading again, slowly, "Whenever my name / is mispronounced, / I want to buy a toy pistol, / put on dark sunglasses ..."

THAT NIGHT THERE was a big party in the hotel ballroom, dimly lit in an attempt to create a romantic atmosphere. The music was cheesy but danceable, although Keesha and I chose to lounge in one of the dark corners, drinking whisky sours and making fun of the sloshed writers careening around the dance floor, bumping into each other. We made bets on who would be successful at finding someone to share their big hotel bed that night. As we were laughing at our own mediocre jokes, John detached himself from the jostling crowd and approached us, a foaming beer in one hand, the other hand open in invitation.

"Care to dance?" he asked. There was no mistaking that the question was intended for Keesha—still, for one brief moment, I thought he might be asking me and I wondered what I would do. I caught a whiff of musky aftershave as he stepped closer.

I looked to Keesha; she tilted her drink and took a big sip before answering him. "I don't dance. I'm sorry."

"You don't dance?" His face was amused, incredulous. He took her free hand and swung it back and forth, smiling. "Really?"

Keesha gently extracted her hand, maintaining her cool. "Really. Sorry." She gave him a half-smile.

John attempted an unbothered grin and shuffled his feet in a silly two-step, spilling a bit of his beer on the floor. "Well, if you change your mind, you know where to find me." He smiled once more and dance-walked jauntily back to the dance floor, disappearing into the drunken crowd. We could see he was trying to play it all off as a joke, something he'd pull in workshop to get a laugh out of us when we seemed tired.

We stared after him. "Uh oh," I said, before Keesha could speak.

"Yeah," she said.

"He likes you."

"God, I hope not." She swirled the ice around in her drink. The DJ put on TLC's "No Scrubs," which caused great excitement on the dance floor—a few people whooped in recognition and sloppily high-fived, some drunk undergrads started jumping up and down. We watched older men in blazers bob their heads off-time to the beat as they circled around their companions, middle-aged women in floral dresses trying to gyrate.

"I think he does," I said.

"Maybe he's just drunk." Her tone was hopeful.

"Maybe," I said.

BACK IN PORTLAND the next day I resolved to work on a story that wasn't going anywhere and had devolved into a tangled mess. I got up, still tired from the conference and trying hard not to feel hopeless, and packed my backpack for a trip to Coffee People, throwing in the most recent draft along with my notebook and a few of my favourite black ballpoint pens.

Two cups of coffee later I had the jitters and nothing to show for it—not one new sentence, not one realization about my characters. I stared out the window at the people passing by—hipsters in old men's Oxfords pedalling rusty Schwinns, parents with babies strapped to their chests and green smoothies in their hands, fast food workers in colourful uniforms hurrying to catch the bus. I decided today was a day to give up, to stop at the convenience store on the way home and get a bag of chips in which to drown my sorrows.

I was known at this store by the manager Alfredo, who usually worked the early shift. Many days I had to run in to get half-and-half for my coffee in the morning or a small tub of raspberry gelato late at night. But it was late afternoon now and another person was working, a young woman I hadn't seen before. She smiled at me as I headed to the chips section. Out of the corner of my eye I saw a tall man in an oversized blue sports jersey lumber toward the counter and thump down a litre of Coke. I didn't hear what she said to him, but he boomed back, "I like you. You've got good energy."

What a weird thing to say to a stranger. I stared at the rows of chips, carnival red and mustard-yellow shining gaudily under the fluorescent lights. I contemplated salt and vinegar, ketchup, or barbeque.

I heard the tall man proclaim, "And you're a giggler. I like that. I like giggles."

I turned to look. He was leaning forward, tapping a neon-green lighter from the display on the counter, smiling. I could make out the scruff of a few days' beard and tousled hair. He looked older than I thought he would be from the sound of his voice. Was this his attempt at flirtation? Was the clerk supposed to be flattered?

The clerk laughed as she bagged the man's purchases. A nervous laugh. I wouldn't call it a giggle.

"Thank you, darlin'," he said as he swaggered out of the store. The little bell tinkled as the door swung shut behind him.

I grabbed a bag of barbeque and headed up to the register. "Real charmer, hey?" I motioned my head at the door.

She laughed, a full laugh this time. "Oh, these guys," she said, shaking her head as she rang up my chips. "These guys."

BACK IN MY cramped studio, it was cold. I creaked shut the window I had left open for air flow and plopped down on my bed, ripping open the bag of chips. Chip after chip disappeared into my mouth as my fingers became coated in sticky orange dust. After a few handfuls I got up and went to my desk to grab a pencil. It was the editing instrument I used when I was feeling most desperate. I clutched it in my right hand, looking at it as if it might tell me something. *Help me*, I thought. *Help me*. But who was I talking to? Or was I praying?

I had a meeting booked with John for the end of the week, a meeting we had set up some time before the writing conference, and I was trying to wrangle my story into some kind of coherence so as not to embarrass myself when we met. But I couldn't focus. My mind kept returning to the night before, John's attempt to get Keesha to dance with him. It had been awkward. Embarrassing. I imagined his grinning red face, his silly little dance. Keesha's carefully contained disdain. I put a spicy chip in my mouth and chewed slowly.

Before I could stop myself, I was imagining him holding out his hand to me. Pulling me into his arms. I laid my head on his shoulder. A quiet song playing, something by Sade.

I shook my head to dispel the image. What the fuck. I shoved a fistful of chips in my mouth and chewed aggressively. I had been spending too much time alone, and loneliness made me weird. I had been trying not to write about my ex, but the more I tried to push thoughts of her from my mind, the more urgently they crowded in. I knew what her eyes looked like but I could no longer picture them, and this felt unbearable. So I hurled myself into fiction, spending days and nights trying to make my stories passable at least, something worthy of another person's time. This feeling often came over me when I was trying to write—this sense of pushing back a huge shadowy hopelessness that always threatened to snuff out my sentences. It was like trying to shove a big black duvet back into the corner of an already crammed closet and the struggle often left me exhausted.

I kept putting chips into my mouth, working my jaw. I knew if I looked in the mirror in that moment I'd have a huge orange circle of chip dust around my mouth, like a poorly made-up clown. And like a clown I'd be frowning, my face pale, a tiredness pulling under my skin.

JOHN'S OFFICE WAS on the third floor of the arts building, a modern building with big windows facing south, although due to the rainy climate there still wasn't much light for most of the year.

I poked my head around the door. "Am I early?"

"Early? No, you're just on time!" He smiled, gesturing to the plush green chair facing his desk. "Have a seat. I'm glad we're getting to meet before our next class."

Unlike his colleagues' offices, John's was clean and well-organized, almost spartan. Orderly rows of books filled the one bookcase and a small stack of student manuscripts sat on a round table near the door. His desk was clear except for a laptop, the Christmas cactus, a travel mug of tea, and a picture of Marilyn and his two young daughters smiling next to a pool.

I sat down, setting my backpack on the floor at my feet and unzipping it to retrieve my story. I felt shy now that I was alone with him. There was something about his presence, this strong energy that filled our small workshop room and now his office. I flipped through my story and paused, pretending to read a few sentences as I heard him rifling around in his desk drawer. When I looked up, he was smiling radiantly and holding out a Hershey's kiss.

"For you," he said. "Because you're working so hard. Marilyn gave me a bag to keep in the office. For you kids." He smiled again.

I wasn't sure how I felt about being called a kid but reasoned he no doubt meant it affectionately. He was twice my age, after all. I glanced down at the desk where his arms rested, the rolled-up cuffs of his white button-up revealing strong tan forearms and hands. Capable hands, was the thought that came, unbidden. I felt a blush climb up my neck. My ex used to tease me, calling me a "hands man," and it was true. After we broke up I fantasized about her hands for months, and these fantasies, which started out erotically, usually ended in tears and despair.

I took the Hershey's kiss and put it in my pocket. "Thanks," I said.

"You're not going to eat it? What, don't tell me you're on a diet."

The diet comment caught me by surprise. He had never said anything like that in workshop. But there was no way I was going to eat the kiss now. I could think of few things more humiliating than eating it while he watched. "I'm saving it for later," I said. "I might need the pick-me-up after I get your feedback."

He laughed. "That tough, am I?"

Unsure of how to reply, I awkwardly shoved my story across the desk. "I'd appreciate any help you have. I'm totally stuck."

He took it and held it with both hands. "I'm sure it's not as dire as you think." Then, rather than start reading it, he set it down on the desk and took a big sip of his tea, looking at me from over the cup's rim. "Why don't we start by you telling me what you're finding challenging and we can go from there."

This suggestion made me even more anxious than having him read the story in front of me, but I didn't know what to do so I just started nervously talking. "Well, there's this scene between two lovers, I mean, they're actually breaking up but it's not totally final yet, and then the one comes over to the other's apartment and he's being sort of passive-aggressive, and—"

"Wait, 'he'? You mean this couple is a man and a woman?"

"Well, yeah, I mean the man is trans and when they met he hadn't started transitioning yet but …"

John smiled enigmatically. "Well, that's interesting." He started leafing through the pages. "Some new content for you?"

"Not really." I watched as he paused on a certain page and started reading. What had I been thinking, bringing this story to him? I looked down at my hands. There was still a bit of orange dust lodged under one of the nails. I started to dig it out with the edge of my thumbnail.

John smiled as he read and his fingers strayed to his lips, which he touched absent-mindedly.

I watched him for a moment, then turned back to my nails, carefully pushing down each cuticle. It was clear to me now in the light of day that my story wasn't very good and I didn't want to sit through the embarrassment of him pumping up the few decent passages as if they were really something and then kindly suggesting a few minor revisions. He would be gentle with my ego. He was good at that.

A nervous sweat broke out under my sweater. I was afraid of what images my mind might conjure up, but I told myself to calm down, to stop overreacting. Just then I saw Keesha's face, an ironic expression. Why had he asked her to dance? Did he really think she'd say yes? In my mind her face softened to a "careful, girl" smile, one she'd given me many times.

I reached out my hand for the story. "Maybe I should just take it home and work on it more. It really isn't very ready to be read. I'm sorry." I hoped he wouldn't notice that my cheeks were red.

He looked up at me. There was something inscrutable in his gaze. "Why are you sorry? This is a great draft. A great draft. I mean, this scene …" His words tapered off as he started reading again. The air in the room felt thick, stagnant. I glanced over my shoulder to see if I had left the door open. It was closed.

"This, um … device … I haven't seen it in a story before," he said.

"What do you mean?"

"The … what do you call it? The …"

A queasiness gathered in my stomach. I wondered if I was imagining things.

"The strap-on." He smiled at finally locating the word. "Yes, I haven't seen that in a story before. It's hot. I mean, it has a temperature. It feels a little dangerous, you know?"

I stared at my fingernails. Sweat gathered under the wool of my sweater. I could feel it pooling in my armpits.

"I don't know," I finally said. "It's not that unusual in my community." Almost mechanically, I took the chocolate out of my pocket, unwrapped it, and shoved it into my mouth. At least I wouldn't have to speak while eating it.

"You need that nourishment now, I guess?"

Was his smile flirtatious? What was happening? The rain started up again and I watched it drizzle down the large windows. "I think I have to go," I said.

"Oh. Okay." He looked disappointed. Then he lowered his voice, his tone slightly apologetic. "I hope I haven't made you uncomfortable." He took another sip of his tea and paused. "I also wanted to talk to you about … I was hoping to talk about sending some work out. My buddy I mentioned, Tim over at the *Crab Orchard Review*, is looking for fresh work. I thought of you."

Before I could summon a reply, he changed the subject again. "Have you seen Keesha lately?"

Why was he bringing her up now? "Um, yeah. I see her all the time."

"She hasn't been by my office yet. Maybe tell her to stop by with that new piece she's been working on? It's pretty dynamite."

I again felt queasy and looked at the door. "Sure, I'll tell her." I held out my hand for the story. He got up from his chair and came around the desk. For one disorienting moment, I thought he was going to try to hug me, but he just handed me the story and then walked to the door, holding it open. "Until next time," he said, smiling his trademark grin.

THE NEXT WEEK both Keesha and I had stories up for workshopping. It was over midway through the semester and by this point allegiances were well-established. John loved us. Samantha hated us. A couple of other classmates were on Samantha's side, and there was one husky blond fellow, Liam, who seemed to be trying out for the role of John Junior and vacillated between praising our stories and then trying to even things out by agreeing with Samantha. Our only allies other than John were Renaldo, whose stories were often praised by classmates for their "authenticity" but critiqued for their "awkward grammar," and Emily, a pale, quiet undergrad who had gotten into the grad workshop based on the merits of her melancholic stories about her alcoholic father. Neither of them spoke often, but when they did, they usually came to our defence.

Keesha's stories mostly focused on Black middle-class life in Chicago and my stories were usually about queer heartbreak. That week, Keesha had taken a risk and tried a new setting—the city we were living in. Only one of us, Renaldo, actually grew up in Portland—his mom owned a popular taqueria on Alberta Street where Keesha and I sometimes went for burritos. I had lived in the city for just a year when I was twenty but was only familiar with parts of the east side and downtown. Keesha's story also tried out a new type of protagonist—a Black professional woman who was looking to buy a house but couldn't get her white realtor to show her any properties outside of a very few neighbourhoods.

I was still unsettled by the meeting with John and tried not to look at him as he sat as usual at the head of the table in a crisp white shirt, a travel mug of Earl Grey steaming beside him. But that day he didn't speak right away—instead he looked around the table and waited. Finally Liam started off the conversation with some general praise about Keesha's ability to capture the essence of the city in the few opening paragraphs. He had barely finished speaking when Samantha cut in. "But in this day and age?" she asked. "I mean, the realtor not showing her places outside of African-American neighbourhoods ... maybe it *could* happen, but realistically, realtors want to make money and she's got the money, so it seems like the realtor would take her wherever she wanted to go."

"I see what you're saying," Liam agreed. "I mean, essentially, I had the same read. I kept asking myself, 'Would this really happen?' And I wasn't sure that it would. I mean, I just couldn't see this happening *now*, in the year 2000, you know? Maybe twenty or thirty years ago ..."

John looked calmly around the table as if gauging whether or not to weigh in. He didn't seem perturbed by Samantha's or Liam's comments, but I felt my blood start to quietly boil. Before either of them could say another word, I broke in. "Having lived in Portland for a year not that many years ago, I find this depiction very realistic," I said. "It's a hugely segregated city. I mean, Black people were actually banned from the state altogether in, I think, the 1800s. I thought it was very strategic, actually, for Keesha to choose Portland as the setting for this story." I looked down at the desk, feeling my cheeks redden as they always did when I disagreed directly with someone. I sensed the eye rolls coming from Liam and Samantha, who no doubt thought that I was just trying to be what they liked to call "politically correct," or that my comments were not objective enough, that they had no merit since I was simply defending my friend.

Renaldo came to my aid. "I agree with Benny," he said. "I found it believable." He spoke softly. "I've experienced similar things, like, when looking for jobs in Portland. It's a weird city." He smiled ironically as if to underline the word "weird."

Even then, John didn't say anything. He stroked his chin and made a few notes on the draft with his green pen. Then he looked up and smiled at us amiably, as if he was our father and he was proud of us for having an adult conversation, just happy to be listening in.

According to the strict etiquette of the workshop, students weren't allowed to speak while their stories were being discussed, so even as the conversation grew more tense, Keesha was barred from saying anything. I tried to meet her eyes to give her a sympathetic smile, but she was looking over John's shoulder, out the window at the heavy grey clouds.

John shifted his chair in her direction. "Well, a lot of food for thought, right, Keesha? We can discuss this more during my office hours, but this should give you something to go on as you begin your revisions. Your fellow writers have certainly given you a lot to think about."

"They sure have," Keesha said, turning her gaze from the window. She smiled at me, ignoring John, who was looking at her expectantly.

"Well, gang, time for a break, okay?" John clapped his hands together like an enthusiastic coach. "I've got a lemon loaf back in my office that Marilyn whipped up this morning. I bet we'd all like a slice."

The workshop didn't improve after the break. My story was shredded by my classmates—not without reason. The ending was flat and I had spent far too much time labouring over unimportant details and throwaway dialogue. Keesha had read my story when we met for bubble tea and noodles earlier in the week and had told me some of the same things, although her biggest issue had been that I kept getting the neighbourhood details wrong. The story took place in Chicago, her hometown.

"It's not the pink line, although I understand the significance of you wanting to use that colour," she told me, pausing to suck back some bubble tea. "It's the blue line, definitely the blue line for that neighbourhood you're talking about."

She'd given me some good suggestions, but I hadn't had a chance to implement them before the class, so I had to hear the critiques again from much harsher critics. And just as he had when Keesha's story was being workshopped, John remained silent. Remotely friendly, seemingly attentive to what we were saying—and silent.

AND THAT'S HOW the rest of the semester went. John kept his distance from us and spoke sparingly about our stories, while he seemed to have gained a deeper admiration for the work of Emily and Liam. Emily's characters were "achingly believable" and "masterfully composed." Liam's work was "very affecting," it held "the humour and pathos of the working class." When John did talk about a story of mine or Keesha's, both his compliments and critiques were equally muted—he was careful not to be too effusive in his praise and careful also not to tear us apart.

When he passed me in the hall, he still smiled and called me by name, but his manner was reserved, and he never again invited me to his office.

You'd think I would have felt relieved by this. John's light had finally shifted—it no longer shone so intensely on Keesha and me. But strangely, I felt hurt and angry. The last story I turned in was very short, written hurriedly the night before. If he wasn't going to take an interest in my work, I reasoned, then I wasn't going to try very hard.

Keesha, though, had a different take. A few weeks after the class ended, we met up at our favourite noodle joint. She ordered her usual large vanilla bubble tea and I had my usual iced green. Keesha produced a collection by Sonia Sanchez that she'd been carrying around in her purse and read her favourite poem to me. I told her about the Audre Lorde essays I'd been devouring. We sipped our teas and slurped our noodles and contemplated our semester. Talk turned to John's class.

"He's basically an asshole," I said. "I mean, he acted like we were so great and then he abandoned us." I had never told Keesha about the uncomfortable interaction in John's office, and I wasn't clear why exactly I hadn't told her.

Keesha threw back her head and laughed. "Good riddance!"

"You don't care?"

"Not a bit." She chewed her noodles. "We dodged a bullet with that one. Did I tell you how many times he tried to get me to come to his office?" She shook her head. "Please." She lifted another forkful of noodles. "Mr. Bigshot. Everyone said he was so great." She made a dismissive *phh* sound.

"He was a little weird," I admitted.

"Weird is right." She grinned at me.

I lifted my cup for a toast. "So much for our foray into fiction, I guess, right?"

IT WAS A hot Sunday afternoon more than ten years later that I got the call from Keesha. I had been out weeding the potatoes and planting more kale in the backyard of the house I shared with my partner and three friends and had to take off my dirty gardening gloves to answer the phone.

"I wanted to call rather than just send you the links," she said. "It's pretty gross."

I read the articles, the stories circulating on social media. They were mostly young, the women. Some were still teenagers, under-grads just out of high school. It was easy to play on their insecurities, to schedule private conferences in his office that turned into beer tastings at the pub that turned into bourbon-drenched evenings at the women's apartments. Marilyn finally left him. His colleagues started to notice that he sometimes smelled of whisky. And this went on for years, until one of the women wrote about it in a national magazine and he eventually lost his job.

Her account of their relationship was chilling. He threatened to have her scholarship rescinded. He left bruises on her arms. He got her pregnant and coerced her into getting an abortion. One night he locked her in a closet. She avoided campus, quit hanging out with her friends. She started drinking a lot. She became very anxious and depressed and attempted suicide. Finally, she extricated herself and left the state. She was only twenty-two when their relationship ended.

After reading, I felt queasy and had to get a glass of ice water and sit down on the couch. I rubbed a bit of dirt from my knee and stared blankly out the window at the sun-baked front lawn, trying to make sense of it.

My first thought was that it was too extreme, that the story must actually be about someone else. For legal reasons, I assumed, the writer had not named John directly in her piece. There were so many stories like this coming to the surface lately—it had to be about someone else. I couldn't reconcile this cruel bully with the teacher I had known. But the details were so specific—his after-shave, the brand of whisky he drank—and as I sifted through them, a picture started to emerge.

I had a flash of John's face, smiling as he sipped his tea. Tilting back his head to laugh at a joke cracked by one of the students in workshop. The time he brought a big stack of *New Yorkers* and *Harvard Reviews* to class and gave us all copies, the time he bought us all beers at the conference.

It had been years since I had thought about the meeting in his office. The scene flickered dimly—a rainy day, a desk, a plush chair. It had been so awkward. I had been awkward. He had given me a Hershey's kiss. Why? I took a sip of water and held a sliver of ice in my mouth, feeling it dissolve against the inside of my cheek.

The sun beamed through the large window, lighting up my legs. I took another big swallow of water. I tried to remember his exact words, what story I had brought for him to read. But I couldn't. All that remained was an anxious feeling, a glimpse of tan forearms and rolled white cuffs.

When I first read the former student's account I was so struck by it that I didn't pay much attention to the writer's name. But as I set down my ice water and picked up my phone to read the story again a face appeared in my mind, smiling shyly. Emily. Emily Johnson. I remembered the way she'd nervously tap her pen on her arm or draw little circles on her thumb while she listened to the rest of us talk. How she'd look up from time to time, eyes alert like she was recording everything and would later use it in some surprisingly scathing story. I remembered her small, careful handwriting, her questions on my drafts. The way her gaze would often turn to John when she'd look up from her lap. She was a really good writer, probably the best in the class. I hadn't really known her, but we had all sat around that table together, we had all listened to John's jokes, his silly stories. We had been in that room together.

I remembered now one class in which he'd loaned Emily an anthology of stories, the almost ecstatically grateful look on her face as he handed the heavy volume across the table to her. He had said something like, "Now, don't read this in the bathtub and let it fall in the water, okay? It's my only copy." Had he winked? I couldn't remember. But I remembered now the feeling, which I hadn't been able to fully acknowledge at the time—annoyance, a tinge of jealousy. And also a feeling of deep discomfort, of wanting to look away.

"A skilled predator," one of the articles said, the one about a girl he had seduced at a private high school years before he ever entered our classroom. This was decades before he ever brought us warm muffins, before he ever loaned us his books, before he ever smiled at us so brightly, like we were the finest students he had ever had the honour to work with.

MY TUMOUR

IN THE LETTER her brother used the phrase "my tumour" several times. "I'm sorry to have worried you about my tumour," he wrote. "I should have thought more carefully about it before I wrote you. I regret telling you about it and I won't speak of it again." He went on to say he was unwilling to tell her about any medical decisions he made about his tumour, if it even was a tumour. It might just be a swollen gland. He realized now, he explained, that telling her meant she would be concerned and would ask him what he was going to do about it. He wasn't willing to share this information, he stated.

He emphasized several times that he appreciated her concern and hadn't meant to worry her. "You may feel angry, sad, or disappointed about my decision not to tell you more," he wrote. "And all I can say is talk to God or whatever you believe in. We each have our own path to walk in this life. This is mine."

Lise had come down to the lobby to get her mail and, seeing the sun streaming in through the large windows, decided to step outside into the day, to sit on the concrete steps leading up to her apartment building while she read the letter. It had been raining for weeks, and she wanted to feel the mid-March sun, weak as it was, on her face, her hands. A second cup of coffee to rest near her feet and sip on would have made the moment perfect, but her half-full French press sat cooling up in her studio.

She turned the envelope over in her hands. Matthew usually decorated them with the most elaborate drawings in rich burgundies, violets, gradations of blue. This time he had covered the front of the envelope with swirls of rainbow and small orange roses. A large blue-green turtle spanned the back, its mouth opened to snap. Beautiful. They were always so beautiful. It was sometimes hard for her to believe he'd actually made them, when she read the words that were inside.

HER BROTHER'S LETTER before this one hadn't been much of a letter—just a scribbled note on lined paper, "for your information," shoved into an envelope with two articles he'd printed out from the internet that detailed the perils of vaccination—the dangerous allergic reactions, children getting autism, the government using it as an opportunity to slip in a substance that would mind-control the populace and create a new world order populated by sheeple, "sheeple," a term she'd heard him use before in conversation. Neither article was written by a doctor; when she looked them up online, she found that neither author had a background in medicine or science of any kind, although they both had posted many photographs of themselves holding guns. These were the experts her brother liked best—disgruntled people on the fringes who believed they knew the real deal, the truth, and weren't afraid to share it.

Matthew had sent these articles to her because she'd made the mistake of mentioning on the phone that her friend Maria was having a baby. He'd immediately grown tense. "But she's not going to vaccinate it, right? It could kill the baby. Give him autism, or something worse."

She should have known enough by this time not to get drawn into this sort of conversation, but she took the bait. "Matthew, seriously? That's been totally debunked. I can't believe you still believe that."

There was a moment of heavy silence. His voice was calm when he spoke again but she could hear the layers underneath, his frustration at being questioned and also his pity for her, that she could be so deluded. "I have a lot of free time on my hands. I do a lot of research. And I learn things, things that a lot of people don't know. Or don't want to know. If you don't want my perspective, okay. I don't have to share my findings with you. But if you care about your friend, about your friend's baby—"

"Goddamn it!" How did he always manage to do this? Why did she always let him? The raw nerve was there, waiting to be tapped. "I'm so sick of all this crazy bullshit! There is absolutely no scientific basis for any of this. Why do you keep reading this crap?"

A longer, more painful silence. When he spoke this time his

voice was ragged. "Don't yell. Don't raise your voice just because we don't share the same beliefs. You can think what you like and I can think what I like. But at least I keep an open mind. At least I give other perspectives a chance."

"Too much of a chance, Matt. Some things don't deserve a chance. These things you read online, these people—they're just spreading fear. It's misinformation. It has no basis in fact."

"I'm not afraid," he said. His voice had descended to cold stone, and although she couldn't see him, she knew all too well the face that accompanied this tone.

"Matthew," she tried again. "I'm not trying to attack you, I'm just concerned—"

"I have to go," he interrupted. "I'll be late for my shift. I'll send you some articles."

"Don't bother," she said. "I won't read them."

"Do what you like," he said and hung up the phone.

LISE HAD ONCE grown a tumour herself. Quietly, unknowingly, over the course of a year following a particularly brutal break-up. One day she was doing neck rolls in the bathroom in front of the mirror, as she often did in the morning, and saw an extra shadow gracing her throat. But it didn't move when she shifted her head. She touched it. It was hard, bulging under the skin.

She made an appointment with her doctor, and her doctor sent her to get an ultrasound, and then she was referred to an endo-crinologist. She walked a very long hall to the end of a neglected wing of the hospital, which was itself rather shabby, and when she arrived, there was no receptionist and no one else in the waiting room. The room was dreary, painted beige and smelling of dust and old magazines. She sat in one of the fake wood-panelled chairs and stared for a long time at a painting of a seascape that's palette placed it in the 70s. She was wondering if someone's great-aunt or great-uncle had painted it or if it had come from a garage sale when the endocrinologist poked his head around the door to the examining room and told her to come in.

The endocrinologist was a young man with short parted hair and a superior air. He asked her to sit on the examination table and then he took out a long needle which he stuck into the lump in her throat. "Just slowly count your breaths," he said. "This is going to sting a bit."

Afterward, he pulled off his blue medical gloves with a snap and threw them in the wastebasket. Then he tried to reassure her.

"Even if it is cancerous, you probably don't need to worry. Most of these cysts are so slow-growing they are non-fatal. Often autopsies reveal cancerous tumours in people's thyroids that they didn't even know about. Didn't affect their lives at all. I'd rather have non-aggressive thyroid cancer than diabetes, let me tell you." He gave a restrained smile, then glanced down at her arm.

She was wearing a bracelet her ex had given her, little square beads with faces of holy people on them strung together on a length of green elastic. She had worn it nearly every day of the thirteen months since the break-up and was surprised it hadn't broken yet.

"Is that *Jesus*?" the endocrinologist asked.

She looked at her wrist and looked back at him. "I don't think so. I think they are maybe Hindu gods and Buddhist saints? I'm not sure. It was a gift."

But then for some reason she continued, "Not that I have anything against Jesus, though."

A glimmer of something—annoyance?—passed over his face. "Are you religious?"

"No." The white tissue-like paper underneath her gave a crinkling sound as she shifted on the examination table. She was still sitting, her legs dangling off the edge, and this made her a little bit taller than him.

"Just don't try to pray the tumour away, is all I ask."

She shook her head. "I don't pray. Not usually." Then she made the mistake of telling him that she had gone to see a Shipibo shaman a few weeks before, a man named Ernesto. She saw the endocrinologist's eyes narrow.

She didn't say more—about the ceremony that took place in a yurt on Bowen Island, a huge yurt made of soft canvas the colour of a cougar's skin. She had arrived in the late afternoon with Lerato, a queer man she had met on a rideshare board, who grew up in South Africa and had been HIV positive for fifteen years. On the ferry over, they'd talked about healing. He had recently given up pot and coffee, starting his mornings instead with a big mug of green tea that he took across the street and sipped from as he puttered around his community garden plot. It was the first time for both of them, doing a ceremony, drinking ayahuasca, and they traded stories they'd heard about others' experiences. Lise told how her friend had seen her beloved dead dog at the foot of her mat, come back to comfort her. Lerato told about his friend who had encountered God—a huge green woman, a giantess by the sound of it, who, when Lerato's friend asked her why the world existed, had lifted one enormous ass cheek and farted.

After the second cup of sludgy brown tea, she had lost her grip on the world. Everything spun for hours—geometric shapes in neon colours pulsated when she opened her eyes and also when she closed them, like star systems from far-away galaxies. Dizzy, she lay on her back, holding the edges of her mat, feeling as if it was a flimsy cardboard sled rushing down a perilously icy hill. At one point she managed to sit up as the shaman came to her and sang at her feet. But soon after he left she started vomiting so hard that it felt like she was tearing out her stomach lining, clutching a bowl between her knees that she had brought from home for this purpose, a stainless steel bowl that usually contained salad.

After throwing up, she descended into a very stoned state of calm. She closed her eyes and saw her father's balding head floating in front of her. She held his stubbly cheeks and kissed the crown of his head repeatedly, telling him he could go now, she was okay. After he left another image rose out of the darkness—she was sitting cross-legged in a circle with her ex and the woman her ex had left her for. The three of them were naked, holding hands and pulsing with light.

These were visions, she realized later. All her friends who had done ayahuasca had told her about their visions, and these were hers—images she could still feel in her body weeks later, ones she could never have conjured up when sober. They glimmered with feelings she had often tried to will into being but had not been able to. She held these visions carefully, like frayed bits of paper she was afraid might float way.

At one point in the endless night she looked across the room and saw Lerato sitting calmly on his mat. He was holding his hands up, palms facing toward her, and she wasn't sure what he was doing but she imagined him sending her positive energy.

When things slowed down in the early hours of the morning she went outside to pee. She had forgotten to put on socks, just shoved her feet in her sneakers, and it was cold. She shivered as she crouched down in the wet field, looking up at the sky. It was still black out and the stars felt so close. She remembered her ex telling her that when something in the sky winked, it was a star. Stable light meant it was a planet.

Finally she slept for a little while, or at least closed her eyes for some time without feeling sick, in a darkness free of spinning shapes, and when she opened them the yurt was still, filled by the quiet blue light of dawn. A white-haired man on the other side of the circle started plucking softly at his guitar, the music like a water she hadn't known she was thirsty for, mournful and contented at the same time.

LISE LOOKED AT the endocrinologist again, his young face already set in the wary lines of a medical professional bent on seriousness, and she didn't tell him about the stone Ernesto had given her at the beginning of the talking circle the morning after the ceremony, how warm and alive it had felt in her hands, and how she had struggled to find words, any words, to speak.

Even though she told him none of this, the endocrinologist gave a condescending smile. "Maybe the ceremony made you feel better, but it won't do anything to help your tumour. And you have to be careful. These plants—some people call them medicine, but they can be really dangerous. We've had people show up at the psych ward after drinking that stuff."

She felt a rush of anger at his tone, his assumptions, and wondered if this was the man she wanted to entrust with her neck. She wondered if she should have the surgery at all. There was a doctor on her block who worked out of a Traditional Chinese Medicine clinic. Some of her friends had had success curing their illnesses with her herbs. Her friend Jeevan had shrunk her ovarian tumours with months of daily visualization. Maybe she could do the same. Lise tried to imagine golden-white light encircling her neck, but in her mind's eye the light reminded her of one of the glow sticks she'd waved at raves as a teenager and the image made her feel ridiculous.

Could the endocrinologist see all this pass behind her eyes? She hadn't read him as a sensitive man yet he seemed to sense something. He looked at her intently. "Don't bother with the shaman again, okay?" He rifled through a pile of folders on his desk. "Leave the tumour to me."

WHEN SHE DISCOVERED the tumour, she did not tell her brother. She knew what he would say. Matthew did not believe in doctors, in dentists, or in anyone who had the potential to make money off of other people's suffering. He didn't really believe in the healing professions. He once went to a counsellor who told him he had some unresolved trauma from childhood but that he was better off than many and recommended that he start taking steps toward getting a girlfriend. Matthew had stormed out of his office.

He once read a book called *Money by the Mouthful*, a book brimming with tales of crooked dentists who performed unnecessary procedures on their unsuspecting patients just to squeeze a few extra dollars out of their pockets. These were the kinds of stories her brother liked best—corrupt politicians, conspiracies of lawyers, therapists who loved Freud more than their own patients.

He had always had a very strong critical mind. In high school, everyone had told him he should be a lawyer, or at least join the debate team. He could out-argue anyone, and he had an uncanny memory for historical facts. He read voraciously and spent long evenings at the public library. There, he encountered books about yoga and vegetarianism, and he started practising both. On his evening breaks at the convenience store, he'd go in the back room and do sun salutations. His co-workers all thought he was a complete nut.

He beçame very influenced by Gandhi and Martin Luther King Jr. and the concept of nonviolent resistance. But then he read that Gandhi was a casteist and MLK a womanizer, and he disavowed them both. This became a theme—there was always a new hero, a new thinker or revolutionary, but they were always discarded after a while—their theories were flawed, they were corrupt, they were imperfect.

But he kept looking. He kept looking. Lise had always admired this quality of his, his ever-searching mind. He seemed to believe the truth was out there somewhere, waiting to be discovered, if only he read enough. He had a thirst, a tenacity that she lacked. Even as a child, Lise had often felt confused and conflicted, like all she had were her feelings, and they never made any sense. She loved to read but was easily overwhelmed. At a young age, she had created an image in her mind—a deep cave to climb into. There in the dark she could remain unseen, and she retreated there often.

In his senior year, Matthew fell in love with Marshall Rosenberg's teachings on nonviolent communication after finding one of his books in the library. Rosenberg came to town on a book tour and Matthew went to see him in a crowded high school auditorium two neighbourhoods away.

When he came home, Lise was studying at the dining-room table, a half-eaten grilled cheese cold on a plate in front of her, their mother already passed out in her bed after downing a box of Gallo.

"You hungry? There's another grilled cheese in the fridge. Mom wasn't hungry."

Matthew went to the fridge to grab the sandwich and then paced the dining room, taking big bites and chewing as he talked. "It just all makes so much sense now. Why we fight. Why everyone fights. And it doesn't have to be that way. It's not even that hard to fix. Rosenberg makes it so easy to understand." He carried on, trying to explain all of Rosenberg's ideas in a rush. As was always the case, he wanted to make Lise understand, to feel what he was feeling and see what he saw. He told Lise he'd cried while listening to Rosenberg talk—it was such a relief to be presented with another way to communicate, a better way. As he spoke, tears rose in his eyes and he stopped pacing. He stood looking at the wall, holding the crust of the cold grilled cheese. Lise rose from her chair and reached out to touch his arm, thinking to hug him, but they were teenagers by then and they never touched each other, so she pulled her hand back.

Lise thought Matthew appreciated Rosenberg because he gave a clear formula, a blueprint for how to navigate difficult conversations, a way to rise above the sticky mire of emotions. Matthew tried to practise the skills with Lise and their mother, but neither of them took it very seriously—they didn't even make time to read the book—and after a while he gave up. Lise expected him to be frustrated with them, but he wasn't really, because his own attention had already started to stray. This was around the time he started reading extensively about global conspiracies, the nefarious workings of world leaders and their henchmen, the deep rottenness at the core of every institution. He'd spend long nights on the computers at the public library, sunk in the dungeons of the internet, in shadowy chat rooms full of other young men spinning story after dark story.

It was also around this time that he dropped out of high school, saying the teachers were all full of shit and they never taught him anything useful anyway. He wasn't necessarily wrong—Lise often felt the same way, but she was determined to slog through and get her diploma and then move out of the state to go to college.

After too many yelling matches with his history teacher, after long conversations with the vice-principal and being expelled a couple of times, after phone calls from the school counsellor that their mother never answered, Matthew just stopped going back. The art teacher had always doted on him, but when she stopped by the house to drop off some of his paintings, he hid in the darkness of the living room and didn't answer the door. He took on more shifts at the convenience store. Later that year, he was promoted to assistant manager and a year after that, he became store manager.

Although her brother quickly tired of him, Rosenberg stayed with Lise, somewhere in the back of her mind, and years later she took one of his books out of the library. She tried to use his techniques when she found herself in a fight with her partner at the time, tried to avoid saying "you" so much, to use "I" statements about her feelings. She believed that reading Rosenberg made her a better listener; rather than yell back at her partner when they said mean things, she tried to listen for the needs and feelings underneath their declarations and to state those needs and feelings back to them calmly, without judgment, to let them know that they had been heard.

But when her most recent ex broke up with her so suddenly, so callously—another woman, a mutual friend, already kissed (maybe more than kissed), waiting in the wings—Lise forgot all of Rosenberg's techniques and simply cried and screamed until her throat hurt and she wanted nothing but to climb into bed and die.

THE ENDOCRINOLOGIST HAD been right, it turned out. The ayahuasca ceremony had not done anything to help her tumour—it hadn't shrunk even a bit.

So some weeks after her visit to the endocrinologist, Lise decided to have the tumour removed. She sat in the waiting room of St. Paul's holding her friend Maria's hand, trying not to notice the large, extraordinarily loud clock tick-tocking on the wall across from them. She clutched a piece of paper with a list of healing statements, simple affirmations that she had gotten out of a book on holistic healing: "I will wake up and be able to eat and drink," "I will wake up feeling healthy and strong," "I will wake up and have a healthy bowel movement within twenty-four hours"—things like that.

Next to the obnoxious clock was a medium-sized wooden cross that Maria couldn't stop glaring at. A survivor of Catholicism, raised in the religion and forced through Catholic school from the age of five all the way up until she graduated from high school, Maria had no love for religious symbols of any kind, but Christian iconography made her especially furious. Lise knew that Maria didn't even like to set foot in St. Paul's, and was grateful that she had made an exception for her. Of all her friends, Maria was the kindest, the most maternal. It was years before she would have her first child, but Maria seemed already well-prepared for the role of parent. Her eyes were bright and calm, her voice patient; she was slow to anger and often the first one to make a joke. As she squeezed Lise's hand, she looked into her eyes and mouthed the words "you'll be fine." Before the nurses whisked her away, Maria kissed her cheek and told her that she'd be there when Lise woke up.

Lise's first awareness was of light—before she even opened her eyes. She heard two nurses talking at her bedside, and the sound of other nurses bustling around the room. Machines beeped, there was the rustling of paper gowns and thin hospital sheets, cart wheels squeaking across the linoleum, and this sense of a brightness behind her eyelids growing steadily stronger even as she was unable to open her eyes.

She was aware of the desire to hold someone's hand but wasn't aware that she had been opening and closing hers until she felt a hand slip into hers, the warm palm and fingers, and she heard one of the nurses say, "Oh, that's what she wanted."

And it felt just right, deeply comforting, like the hand of a partner or a dear friend—but she still couldn't open her eyes. Too quickly, the hand was pulled away. She opened her eyes and the nurse smiled at her. "Awake now? Let's check your blood pressure." She slid the band around Lise's upper arm and started to puff it up.

Lise wished Maria could come in to brush her bangs away from her forehead, to wrap an arm around her shoulders. She felt traces of sweat at her hairline even though she was very cold. The room seemed loud, chaotic, although when she looked around, the beds were mostly empty and there were just a few nurses rushing around—not really that many people. Still, she felt scared and exposed. And very thirsty; she'd had to fast before the surgery and hadn't even had coffee or juice that morning. There was a small paper cup of water and a small paper cup of orange juice on the cart next to her bed, but she couldn't quite reach them, and didn't feel able to speak yet to ask the nurse.

Across the room under a high window there was a largish cross, a loin-clothed Jesus slumped on it, his bent head crowned in a ring of thorns. In the fluorescent light of the room, the copper cross gleamed, and she found it lurid, creepy. This tortured-to-death man—was he meant to comfort the patients, vulnerable and confused in their first moments returning to consciousness after the near-death of anesthesia? How horrible. How stupid. Inexplicably, she felt tears well up and she blinked them back. Even though only her throat had been operated on, her entire body felt tender, and she wished she were already at home, curled up in her own bed.

"The surgeon read the healing statements as you were going under, just as you asked," the nurse told Lise, seeming not to notice her emotional face. She laughed. "I bet he's never had to do anything like that before." Then she caught herself and resumed a professional expression. "He said the surgery went well. Very well." She deflated the blood pressure cuff and slid it off Lise's arm, patting her hand. "Your friend is waiting for you outside. When we move you to another room, you can see her."

IN ADDITION TO sending her articles about various conspiracies and catastrophes in the world, Matthew also sometimes sent her comics that he drew himself that featured a little monster character with hair coming out of its ears. The monster wore Matthew's convenience store uniform—a pink polo shirt with a little soda pop emblem—and a tiny nametag that read "manager." This monster was always getting involved in ridiculous high jinx—fending off thieves with cleaning spray, accidentally setting the magazine section on fire. But some of the plotlines were more telling. The monster comes home to a larger monster slumped on the floor. The little monster tries but can't manage to lift the big monster up to carry her to bed. He props a pillow under her bushy head, floats a blanket over her humped back and horned feet.

The monster Matthew drew to represent himself was rather adorable and reminded Lise of certain lovable protagonists in children's books. But it also reminded her of a dream Matthew had some months after their father died of colon cancer, when they were young teenagers in their first and second years of high school.

In the dream, their father had come back, and he and Matthew were roofing a house together—a funny detail that seemed to reveal some secret fantasy of masculinity on her brother's part, as roofing was an activity neither man would ever do in real life; neither of them were in the least bit handy. It was a hot day and they took off their shirts, hammering and sweating together under the beaming sun.

But then her brother realized something and he turned to their father. "Wait a minute—you're dead," he said.

And their father smiled and said, "Yes, but it's okay. I'm here now. Everything's okay."

And her brother felt soothed, and they stepped toward each other and hugged. When Matthew told her the dream, he had emphasized this part—how happy he was that their father was back and how glad he was to hug him, how relieved. But as he held him, Matthew felt bulges start to push up under his hands, huge tumour-like shapes rising out of their father's back. He released him and quickly stepped back, looking up at their father who was expanding horribly, his face contorted by knobby protuberances, his skin turning greenish and scaly as he transformed into a hideous monster. Matthew woke up terrified, unable to catch his breath, his blanket pulled over his head.

She had never forgotten this dream and had asked him a few times over the years what he thought it meant—did he really think their father had been a monster? Although not a drinker like their mother, their father had a temper he struggled to control, and had beaten both of them from a young age. As the boy and the older one, Matthew bore the brunt of it.

But Matthew never cared to answer her question—or pursue any line of thought that included analysis of their parents. He preferred other conversations, on topics like the economy's next crash and the aliens who would engineer it, or the recent school shooting and how it was a hoax to take people's gun rights away—a bizarre stance, considering that her brother had never had any interest in guns or owned a gun of any kind.

THE LAST TIME Lise had seen her brother was about six months before she received his letter about the tumour. She was visiting Portland for a few days, staying with friends, and stopped by his convenience store to see if they could take a walk on his lunch hour.

She hadn't told him she'd be in town, and when she walked through the door, he didn't notice her at first. He was in conversation with a customer, a regular by the sound of it, an older woman with white hair and a gravelly voice who was buying a carton of cigarettes. Matthew was telling her about a powdered vitamin mix she could get at the food co-op a few blocks away that would help clear out the mucous in her lungs.

"I don't smoke, but I used it a few times when I had a cold," he was saying. "It works."

Matthew knew a lot about a lot of things; vitamins and supplements had long been one of his research passions. When Lise had been dumped by her cheating ex, she had told Matthew in a letter that sometimes she couldn't function, that she'd call in sick to her non-profit job and spend whole days in bed crying. A week or so later her buzzer had rung—Fed-Ex, with a package containing a large bottle of multi-B vitamins and a note from Matthew saying he'd read that they replenished the body after times of emotional stress.

The white-haired customer headed toward the door and Matthew looked up and saw Lise. His face lit up and he came from behind the counter and walked toward her, reaching out as if to hug her. But then he just patted her arm as usual and said, "So you're in town? Good to see you." As was always the case it wasn't just happiness he radiated—there was an anxiousness too, as if he worried his emotion might be too big for the occasion, as if he was pleased but had to hold back some of his pleasure. It always made her feel sad to see this in his face.

Matthew's hair was longer than she'd seen it in years, pulled back in a ponytail. Lise had always envied his hair—thick and dark, inherited from their mother. Lise had ended up with their father's thin blond hair and worried she might bald early like he had. A few strands fell around Matthew's face; he was starting to get streaks of grey. Standing so close to him, Lise could smell that his work uniform hadn't been washed in a while. His manager tag was pinned at an angle, no doubt dislodged from its usual position due to the many times he'd pulled the shirt over his head.

He walked back around to the other side of the till and pulled a book out from under the counter, holding it up for her to see. "I recently ordered this online. Can't get it in the bookstores or the library. It's a real page-turner. I haven't been able to put it down."

He came back around the counter and put the book in her hands. The cover showed a bunch of puffy clouds against a technicolour blue sky, the sun shining through them. A white man in a turquoise jumpsuit was sitting in a white chair perched on the clouds. She was immediately put off by the image and turned the book over so as not to have to look at the man's face. The back cover swam with clouds and blurbs.

"Some of the customers are really interested in this one, some are really curious. Some don't want to hear it." Matthew shrugged. "But a lot of people know something's going on, that the government just isn't right. This guy—" he pointed at the cover "—he really explains things very clearly. What's actually going on." He went on to explain that, while travelling in South America, the man fell into a trance and started channelling a disembodied spirit who told the man a number of secrets about Earth, the most revelatory being that all of the major governments and institutions were run by lizard-beings who got their power from torture and mind control, the drinking of blood. Something about terror changed the chemical composition of their victims' blood and made it especially delicious to these lizard-beings, her brother explained. They couldn't resist it, and it gave them the strength needed to control the world. Lise had heard a lot of outlandish theories from her brother over the years, but this one was by far one of the most repugnant. She couldn't look at his face as she pushed the book back into his hands. "Thanks—I've got a lot to read these days. Maybe I can get it another time." She looked back at the register, then toward the door. "Should we take a walk? Is there someone to cover for you?"

He tried to hand the book back to her. "You might not be able to get it up in Vancouver. You can just borrow it for a week or two, send it back when you're done." He looked at her, but her stricken expression must not have registered—or he read it as something else. "Just give it a chance. Keep an open mind. You might be surprised what you learn."

She found herself taking the book and putting it in her backpack, already imagining herself dumping it in the garbage can at the station before she boarded her train home.

Outside, spring was starting, clumps of daffodils and crocuses pushing up in front yards, trilling birds in the trees they passed. Once they got off the busy street, the air smelled better, like mud and plants, early blossoms. The solid Portland houses glistened in the early afternoon light, painted in purple, teal, orange. Some had porch swings or hanging flower baskets, others had bicycles locked to front gates and rows of lettuce and chard starting to peek out of the grooved soil of garden plots.

Lise matched her brother's steps and thought about how she was going to phrase the question she wanted to ask. Finally she came out with, "Mom still falling down a lot?"

At her question, she felt something tighten in Matthew, an almost flinch. She was used to this response—it meant he didn't want to talk about something, and often it was followed by him going silent or abruptly changing the subject. But sometimes he surprised her. "Not so much. Not since I had a talk with her." He paused to look at a bunch of velvet-chested robins hopping across a front lawn. One pulled a fat worm right out of the dirt and held it writhing in its beak, then swallowed it in one gulp. "I told her no more vodka. I can't keep picking her up—I'm not strong enough. Sooner or later she's going to break a hip or something. It's only a matter of time. She agreed to stick to wine. It's been better."

Lise nodded. "You buy it for her?"

He looked embarrassed and started to walk again. "Not anymore. There's so many places you can order by phone now. She just gets it delivered."

They crossed back to the busy street and started to walk toward their old high school. They passed a bus shelter where Lise and her friends used to smoke cigarettes and drink Big Gulps after school, a dismal place to hang out, she had realized even then, the cigarette butts and coffee lids crushed amid dusty weeds growing between the cracks of the sidewalk, the exhaust hot in their faces as cars roared by. But there really hadn't been anywhere else to go, anywhere better, that is.

They stopped at the chain-link fence encircling the high school's track. Classes were still in—only a few students could be seen hanging out on the bleachers, passing around a joint, it looked like. Several after-lunch stragglers hurried toward the wide front steps, clutching phones and backpacks. She and Matthew stared at them through the grid of the fence.

In the rotunda in front of the high school was a statue of George Washington, the school's namesake. Matthew's voice took on the knowing tone he often adopted as he said, "Old Georgie. Old George Washington. Did you know he was a slave owner?"

"Weren't they all?"

"He was one of the worst. Notoriously cruel. And greedy as hell. Notoriously greedy."

"I wish all the schools weren't named after these guys," Lise said. "I hate thinking about them."

"I know," Matthew said. "And their slave-owning is just the tip of the iceberg. They were all Masons too. Satan worshippers."

"Satan?" She had that sinking feeling she often got when spending time with her brother. She never knew where the conversation would go, but she did know that sooner or later it would go somewhere she didn't want to follow. She'd learned to brace herself against his arrogant tone, his condescension, but she hadn't figured out yet how to talk over it, or under it, or around it. She'd tried for years and all her efforts hadn't gotten her very far. "You don't think Satan exists, do you?"

"Oh no." He chuckled darkly. "No, no. I mean, not in any Christian sense. But the Masons do. They believe in him. They bow down to him. They conduct sacrifices. All of them. Even Obama." His tone picked up an urgency, and he looked at her face intently, as if he could convince her that what he was saying was the verifiable truth if he just stared long enough into her eyes. He shook his head. "It's so sick. That these are the people running our government. Our world." To her surprise, his eyes filled with tears. She hadn't seen him cry in years. "I just don't know what to do about it sometimes," he said, his voice hoarse. "This world is so sick."

Before he could stop her, she put her arm around his shoulders and hugged him to her side, nestling her face into his shoulder. "Matthew, you have to stop reading this crap," she said, her voice muffled against his shirt. "It's making you too depressed. It's not helping you at all. It's not helping anyone."

He didn't say anything. He let her hold him for a minute. She heard him sniff a couple of times. His body was tense against hers, the muscles felt coiled and ready, as if he was about to break into a run. But then he removed her arm and stepped away. "That's what you think," he said, wiping his eyes with the sleeve of his shirt. "I help a lot of people at my work. I help them to understand what's really going on."

She felt the familiar feeling of hopelessness sinking down from her throat and settling into the pit of her stomach. It always made her feel so cold. She always felt so tired after hanging out with him.

IN HIGH SCHOOL she and her brother used to go on Saturday afternoons to an art house cinema downtown. They'd jump the number 4 bus and then walk a few blocks up Fifth Avenue to catch films they couldn't see in the big blockbuster outlets, French and

Italian, or indie numbers made in Montana or Rhode Island on a shoe-string budget, featuring people who had never acted before, people with blemishes and bellies who seemed to their teenage eyes so believable, so real.

Lise liked the pace of these films, the slow close-ups that allowed the viewer to really stay with a face, to get to know a pair of grey eyes or a mole on a cheek; the long shots of drenched artichoke-green fields or cities in dying blue light. Everything was beautiful because it was so different from her own life, and she fell into these films like an exhausted person plunging into sleep.

One Saturday a few months after their father died, Lise and Matthew left home in the early afternoon, forgoing the bus to walk all the way downtown to see a French action flick. They were trying once again to escape the dreary house, the smell of mildew and gin, their mother's slurred stories dragging the day out until it blurred into evening.

The film was action-packed, full of chase scenes, pounding music, indecipherable dialogue, and romantic interludes. The hero had spiky bleached-blond hair and looked good in his white jeans or tuxedo as he raced down stairs and into trains, as he spoke his silky language. He loved music; he loved an heiress; he wanted to form a band. In the end, he got shot and the heiress cried with his bloody hand on her cheek. But then a minute later she was fighting off thugs and he was still alive, it seemed, singing along to the music.

The effect of this movie on Lise and Matthew had many layers, but the most prominent one was: it made them feel cool. They left the theatre with that feeling, walking through the sleepy Portland streets in a pleasant daze, as if they were walking through Paris, as if it was possible that they too could live shadowy but glamorous punk lives in subway corridors, form rock bands and woo beautiful women with their scrappy spike-haired charm. The fact that their own city had no subways made the film seem even more edgy, unhesitantly urban.

It was an early fall day and it had rained while they were in the movie, but by the time they left the sun was out, streaking every wet thing with gorgeous light. After the film, everything their eyes glanced upon seemed like a framed shot, and they kept touching each other's arms to point things out—the Hawthorne Bridge glistening against a backdrop of lit clouds, the long row of crows conversing on a telephone wire, the shivering river reflected in a tower's glass, the vibrant green of Waterfront Park's grass. Everything seemed so achingly alive. The coffee shop on the corner, some tall woman in a black coat stepping out with her espresso—she could be French, she could look their way and smile, wink, fall in love with one of them.

They started to walk over the bridge, still pointing out possible shots. Lise was hungry, and hoped they might stop for tacos or burgers on the way home, but she didn't have any money and didn't want to ask her brother to treat her—he always had more money than she did because of his job at the convenience store. They stopped halfway across the river to look down at the water, the rippling slips of light like little rafts riding the swells.

Matthew turned to her and smiled. "I'm going to get his haircut," he said. "And bleach it too. I think it will look good." He gestured to his own hair, cut in the only basic short style their mother knew.

"You should totally do it," Lise said. "And get a trench coat too. He looked so cool."

"I'm going to," he said.

He didn't follow this with "and get a girlfriend," but Lise knew that was what he was thinking. The heroine in the film was slim and sophisticated, with the liquid brown eyes of a French starlet, expressive in her every movement. Lise had found her beautiful as well, although at that age she hadn't understood her crush, had focused only on the rebel blond hero.

SITTING ON THE front steps in the early March sun with no coffee and her brother's cold letter, Lise remembered how earnest Matthew had been when he turned to her that afternoon on the bridge, and how much she had believed him, believed he would become a daring man living in a glamorous city, friends with saxophone players and subway-dwellers, boyfriend to some stunning woman who was his perfect match, who wasn't afraid to shove and run and yell. Even now, she could envision this version of Matthew, his bleached hair sticking up at all angles, accentuating his clear brown eyes, his clean skin and expectant grin. She looked at the envelope again, the large blue-green turtle with its open mouth, the rainbows arcing over her name, the little orange roses she wished she could touch. She held the envelope up to the sunlight and, closing her eyes, she sent her brother a prayer.

THE DEAN REGRETS

"WE HOPE EVERYONE is having an excellent start to the semester! The Arts and Humanities Department is once again hosting Coffee with the Dean this Thursday, our January edition. Please feel free to stop by with your ideas and your concerns. This is a great opportunity to talk with the dean about what's happening. The coffee's free and the doughnuts are plentiful! Be green and keen: bring your own cup. We'd love to see you!"

Brandi is reading this message off her phone, using over-inflections to emphasize the exclamation points. "Well, doesn't that sound terrific," she says, slamming her phone down on her desk. "Who the hell writes this shit?"

"The dean?"

"Yeah right. He can't even be bothered to sign a contract. Ashanti probably had to do it."

"Should we go get some free coffee?"

She shrugs. "You can go if you want."

I've been Brandi's desk neighbour for seven years; she's been here a couple of years longer than me. There are four other desks crammed into this room, a box-like space with small high windows and a permanently stuffy smell from the radiators. It can get claustrophobic. I pick up my travel mug. "It's too hot in here. I'm going to get some coffee."

Brandi pats her thin strawberry-blond hair as if to fix it. Her hair is always staticky, and no matter what she does, it always sticks out from her head. "Okay. If you insist. I'll come with you."

We end up at the union office instead, in the peach-walled lounge, looking out of the big windows facing the quad. The union office also has free coffee, but better free coffee—dark roast, organic half-and-half—and here we won't be forced to make small talk with the dean. I've been avoiding him ever since his office sent out a survey on workplace satisfaction a few weeks ago. I had filled it out honestly, checking ones and twos for every box, but when I told Brandi, she chided me for believing it was really anonymous and reminded me how important it is to stay on the dean's good side.

Brandi shoves a doughnut hole in her mouth and chews as she looks out the window at the undergrads in their heavy backpacks, slumping by in the snow. A lot of them are from warmer countries—Taiwan, Singapore, India—and are only wearing thin jackets and sneakers. The quad's main attraction, a big fountain with some cavorting concrete nymphs, has been turned off and the shallow pool is frozen. "Even the nymphs look fucking cold," Brandi says through a mouthful of doughnut.

Donna, one of the union reps, storms in. She's one of those people who seems to be in a permanent state of anger—if she were a cartoon, she'd have steam coming out of her ears. Today she's in a high turtleneck, maroon, which emphasizes the redness of her round face.

Brandi swallows the rest of her doughnut. "How's bargaining?"

Donna starts in. "Horrible. Horrible." She huffs around the room. "This round has been like squeezing blood from a stone. We can't get them to agree on anything. Trying to claw back sick leave, parental leave …"

Brandi nods in a way that seems sympathetic.

"And dental's off the table now. Totally off the table."

"Well, we adjuncts don't get shit anymore, so it's hard to feel too sorry for the tenured bastards." It's hard to tell from the tone of her voice whether or not Brandi is joking.

"We get coffee." I raise my travel mug to toast her and Donna, then take a small sip. The coffee is delicious, rich and dark, but so hot it nearly scalds my tongue.

"Remember when we had dental?" Brandi turns toward me. "Seems like a lifetime ago."

"I never got it," I say. "Before my time."

Brandi gives a fake "I'm-a-model" smile and points to her teeth. "See these? From the old plan. It paid for braces."

Her teeth do look pretty good, straight and fairly white. Mine are permanently yellow from too much coffee and not enough flossing. I've had a snaggletooth since childhood that I could never afford to fix—it juts out from the left side of my mouth whenever I smile or laugh. Luckily my girlfriend Lila finds it cute; she likes to lick it and call me her little she-wolf.

Donna interjects, "We've tried. We've tried so many times. And we'll keep fighting for you, for all adjuncts. We will. But it's a hard fight—I mean, the employer won't give us a *bone.*" She looks angrily out the window at the quad as if she wishes the president and provost were walking by this very minute so she could rush up to them and shake her fist in their faces. "It's disgusting," she concludes.

I nod in agreement while trying to figure out how to make a graceful exit. Brandi has wandered back to the coffee table and is grazing the doughnut box, taking her time making a selection. I know Donna is right, but I've always found something repellant about the way she carries on, something insincere. She used to be our English colleague, and at our meetings would passionately argue for the rights of disadvantaged students, but I could never pay attention to her speeches—as soon as she started talking, I'd drift off. Now she has channelled all of her fire into fighting the administration. She enjoys the drama of it all a little too much, is the problem. Listening to her is exhausting, and so even though I want to know what is going on, I usually try to keep my distance.

Brandi comes back over clutching two chocolate doughnut holes. She pops one in her mouth and chews, eyeing Donna. I can tell she's about to ask one of her piercing questions, starting a conversation that could last an hour. It's the perfect opportunity to excuse myself and I take it, mumbling something about grading papers as I hurry out of the office and back into the cold. Outside,

I slow down and try to take careful steps so as to not spill any coffee in the snow.

THE NEXT DAY I accompany Lila on a shoe-shopping expedition over to the west side, where, in a store featuring exquisite shoes made out of expensive Italian leather, we run into the dean. He is already sitting, looking calmly down at the head of the nervous young salesclerk who is bent over his foot, adjusting his argyle sock as he attempts to slip an oxblood wing-tipped oxford over the dean's toes. I immediately turn back toward the door, thinking I can escape without being seen, but Lila is already across the room, calling at me to come and admire some unaffordable silver flats. The dean looks up and spots me, his ever-ready smile—what I think of as his politician's smile—flashing across his face. "Laurel! Fancy seeing you here. Shoe shopping, are we?"

"Just hanging out with my girlfriend." My voice lilts weirdly. I don't know why I always have to be so awkward around administrators. Once I dumped half a cup of coffee on my sweater just because the provost looked my way as she passed the cafeteria.

Lila comes over and puts her arm around me, holding the shoe in her other hand. "This is Lila," I say. Then, gesturing to the dean, "Lila, Dean Johnson."

"Roland," he says, holding out his hand to her. He can't stand up because the poor clerk is still trying to get his feet into the oxfords.

"Nice choice. Classic." Lila points at the shoes.

"You think so?" I can tell he has already been taken in by her easy charm and I stifle an impulse to roll my eyes.

"Yes, definitely. They look at little tight, though. Of course, new leather is always tight." She taps the silver flat against her palm as she says this. Another sales clerk appears and offers to get her the shoes in her size. Lila follows her to the other side of the store.

The dean has stood up and is strolling around, testing out the shoes. He pauses in front of a full-length mirror and points one toe, then the other. He stamps his feet and walks back and forth in front of the mirror. "I just can't decide," he says.

I'm a bad shopper myself and not the best at giving retail advice, something Lila has criticized me for more than once. I always say everything looks good, or else I try to figure out what the shopper wants me to say, and I say that. I use words like "flattering" or "unflattering," "trendy" and "timeless"—words I've heard Lila and her friends use. I'm trying to figure out if the dean wants me to say something, or if it's okay to just nod with a vaguely appreciative look on my face.

He turns to me and smiles. "It's great to run into you."

Is it? I think. And then I remember to smile. "It's nice to see you too."

"I've been meaning to reach out to some of the faculty, set up some meetings. We're contemplating making some changes since the survey. It was very informative. We learned a lot about how we can better meet people's needs."

Meet people's needs. This is the speech of therapists, and of administrators trained in the new corporate touchy-feely speak. And the use of "we." Very Dean Johnson. He never says "I" if he can help it. That way, when the axe falls, it's not his axe, it's "the axe"—or rather, it's not an axe at all, it's just a very unfortunate result, a very unfortunate circumstance, a very unfortunate gap in the budget. I nod and smile, wondering how to extricate myself from the conversation. "The shoes look great. I think you should get them."

The clerk, who has been standing a few feet away, steps closer and agrees, "They look great on you, sir. Very classic."

The dean turns back to the mirror, pivoting on his heel. Even though it's a Saturday, he's dressed in a well-cut green suit and a yellow silk tie. "All right. You two have convinced me. I'll get them." He looks back at me. "Thank you." He smiles again. He must get those teeth-whitening treatments. "We heard from everyone. Lecturers, tenured, adjuncts, full-time, part-time—everyone. And most people are happy. But even what's good can be improved. What do you say, come by my office in the next couple of weeks? You can make an appointment with Ashanti."

I mumble that I will and thank him—I'm not sure why—before hurrying to the other side of the store to admire the shoes it looks like Lila, against all financial arguments on my part, is now determined to purchase. "It's my money," she says firmly when my voice veers toward a whine, and so I shut up.

A WEEK LATER I arrive at the office on Monday morning to find Brandi looking sombre. She's not one to drop bad news gleefully while watching your face for a reaction, as Donna loves to do. But nor is she one for neutral language or avoidance. "The budget is a fucking mess. The provost says the school is a sinking ship. I guess the province is too fucking busy giving tax breaks to oil and gas companies to bother helping us out." She heaves out a sigh of disgust. "Only money from international students is keeping us afloat."

I tell her what I felt when I walked onto campus—something in the air, something palpable. People scurrying around in the falling snow, looking cold and upset. Administrators and instructors staring grimly into their coffee cups to avoid meeting anyone's eyes. Fear, I guess it was. Now, I shiver in my wool coat, even though the office is hot and dusty as always.

"There will be more lay-offs. We'll probably lose our jobs." She looks down at her desk, pulling at her wispy bangs with her fingers.

"But the dean asked me to come meet with him this week," I say stupidly.

Brandi looks at me with consternation. "Shit. He's starting already?"

"Not about lay-offs. About, you know, the survey, 'improving our experience here,' all that crap."

She shakes her head. "Sure. Then you show up and he's like, 'Actually, you're fired! Um, I mean, here's your lay-off letter.'" She cackles. "I told you not to be honest. When they ask for feedback you do one thing: lie lie lie. And smile smile smile." She bares her teeth in a humorous grimace. "This is what I look like every time I walk past the dean's office. Anyone asks? I'm always smiling."

I take off my coat and place it over the back of the chair at my desk. A bit of winter light seeps down from the small high windows. The office doesn't have an overhead light, only a few lamps on the desks, two with burnt-out bulbs, so the place is always dim, even in summer. The desks are corporate-generic, the chairs uncomfortable, both probably purchased at a discount at some office furniture warehouse. Long ago, Brandi commandeered the only chair with wheels, and she loves to glide around the room, visiting whoever might be trying to grade at their desks. Often, though, it's just she and I in here.

At the desk I share with three other adjuncts, there's a calendar from last year that's still up, open to September, a picture of rolling hills of orange and gold, an insurance company's slogan at the bottom. The only other decoration is a framed photo of a little black-haired girl in blue shorts, laughing on a swing. Meijane, a former adjunct, brought it here when she first started, thinking her daughter's smile might cheer us all up. But Meijane had only lasted a year, and when they abruptly stopped giving her classes, she never came back to the office to claim the picture. Meijane was smart and accomplished, and Brandi and I couldn't figure out why they hadn't kept hiring her. Were there student complaints? That seemed unlikely. Had she gone crying to the union about something and word got back to the dean? That seemed even more unlikely. Meijane had a self-possessed air; she kept her own counsel, didn't gossip or complain. "Maybe she was just too good for this place," Brandi said.

Meijane was rare; most people don't leave personal effects in the office. Our colleague Viktor keeps a little Shrek action figure on the shelf above his desk. He sometimes kisses it for good luck before heading into class or makes it talk in funny voices. Last week he had

Shrek jumping up and down on a pile of student papers, whimpering nasally, "Why me? Why me?"

Brandi is here more than anyone, but her only decoration is a quote from Walter Benjamin, written on a yellow index card and tacked to the bulletin board above her desk: "What draws the reader to a novel is the hope of warming his shivering life at the flame of a death he reads about." Ever since I've known Brandi, she's been a secret writer, scribbling away at her novel wherever and whenever she can, between classes, on weekends, on the bus to and from work. She's only ever let me read a few pages, but they were pretty good. When I told her that, she wouldn't let me read anymore. Sometimes we get a drink after work, and with a bit of wine, she becomes more expansive, telling me details about the next scene she's going to write. Her protagonist, Ellen, is uncannily like Brandi herself, but a bit more glamorous and a bit more rich. Recently Brandi recounted a scene in which Ellen vacations in a small fishing village in Mexico and has an affair with a scuba diving instructor, something Brandi herself would probably like to do. Last week she told me that she might try to get an agent once the manuscript is finished.

Well, she'll have plenty of time to finish it now, if we both get laid off. I sit down at my desk and put my face in my hands. The smell of the dust burning in the radiator is nauseating. I feel sweaty and sick. My mind reels, trying to find solutions. Maybe Simran can get me some classes at her ESL college. Maybe Jacob needs a grader—he has those huge lecture classes and is always grumbling about how he never has enough graduate students to help. I wonder how much

EI we might get this time—the province cut the amounts recently, someone told me. Maybe I can sub for Casey. Their college was hiring last month. I should have applied.

Brandi's anxiety seems to have quickly dissipated—she's the queen of compartmentalization—and somehow she's already back to her efficient self, typing rapidly on her laptop. "Sorry—just have to answer this email from a student." After a minute or two, she stops typing. "Jesus Christ," she says. She looks at me. "Brace yourself. Another memo from the dean. Two weeks in a row—this has to be a record." She reads: "In my last memo, I promised a big picture look at our faculty. I'm writing today to give some thoughts about all that we have accomplished in the Arts and Humanities. We have a lot to be proud of!"

"Give me a break," Brandi snorts. Then she continues: "It's not possible to write about our accomplishments over the last year without mentioning our incredibly dedicated faculty. The people power we have here is something else! Recently our English instructors have created a faculty exchange program with Xiangtan University, History professors are writing textbooks with their students as part of our open education initiative, and in Fine Arts we have a new co-op program in which faculty help upper-level students find placements at local galleries to gain real-life career experience."

Brandi rolls her eyes. "Great. More instructors doing extra work for free. As if that's news. Oh, but here we go … he's getting to the survey now. 'Our recent survey showed that eighty-five percent of you are "very happy" with your current positions and eighty percent of you are happy with the institution overall. We aim to make that one hundred percent! In the next few months we will be unveiling some new initiatives that we believe will greatly energize our faculty. Stay tuned for more updates!'"

"Initiatives like handing out pink slips?" Brandi says. "What a crock of shit. Typical. Of course he didn't mention the lay-offs."

"Are they for sure?"

"Donna says so."

I pull out a bunch of student essays; they are limp, damp from the snow melting into my bag. No matter how shitty this news is, I still have to get my grading done.

Viktor bursts in, wearing a blue medical mask over his nose and mouth. His intense brown eyes dominate his face.

Brandi and I both look at him, and then Brandi bursts out laughing. "What are you wearing?" she asks.

"Coronavirus. Have to stay safe."

"That's ridiculous," Brandi says. "You're not at risk. There are like, what, two cases in all of Canada?"

"Three. I have a lot of international students. I'm not taking any chances." Viktor pulls a rolled-up newspaper out of his coat pocket and tosses it on Brandi's desk. "Read this. It's more dangerous than you think."

He looks at my stack of wrinkled essays. "Back at the grindstone, eh? They get worse every term. I mean, some of my students, they're from other countries, and they can't even speak English at all. It's a joke. Listen to this conclusion." He rifles around his bag, pulls out an essay, and reads a few sentences. "Talk about tortured grammar, right?" He shakes his head, grinning sardonically.

"It sounds like a poem," I say, although I'm annoyed. Viktor immigrated from the Czech Republic in his teens and must have at some point had his own struggles learning English, but he seems to have forgotten all that now. Like most of us, he left grad school before getting a PhD, which is why he's stuck in this crummy office with the rest of us adjuncts. Sometimes he says he's going to go back and finish his dissertation on Orwell—he'll wax poetic, drop a few mentions of masculinity theory, but these proclamations usually taper off with a sigh as he acknowledges how much work it will be and how little time he has.

Brandi looks up from the article she's scanning. "It's an administration issue, Viktor. Don't blame the poor students. They've been incorrectly placed. It's an assessment issue. The university needs to deal with it."

"I don't blame them," says Viktor. He lifts his mask, I guess so that we can hear him more clearly. "I don't blame them at all. I just don't want them in my class." He picks up the Shrek figure and makes it dance, sing-songing, "It makes my job so hard, oh … it makes my job so hard, oh …"

"Boo-fucking-hoo, buddy." Brandi tosses the newspaper onto Viktor's desk. It's clear she's only given the article a cursory glance. "We're probably all being laid off again, so you won't need to worry about your dumb students anymore because you won't have any."

Viktor doesn't look surprised. From the steaming cup of coffee he's placed on his desk, it appears he's probably just come from gossiping with Donna in the union office. He takes a sip of the coffee and pulls the mask back down to cover his mouth. "Last time I got laid off I hiked Mount Seymour every day. Got really fit. It wasn't too bad."

"That's because your wife is a lawyer," Brandi says. "It's different for us singles."

"And those of us whose partners don't have much money," I add. "No one to bail us out."

"No one," echoes Brandi. "We're on our own."

THE NEXT WEDNESDAY finds me slumped on the brown couch outside the dean's office, listening to Ashanti fielding calls from students who have gotten wind of the budget cuts. I hear her say at least five times that she doesn't have that information, that the administration hasn't announced that yet, that updates will be posted on the website. She is always so controlled and polite—I don't know how she does it. I scan through emails on my phone. A bunch of my students are sick with the flu; another plagiarized essay; Donna announcing a meeting tonight at the union office (she lets us know, with a winky face, that there will be "liquid refreshments"); Viktor asking if anyone's called Facilities about getting more light bulbs for the office. I'm just about to reply to him when Ashanti looks up at me. "He's ready for you now."

I've only been in Dean Johnson's office a couple of times, but it looks pretty much the same as it did when it was Dean Rodriguez's office. Tall, south-facing windows that let in a lot of light, two comfy grey chairs facing each other with a small table between them. I recognize the pillows as the ones Dean Rodriguez got at the start of her tenure, small and rectangular with geometric patterns in forest green. There is a new addition, however: a small gold-painted Buddha statue adorns the table.

"Laurel." The dean gestures for me to have a seat. "Thanks for coming in." He's more subdued than usual, and I wonder if he's preparing himself to deliver some bad news.

"Is the Buddha statue new? I don't think I've seen it before."

"Oh, it's just something my wife picked up for me at IKEA. Bring a little Zen into the office, you know." His laugh sounds a bit nervous.

I wish I had worn my coat; this office is always cold. Dean Rodriguez used to keep a shawl here that she would wrap around her shoulders while she worked, but that is one tradition Dean Johnson hasn't carried forward. I smile, imagining him in a paisley cashmere shawl. It wouldn't look bad on him, actually. In the corner by his desk is a small space heater but it's not plugged in.

"Would you like some tea?" the dean asks. "I could ask Ashanti to brew a pot."

Dean Rodriguez always had a pot of tea on the go and served it in cups with whimsical designs, sparrows perched on branches singing their tiny hearts out to clusters of red berries. I wonder if Dean Johnson has inherited the cups as well or if Dean Rodriguez took them with her to her new job in Victoria.

The two deans really couldn't be more different. Dean Rodriguez gave you tea, but she didn't pretend to be too nice, and she would tell you more than most administrators would—people found her honest. Dean Johnson doesn't inspire the same assessment. Gossip around the office is that he's not "leader material." Some go so far as to call him a yes-man or the administration's lapdog. Usually the gossiper tries to end on a positive note by saying he's nice, though, very nice.

"No thanks," I say, gesturing with my travel mug. "I got coffee at the union office."

"The free coffee is great. Did you get a chance to talk to Donna while you were there?"

"No, but I got the email the union sent out. It didn't have many details."

"Yes." He looks thoughtfully down at his shoes. They're the oxblood oxfords I saw him trying on at that store on the west side. "Well, we've been a bit in the dark as well. It's all happened rather quickly. The president and provost held a special meeting last week—"

"Are we getting laid off again?"

My directness seems to make him uncomfortable. He shifts in his seat and crosses one leg over the other. As usual, he's wearing really nice socks; this pair is striped, gold and slate. "Well … there's going to be some job loss." He quickly corrects himself. "I mean, work reduction. There will be some work reduction." It's as if he's suddenly remembered the right words to a script.

"Will my work be reduced? Brandi's?"

"We don't know for sure yet, Laurel. We're figuring all that out. We need to see who might be retiring … see if we can give some incentives to retire early … the budget is still in flux. We'll let you know as soon as we can."

I nod blankly and sip my coffee. He seems to be waiting for me to say something, but I don't know what to say.

"Do I wish I had all the answers? Yes, Laurel, I do. People have been coming to my office all week. I wish I had more information for all of you." He pauses, tapping his fingers on the arm of the chair. I stare at his face. He's wearing glasses that I haven't noticed before—turquoise frames, a bit flashy. He looks genuinely pained, and for a moment I feel a flash of sympathy for him.

I nod again and stand up. As I do so I remember the reason we are supposed to be meeting—the survey. But I'm not about to bring it up if he isn't going to. My stomach rumbles. I should have eaten breakfast and I shouldn't have left my coat in the adjunct office—it will be a cold dash over to the student-run café. I put out my hand. "Well, thanks for your time. Let me know more when you know."

The dean rises also, taking my hand and shaking it. "Of course. Thanks for stopping by." He gives me his this-is-an-unfortunate-situation smile. It's a little less brilliant than his everyday one.

BACK IN THE office, it's dark. I click on the lamp on my desk, but no luck—another burnt-out bulb. I try Brandi's and it flicks on, casting a warm circle of light. The recycle bin between our desks is stuffed to overflowing; a few crumpled papers have fallen onto the floor. It rarely gets emptied; the cleaning staff are overworked and don't always make it to our office. Brandi is usually the one who drags it down the hall to dump it in the big bin, but she must be too preoccupied with everything going on to notice it. The radiators pump out heat along with the smell of charred dust. I sit down at my desk and slowly unwrap the tuna fish sandwich I bought at the café. It's a little soggy, but at least it's something.

There's the scratching of someone trying to get their keys in the lock. The door swings open—it's Brandi, looking worse for the wear. Her staticky hair haloes about her head and her eyes are red-rimmed. A drop of snot hangs from the tip of her pointy nose. The only other time I've seen her cry is the last time we got laid off, three years ago. "You okay?" I ask.

"It's official." She holds up a white business envelope. "This was in my mailbox. I saw one in yours too." She sits down heavily at her desk, not bothering to take off her dripping coat. "Those mother-fuckers," she says. "Those goddamned cocksuckers."

"What?" I set my sandwich down on the desk. "I was just meeting with the dean. He didn't say anything. He said he didn't know whether there'd be lay-offs."

"Well, he lied," Brandi says.

"I can't believe this," I say. "I was just in his office." I feel like an idiot. "I should have pushed him harder. I should have been rude to him."

"It wouldn't have done any good," Brandi says. She looks up at the small windows. A small stream of light drifts down, illuminating the thin skin of her face. She shakes her head. "Those mother-fuckers," she says. Her voice sounds almost cheerful.

THE BUS RIDE home is usually one of the least pleasant parts of my day. The number 32 is always late, crowded and stinky. There's inevitably at least one incredibly drunk or high person yelling and making a scene. I often have to stand, sometimes with my face in a rank armpit. I always get jostled. To escape, I listen to podcasts or read news. If I'm lucky enough to get a seat I grade papers on my lap or look out the window and think about what I might make for dinner. Most nights I text Lila to see if she wants to come over or if I can stop by her place with groceries. Tonight she is making me spinach lasagne because of the bad day, the bad news.

After waiting for twenty minutes in the freezing cold, I'm crammed in between a turbaned grandfather balancing a cane between his knees and a sweaty-smelling youth in a black leather jacket. I take out my phone and open my email. There's a message from the dean, sent earlier in the day, entitled "My Weekly Memo."

"The dean's office has decided to start sending out weekly memos to keep everyone abreast of things," he begins. I think about how proud he must be to have used the word "abreast" in a message. "Behooves" is another favourite of his. "It behooves us to think ahead," he likes to say in meetings.

The message goes on to mention a couple of pedagogy trainings that might be of interest and a bake sale Fine Arts is having to raise money for their ceramics program. This is followed by: "Many of you were looking forward to Beers with the Dean, to be held at the new brewing facilities in the Clark Building next week. Unfortunately, this event has to be postponed until next semester. I regret that we can't toast each other with microbrews made by our very own talented student brewers, but I'm sure we'll enjoy those beers even more in May!" Beers with the dean? This is the first I've heard of it. But I did hear from Brandi that the brewing program might be axed.

The memo ends with what I guess is supposed to be a pick-me-up, an announcement that today is "World Biscotti Day," with a meme of a dancing chocolate-dipped biscotti. There's also a cartoon graphic of a person in running shoes leaping over a mountain chasm, with the slogan "Wednesday is Hump Day! You're almost over the hump!" These are followed by the dean's final words: "Thank you to everyone for your hard work and patience in these challenging times."

I close my email and look out the window. I know I should be texting my friends, trying to line up some more work. But I'm too tired for any of that right now. Out the window, the snow has started falling again, hard little flakes in the blueing light. The bus slides as it slows down, bumping the curb. There are big groups of people waiting in the cold at every stop, stamping their feet and blowing on their hands. We pass a sweets shop, a tandoori place, a Szechwan kitchen. Fast food signs pulse neon, promising cheap grease and salt. I just want to go home and lay my head on Lila's shoulder, let her stroke my hair. Maybe we'll have a little wine with the lasagne, watch something mindless on Netflix.

Tomorrow I'll call my friends about work, see what I can rustle up. I'll call Brandi too, see how she's faring.

In these challenging times.

THE BROTHERHOOD

DAVID WANTS TO pace but doesn't want to draw attention to himself, so he shifts from one foot to the other, pacing in his mind. He's always the first one to arrive. He checks his phone; it's already five past. Around him, dust and debris swirls. A yellow fast food wrapper clings to his pant leg and he kicks it off. A few yards away, an old woman with a large bag of groceries sits in a bus shelter yelling into her phone and smoking a cigarette. The smell is enough to make him want to choke. A long line of semis spews out noxious exhaust. David feels his lungs tighten and he coughs into the crook of his elbow. He forgot his handkerchief again.

Behind him the columns of the old lodge are still standing, although the stone steps are falling apart and the windows have all been bashed in. Someone has chipped off the symbols above the door and spray-painted swear words on the facade. Cars roar past it nonchalantly, as if the lodge is just an old ruin abandoned in an overgrown field.

David looks up to see Paul barrelling toward him, dressed as always in a double-breasted suit, sweating as if he's just stepped off a treadmill. His splotchy face is more bloated than it was last year and he's out of breath. Still walking, he passes a hand over his forehead and shakes it into the street. David sees the silver ring glinting on one of Paul's fingers and realizes that he once again forgot to wear his. He hopes Paul doesn't notice. The ring is back in his apartment, stuffed in the pocket of the brotherhood robe hanging in the back of his closet.

Paul halts in front of David and looks around as if he thinks someone might be watching. But no one is, and so he reaches out for the handshake. It takes them a few tries, but they finally get all of the movements right. They mutter a few words that sound like Latin under their breath while staring down at the ground. Only after they finish do they look each other in the eye.

"My brother," Paul says, slapping David on the arm.

It always makes David a little uncomfortable when he uses this sort of language, but he knows Paul can't help it.

"Have you heard from Jeremy?" David asks.

Paul looks around, sweat running down his cheeks. "No. Do you have a handkerchief?"

"No. I forgot mine."

"Oh." Paul rubs his face with both hands and laughs. "Well, that should take care of it, I guess."

Just then Jeremy appears, dressed as usual in a beige trench that resembles the uniform of the secret service men who used to attend him. Jeremy examines David and Paul from head to toe but doesn't meet their eyes. After the handshakes and the mumbled words, he gives a strained smile.

"My brother," Paul says. The greeting sounds forced. "We meet again."

"So we do," Jeremy says, his voice flat. After three bouts of cancer, his skin is a dim white bordering on grey. The flesh hangs loosely off of his cheekbones.

The old woman in the bus shelter gets up and tosses her cigarette into the gutter, still screaming at someone on her phone. Horns blare; there is yelling and cursing from the passing cars, thunderous music from a cab's blown-out speakers.

"I don't know why we always end up in this goddamned hell hole," Paul says, looking down the block at the trash-strewn sidewalk.

Jeremy shrugs.

"It gets worse every year. I mean, look at the temple." Paul gestures at the crumbling lodge, then turns to face a burnt-out building across the street, its bubbly red paint streaked with soot. "And Garcia's." He shakes his head. "Our booth. Those martinis." He smiles nostalgically. "Remember the gelato parlour? Remember Mario? The biggest scoops! Jesus. What I wouldn't give for a dish of praline. He used to say we were his favourite customers."

"He was afraid of us," Jeremy says, pulling a cigarette out of his suit pocket and lighting it.

David starts coughing, waving a hand in front of his face.

"Oh yes, sorry. I forgot." Jeremy flicks the cigarette to the curb. His voice lacks any trace of apology.

"Our brother's asthma has really been acting up, poor sap," Paul booms.

A whirring sound approaches and a large sphere floats into view. It looks like it is made out of soapy water, like one of the bubbles David used to chase through the park as a child. But it is huge, the size of a city bus, and it glides like an enormous translucent jellyfish moving through water.

In the sphere are the shimmering forms of young people sitting in a circle next to a fast-moving river. They are discussing something, illuminated in a peachy sunlight that David can tell just from looking is the perfect temperature. A breeze stirs a young man's long black hair. One of them is saying that the stocks are returning, that just last week they saw salmon spawning in a creek bordering their community's land. Another is asking if anyone wants to go to see the latest Tailfeathers movie at the Urban Forest Film Fest. As the bubble drifts away, David hears another one saying yes, they'll pack pears, sandwiches, and can they bring their grandmother.

The three men stare at it for a moment and then turn back to each other, Paul shaking his head. The sun bears down on them, greasing the faces of David and Paul. Paul wipes his hands over his cheeks again, trying to rub in the sweat. "Eight o'clock and it's already scorching. Next year let's meet at seven."

The other two men don't reply.

"Do you have a handkerchief?" Paul asks Jeremy.

"Only one," Jeremy says, taking it out and dabbing his dry face before pocketing it again.

"So, shall we start?" David asks. His voice is hoarse from the fumes and smoke. "I'm sorry I didn't have time to make an agenda. Does anyone have anything to report since our last meeting?"

Jeremy gives him a blank look. Paul's expression is sheepish as he says, "I tried. I reached out to my old contacts—or tried to get my secretary to." He shakes his head in frustration. "But she quit. Said she'd be better off as a shift supervisor at McDonald's. Just walked out. I think she was pulling my leg, though—she probably started her own business or something. I saw her later in one of the spheres."

"I thought McDonald's went out of business after that sick cow thing," Jeremy says.

"They rebranded. Selling soy burgers now. Going like hotcakes. Christ! I wish I'd gotten in there when the getting was good, snagged a few shares." Paul looks off into the distance. "Foolish. Damn foolish of me."

"Let's get down to business," David says. "Who took the minutes last time?"

Jeremy and Paul look at each other.

Just then, another, larger sphere bounces by, pulsing goldenly. Blue and green club lights burst inside it like fireworks. Flickering images of people writhe to the beat of a halcyon song, laughing and jostling. Several people are on bikes, peddling vigorously to generate energy for the turntables and speakers. Even the bikers seem to be dancing, weaving their heads to the music. David sees one woman with purple and black hair lean in to kiss another woman who isn't wearing a shirt. The music shifts to a heavier beat and the crowd starts jumping up and down, screaming gleefully. The DJ tosses their locs and raises their hand in the air, making a fist and pumping it as if they're at a political rally.

The sphere bounces away and David hears Paul complaining. "It's too hard without secretaries! Nothing pretty in a skirt—there's no reason to even go to the office anymore." He looks off at the noisy street before adding quietly, "My living room is my office now."

"Secretaries?" Jeremy says. "I'd settle just for my old car and driver. Or even just a car of my own. I'm not picky—a second-hand Lamborghini even."

"I miss all of my cars," Paul says. "Every one of them. I used to have my driver take me up to see those blue mountains, the purple light on those hills after we cleared them—beautiful sight." He whistles under his breath. "I made a pretty penny on that one."

"I'd get flown to Geneva," Jeremy reminisces. "Paris. Some kind of summit, a little Bordeaux with lunch, a little business on the side …"

"We need to focus, people." David's voice is strained. "I didn't take the minutes last time. I would remember. Do you have them, Jeremy?"

Jeremy doesn't bother to pull out his phone. "No."

"Can anyone remember what we agreed to?"

"I don't think it matters at this point," Jeremy says.

The sun beats down mercilessly and the smell of putrid meat from a nearby hotdog stand is suffocating. Paul's blotchy face is starting to burn. "Jesus, where can we get a steak? I'm starving," he says. "There used to be a great steakhouse right over there." He points toward a trashy convenience store bordered in neon. "Whatever happened to it?"

"Neighbourhood changed," Jeremy says. "Sick cow disease, remember?"

Paul shakes his head. "I forgot. I'm always forgetting," he says mournfully.

"Half a dozen triple bypasses would make anyone forgetful," Jeremy says.

"I could have half a dozen more," says Paul. "I'm still going." He lifts his jacket and heaves his belly up with his other hand. "Dad's belt. One hundred percent crocodile. Still got it."

"So?" Jeremy says.

"It's my good luck charm. Still got it. When Dad left the brotherhood, I got it."

"You mean when he died?" Jeremy asks.

"We're going to need more than your father's lucky belt," David says. He's trying to stay patient. He attempts an upbeat, convincing tone. "We need a new plan. A strategy—" He stops speaking and looks up as the whirring of another sphere approaches. Inside are glimmering people tending a tangerine orchard. There's the buzz of a thousand contented bees. David imagines he smells honey, thinks of being sick, swaddled in a blanket and sipping a huge mug of lemon tea.

The old woman at the bus stop rises to her feet and starts yelling at the sphere, gesticulating. By the way her arms are raised David can't tell if she wishes she could punch a hole in the sphere or if she's beseeching the people inside to take her with them.

"If only we could get in there." Paul points emphatically. "That's where we belong. In one of those. Doing our work. Making changes."

"They won't let us in," Jeremy says.

"All we need is a little money, a little cash flow, and we can get one of those billboards up again. You know? Catch them by surprise as they're bounding past. Something bold, like 'DON'T BE AFRAID.' Then slip in a few subliminals, you know, dungeons, someone hanging from a sheet, shot in the head ..." Paul trails off.

"They can't see that stuff anymore. It's useless," Jeremy says.

"What we need is another ceremony," Paul says. "Something to get them on our wavelength again. One of the old ones. Tried and true. One of the ones we used for decades." He turns to face the lodge again, looking at it as if his very gaze will turn the lights back on, raise the glass in the windows. A semi full of cars rattles by, the sound deafening.

"Centuries," Jeremy says. "The brothers have used them for centuries. But they're all useless now. We've tried, Paul. Remember?"

"And we were almost there! Almost ... we just need another stab at it." Abruptly, he stomps up the stairs to the lodge and yanks at the door, but it's locked. He shakes it repeatedly and then finally lets his hand drop, turning back to them with a look of barely concealed rage.

"We have tried, Paul." David thinks of their last meeting a year ago at this same stinking corner full of dust and smoke. They'd attempted a ceremony, walking in circles around the temple as they chanted one of the old spells. It was one he didn't know the words to, but he mumbled along, following after Jeremy and Paul. Paul had insisted that they bring their brotherhood rings and press them periodically to their lips. They must have looked ridiculous, but no one passing by seemed to care.

At one point Paul had interrupted to demand, "Do you feel it? I feel it! Something is changing. I feel the vibration." He held out one chubby hand and looked at it for confirmation. "We'll reach them this time. We will!"

But David had to confess he didn't feel any change. He did feel slightly afraid of Paul, his fanatical blue eyes watery and too bright. Jeremy was lost in his own world, eyes closed, droning on with his arms raised in the air like an evangelist.

Paul returned to his circling and chanting but the momentum was lost. David kept glancing up at the decrepit lodge, wondering what they were doing. He felt as foolish as he had at his initiation ceremony, where he'd been blindfolded, taken to the basement of the lodge, and made to walk a plank balanced on a couple of folding chairs. After that he'd been forced to put his hand in a mousetrap while chanting nonsensical words. The entire night had been an exercise in pain and humiliation, and David had wondered if it was worth the promotion he'd get at work, but he'd continued on, too embarrassed to shrug off the blindfold, to call it all stupid and leave.

Jeremy finally came out of his trance and looked at Paul and David like he didn't know who they were. Finally he said, "It didn't work, did it?"

A couple of years before that they had tried a different strategy. Jeremy had managed to cajole a loan out of one of his former cronies and for a very large sum they had hired a young person with pink hair and a nose ring to unleash a social media campaign across several platforms. But the campaign fell flat on its face. People didn't respond in the same way they once had—they seemed immune to the sure-fire tricks, the easy clickbait. Even Paul had to admit that he couldn't feel any difference in the atmosphere, that the energy around them wasn't any more fraught.

This was toward the end of David's tenure at the insurance company, where he had already noticed things starting to shift. His colleagues laughed more and shared snacks with each other, delicious things like homemade samosas and maple walnut fudge. He overheard them telling stories about helping strangers on public transit or meditating next to a swimming pool in a city park. David tried to use the tricks he'd been taught by his brothers, simple mind-control techniques to undermine others and make them doubt their sense of their own realities, but he noticed that the tricks were becoming less effective.

One afternoon he was practising on a colleague as they were getting coffee in the break room, looking steadily into her eyes as he told her a blatant and mean lie in the smooth voice he'd honed to a perfect pitch. She simply shook her head in disbelief, laughed, and walked away.

Anyone could see that things were changing. Instead of the familiar drone of constant worry and anguish, at times a bright, clear feeling would flare up and cut through an interaction in the office or across a crowded downtown square. There were rumblings—talk of people being happier in other dimensions, of creating "a better world." David scoffed, but he also thought these rumblings were probably the reason their plan hadn't worked, although he hesitated to share this realization with Paul and Jeremy.

PAUL IS PACING, his sunburnt face scrunched up in concentration, his blue eyes almost rageful in their intensity. His voice rises over the blaring traffic as he cries, "But have we tried them all?" He looks from David to Jeremy intently, trying to meet their eyes. "Remember that one from The Book, the one we use only in dire circumstances? This is a dire circumstance!" He scans the intersection. "All we need is one or two, a couple of people no one will miss …" Stinking cars stream by tired pedestrians huddled at corners, waiting for the lights to change. The old woman has long since boarded her bus and a man in a mechanic's suit now sits on the bench, his face anxious as he taps on his phone. He doesn't seem to notice the spheres slipping by, glimpses of other worlds full of people going about their days, weeding gardens, chopping tomatoes and garlic for pasta sauce, having arguments with neighbours, stopping to pet a cat as they walk to work or struggling to convince their grouchy first-grader to put on their shoes for school.

Another ceremony from The Book. David feels sick thinking about it. He's heard Paul and Jeremy and some of the other long-time brothers make allusions to advanced ceremonies known only to a handful of upper-level initiates. He's always shied away from the whispers, afraid to hear more, telling himself he doesn't really believe them although he has a dim sense of the spells, the energies they are supposed to create. Fear rises like a cold draft up the back of his neck as another wave of nausea roils in his stomach. "I never did that one," he says. "I don't know anything about it."

"And they let you stay in the brotherhood?" Paul is incredulous.

David shrugs. "They were desperate for members." He had been recruited by his boss at the insurance company who later left his position and was rumoured to have been seen in one of the spheres. David had always wondered how he made it there, what his angle had been. His boss had seemed just like the other men, ambitious and cruel. But maybe there had been something different about him, maybe he had been hiding something.

"There were only a few of us left, and most of us had lost our jobs," Jeremy reminds.

"So if there's no way to fix this then what are we doing? Why are we still holding meetings? If we're never going to get in, why are we even doing this?" Paul's voice is strangled, a deep red rising under the blotches on his face. Sheets of sweat run down his cheeks. He teeters on his feet.

David steps forward and catches his arm, steadying him and leading him toward the temple stairs. "Careful there, Paul. You don't want another incident. No one wants you going to the hospital again. Calm down now. Breathe."

Paul sits down heavily on one of the steps and slumps forward, head between his knees, breathing erratically. Large drops of sweat fall to the pavement. David hesitantly places his hand on Paul's back, and then pats gently. The sun and the sickening gasoline fumes are starting to make him dizzy and he's tempted to bend over for deep breaths as well, but he knows any deep breathing on this corner will just make him feel worse. "Take a few breaths now, Paul. That's it. You're going to be okay. You're going to be just fine."

Jeremy has stepped a couple of paces away and is trying to surreptitiously smoke a cigarette, blowing the smoke over his shoulder in the direction of the bus shelter. David glares at him, but he pretends not to notice.

Paul finally straightens up, sucking in big mouthfuls of air. His face has resumed its normal blotchiness. He shrugs off David's hand. "I'm fine," he says. He adjusts his tie. "Never felt better, in fact. It's just the heat. It gets to a man." He chuckles weakly and stands up, looking around. "How about these people?" He nods at the traffic. "They're stuck here too."

Jeremy finishes his cigarette, tosses the butt in the gutter, and steps over to rejoin them. "They could probably get in more easily than we could," he says.

"These people?" Paul shakes his head contemptuously. "They don't have anything. They don't have our ceremonies."

"Exactly," says Jeremy.

David thinks of mentioning his former boss, but stops himself. Instead he says, "You made a good point a minute ago, Paul. About why we keep up these meetings. I've been thinking in a similar vein recently."

"Me too," Jeremy says. "Maybe it's time we tried a different strategy. Tried going solo, for example. See how well we might each work alone." He takes out his handkerchief and dabs his dry mouth as if he's just finished a meal. Even in the bright sun he still isn't sweating. David notices that Jeremy also isn't wearing his ring. Paul looks at the handkerchief as if he'd like to eat it.

"Alone?" Paul's indignation is palpable. "Alone? We didn't join the brotherhood to go at it alone! We're in it together, brothers. Until the end."

"I would say this is the end." Jeremy's tone is matter-of-fact. "We've tried everything. These meetings are pointless." He reaches into his pocket for another cigarette and then thinks better of it.

Just then there is a commotion in the street. Brakes squeal; metal slams metal. Two men jump out of their cars and start bellowing at each other, pressing their fingers in each other's chests. A car alarm bleats hysterically. A bus rips over a curb and jams on its breaks, nearly running a red light. A sullen young person in expensive leather boots pushes a shopping cart piled high with retail bags straight through traffic as cars dodge them, honking their horns.

The three men stare at this scene for a while without speaking. Finally David says, "I have an idea."

The other men look at him.

"We joined, and we can leave too. I mean, there must be a ceremony, a spell or something. It's been a while since I checked The Book, but I bet there's one in there."

"I was just going to vaporize," says Jeremy. "Disappear. Take up residence somewhere else."

"Where?" Paul says. "No one will have us. Even the colonies aren't colonies anymore. We're locked out."

"I think it's important that we stay positive," David says. Another wave of disgusting gas and smoke passes over them and nausea churns in his stomach. "And practical. Who has a copy of The Book on their phone?"

Paul rummages around in his pockets as Jeremy, phone already out, calmly scrolls down a series of pages. "I seem to recall there was something around page 211," he says.

A few spheres hum by, full of seemingly happy people doing mostly simple things. David shifts impatiently, feeling light-headed. He senses the lodge looming behind him and has the sudden fear that it will come crashing down, burying him in dust and brick.

"Ah," Jeremy says. "Here it is. Chapter 22: *Leaving the Brotherhood.*" He reads silently, his thin lips pursed. Finally he says, "It's not good."

"What does it say?" Paul leans in and tries to read over his shoulder. Jeremy takes a big step away from him.

"It looks like we'd be better off going our own ways." He pockets his phone quickly. Looking at Paul, and then David, he nods. "Best of luck to you both." He strides quickly down the block and disappears.

"Shit," says Paul. "It can't be that bad."

Out in the street the fight between the two drivers has escalated. They are now shoving one another and screaming obscenities about each other's mothers and wives. One man spits in the other's face and in return the man punches him in the nose. The punched man squeals, blood pouring down his face, "You stupid mother*fucker*!" He wraps his hands around the other man's throat. Paul watches them as if transfixed.

A sphere sails by, lit by fireflies. David sees the long white carpet of the moon's light stretching across the ocean, thinks he smells a campfire. Children and dogs run down the dark beach, leaping up and falling on the damp sand. He glimpses people gathered around the flickering fire and thinks he can taste the salt on the potatoes they are roasting. He imagines the stories they are telling each other and wonders if he or his brothers are in any of them.

SISTER

WHEN WE FIRST started dating, Elise always wanted to consult the tarot or the I Ching about our relationship. She'd invite me over for a sex date, but when I arrived there would be a pot of steaming red clover tea and flickering candles on the coffee table and she would be fanning her tarot deck in her hands, saying she had just a few questions.

One night, she tried to convince me to go to a meditation class with her at the local Buddhist centre the next day, and when I didn't agree to it, she tried to push me to take part in a past life regression workshop with her at Unity Books and Charms the following week. "Just think," she said, "we could find out the lives we've lived together before."

"This life is enough for me," I said, reaching over to kiss her deeply, sliding my tongue over her teeth in the way I knew she liked. I started unbuttoning her blouse, my fingers stroking her nipples.

She responded by slipping her hand down the front of my pants and the conversation was abandoned for another kind of conversation, one I actually had an interest in.

After a few months, I finally had to tell Elise that I would never share her fascination with the woo-woo. I decided that my approach needed to be blunt in order for her to take it seriously, and I decided to take her out to dinner to tell her. As we chomped on mushroom tacos at our favourite Mexican restaurant, I confessed: "I don't want to read horoscopes with our morning coffee. I don't want to go see a psychic with you. I'm sorry."

She kept chewing calmly, watching my face.

"I love you, but I just don't believe in any of that stuff. I'm sorry."

I had expected a fight, but she took it surprisingly well. She smiled at me and took a sip of lemonade. There was an endearing smear of guacamole on her cheek that I wanted to lick off. "Okay," she said. "I mean, I can't force you. If you don't believe, you don't believe." She shrugged. "But you don't care if I still do it though, right?"

"I love that you do it," I half-lied, setting down my taco and wiping my hands with my napkin before I reached out to rest my hand on hers. "It's part of who you are."

BUT THE TRUTH was that sometimes the woo-woo stuff really scared me. After we moved in together, Elise would sometimes come home from visiting her long-time psychic and tell me unsettling things. One time she shared that the psychic had contacted a past life in which Elise was a Roman soldier who had murdered his wife and then spent centuries as a spirit mourning at her grave. Another time the psychic was visited by Elise's dead grandfather, who revealed he was not ready to incarnate again and wouldn't be for some time—he hadn't yet fully processed why he had spent an entire lifetime hurting his own children.

Sometimes I'd come home and the entire apartment would be sunk in inky darkness. I'd hesitate at the doorway, calling Elise's name, nervous as if at the threshold of a stranger's house. I'd find her lying under a blanket on the couch, "communing," or sitting blank-eyed in front of her shrine in the spare room, not having bothered to light candles. Sometimes she would be wrapped in a shawl on the couch, whispering on the phone to her best friend, Serena, and when I clicked on a lamp, she'd shudder and blink, as if I'd yanked her out of a comforting cave into the harsh glare of sunlight.

ELISE AND SERENA had been friends since they were teenagers. Both came from amazingly dysfunctional families that somehow managed to stay intact long enough to lurch the girls through childhood and young adulthood—and then they were free to escape to university, where they had the good fortune to get rooms on the same hall in the same dorm.

Their interest in the woo-woo was part of what drew them together. Elise had been the kind of teenager who read tarot in her dark bedroom, purple scarves draped over the windows and lamps. She was the kind of teenager who saved money from her fast food job to go to gem shows and buy crystals she believed held healing powers. Serena had similar proclivities, although she came from a smaller town, one that didn't have an occult bookstore. This was before the internet, so she had to go to the neighbouring college town to get her divination cards, her books on reincarnation and channelling. They had "a profound connection," Elise had told me more than once. I understood this to mean they were more or less in love with each other, albeit platonically.

ELISE AND I had been together for a couple of years before I finally met Serena. She and her boyfriend, Bodhi, arrived on the train from Seattle one May afternoon, and Elise went down to the station with a bouquet of lilies to pick them up. I thought the flowers were a bit much but didn't say anything to Elise. I hadn't managed to keep my mouth shut the night before about the chocolate torte with a red heart on it that she had purchased at Fratelli's—I harped on the price and told her it looked like some cheesy Valentine's Day cake. The argument turned to money, who made more, who had the right to spend what on what. It was a stupid fight, one that could have been avoided if I had only had a little more restraint, but I was keyed-up, nervous about Serena's visit. I had heard so many stories—too many stories, perhaps.

When I got home from work that evening I found Serena and Bodhi lounging on pillows on the living-room floor and sipping tea while Elise bustled around in the kitchen. Elise had already toured them around the neighbourhood, taking them for croissants at her favourite coffee shop and cheese at the Cheese Grotto, stopping at the local pot shop to get a small stash for Bodhi. Serena rose to greet me, but Bodhi stayed sprawled, smiling up at me and extending his hand from the sleeve of his striped tunic-sweater.

Serena looked just like her pictures except a bit older around the eyes where a few small wrinkles were starting to form. Her hair was long and dark, flat down her back as if ironed.

She held on to my hand when I gave it to her to shake and looked into my eyes. I felt like she was trying to read my mind or perhaps more accurately read Elise's mind—that she thought by looking into my eyes she could glean why Elise had chosen me.

Then she unexpectedly pulled me in for a hug. "It's so nice to finally meet you," she said.

Surprised, I hugged her back. "I know." I looked over her shoulder at Bodhi who was grinning at us. I didn't know what else to say, but finally came out with, "After all these years."

"All these years," she echoed. "I've been waiting to meet you. Elise's one. I'm so happy."

LATER THAT NIGHT we imbibed a lot of cheap red wine and put back a huge pot of pasta slathered with olive oil, garlic, and lemon zest. Then—after Serena and Bodhi had sufficiently oohed and aahed over it—Elise dished us up huge slabs of the chocolate torte. After we finished, Bodhi set down his napkin and announced he was going to take a walk around the block to smoke his nightly joint. Serena said she'd accompany him for some fresh air (she didn't smoke).

After they left, Elise and I sat on the couch, enjoying the last few sips of wine in our glasses. It was a warm spring night and we had the windows open to let in the smell of blossoms. Usually our neighbourhood smelled like old beer and puke, gasoline and garbage, but for this one small slice of the year, the air was redolent with honey, green branches, and new leaves.

This was the era of answering machines. The phone rang four or five times and then the machine clicked on. We sipped our wine and listened to Elise's cheery voice tell the caller we might be sleeping or we might be out, but either way, they should definitely leave a message.

The beep, and then a stranger's voice. "Hello? Bodhi there? Hey, fag. You said it's okay that I call you here, right? It's Jason. I'm only in town until Sunday. Call me tonight. Later."

Elise and I looked at each other. The sink dripped slowly, and I could hear the traffic from the busy street one block over. Before either of us could speak, the phone rang again.

"Hey, bro, forgot to say. I'm at the Westin downtown. Room 314. In case I'm out—"

Before I even knew what I was doing, I'd picked up the phone. My greeting came out like a command. "Hello."

"Hey, uh …" He laughed a little. Was he drunk? High? "Bodhi around?"

"No," I said coldly.

"Oh. Well, tell him—"

"Listen," I cut in. "My girlfriend and I don't appreciate you leaving that kind of language on our answering machine. It's not cool."

"What?"

"That word. 'Fag.' It's not okay."

"Oh. That. I didn't mean anything by that." He laughed his weird high-drunk laugh again. "It's just, we call him that because he writes poetry."

"I don't think it's funny." My words were encased in ice. "It's homophobic, actually, and you left it on me and my girlfriend's answering machine."

Elise was watching me from the couch, not drinking, holding her wine glass against her chest.

"What?" His voice was suddenly angry. "I'm not homophobic! My mom's a lesbian."

This was surprising enough to stop me for a moment. It wasn't that I was surprised that his mother was a lesbian, necessarily, but I found it strange that he thought this was any sort of defence. "Listen," I said, trying to keep my voice calm.

"No, *you* listen," he interrupted. "It was just a joke. Bodhi's my friend. And I don't need this. Just tell him to call me when he gets home." Before I could say anything, he hung up.

I held the receiver, staring at it as if it might explain what had just transpired. Elise came up and put a hand on my shoulder. We stood there for a moment and then we heard the door open. Bodhi and Serena came in, the smell of weed wafting from their clothes.

"Nice night out." Bodhi gave a spacey grin. "I like your neighbourhood."

I was too angry to look into his bloodshot eyes so I looked at the big living-room window. The blinds were up and we were reflected as if staged for a tableau: Elise and I hunched slightly forward, Serena and Bodhi loose-limbed, magnificently relaxed. My hands were so tense that they were nearly curled into fists. I willed myself to unclench them.

"I'm glad you had a nice walk," Elise said, ever the peacemaker. Her smile was strained, but neither Serena nor Bodhi seemed to notice. "Would you like a nightcap?"

"Sure," Bodhi said.

We had finished all the wine and all we had on hand was some crappy vodka left by a friend after a recent party. Elise took a can of orange juice from the freezer and set it in a pan of hot water to thaw in the sink as she poured shots of vodka into four glasses. I could see by her slightly stilted actions that she was upset but was trying to make it all nice and normal.

On the couch, Bodhi prattled on about how much he loved Vancouver. "People are so nice here. So chill. They just smoke dope in the streets like it's nothing. No one gives a shit. It's like the cops are so chill too that they might even light up with you." He giggled. Serena sat close to him, her arm around his shoulder, smiling.

I sat down in the worn IKEA chair facing them. "You smoked?" I asked Serena, even though she had already told me she didn't smoke.

"Not tonight," she said. "The energy of the stars and the lights on the mountains were enough for me." She had said a few mystical-sounding things like this already that I had tried not to find annoying. She looked sublimely happy as she patted Bodhi's leg and gazed around the room at our drab thrift store furniture and bright paintings donated by friends.

She and Bodhi had only been involved for a few months. Before that, Serena had been single for two long and lonely years. Her anguish over not having a partner was a frequent subject of her and Elise's conversations. They would cast the I Ching and spend hours on the phone discussing the minutia of the reading, what it said about Serena's willingness to let love into her life. That was the language they used. "What am I doing to block this?" Serena would lament, her voice leaking out of the receiver. "I'm trying so hard to be open." These conversations often went on late into the night. More than once on the way to bed I heard Elise assuring Serena that she would find him, he was waiting for her, it wouldn't be long.

And then she had finally found him.

"You will love him," Serena had gushed to Elise on phone as they planned the visit.

Elise had assured her that she would. "Anyone you love, I love," she had said.

WHEN I FIRST started dating Elise, I had been jealous of her and Serena's weekly phone calls and long emails. They usually met up once or twice a year to attend a psychic fair in some distant city or sit a meditation course together. Coming back from these excursions they were always starry-eyed and more friend-in-love than ever, and would talk two or three times a week for the first month following their return.

Serena would say things to Elise that I found upsetting. One time I discovered a card Serena had sent her with a picture of a sunflower on the front. "Your brightness exceeds even the glow of this flower," she had written inside. "I love you more than anyone." She had signed the card "your spiritual wife." When I confronted Elise with the card, she didn't respond in the way I hoped. Rather than admitting that the message was over-the-top and agreeing to ask Serena to cool it, she told me in no uncertain terms that she wouldn't countenance any jealousy on my part. "She is my sister," she said, her eyes radiating a blue made more intense by the tinge of anger. "If you can't understand that then ..." She didn't need to finish the sentence. And I loved Elise, so I decided to shut up and stay.

ELISE CAME BACK from the kitchen with two slushy screwdrivers and set them on the table in front of Serena and Bodhi. As she went back to get ours, I leaned forward in my chair—I just couldn't contain myself any longer. "Your friend called," I said, looking intently at Bodhi's slack face.

He perked up hearing this. "Jay?" he said.

"Jason, he said his name was."

Elise came back out with our drinks and handed me one, setting hers on the table. I took a sip; the orange-boozy slush burned slightly as it slid down my throat, and I watched Elise drag a chair from the kitchen and position it to face the couch. She sat down. "Marin had to tell him he was being inappropriate," she said. Her voice was calm, giving nothing away.

I looked to Bodhi's face for a reaction, but there wasn't much of one. He looked a bit dazed as he slurped his drink.

Elise continued, "Basically, your friend left a message calling you a fag. He meant it as a term of endearment?"

Bodhi still didn't say anything, and from what I could tell, he didn't seem chagrined or surprised. Serena patted his leg and smiled at us all passively, as if the conversation had nothing to do with her. I could sense Elise waiting for a response from her friend. I didn't have to turn my head to know that her cheeks were flushed.

Finally, Bodhi responded. "Well, I could be gay, you know." He gave a little laugh. "I mean, isn't everyone, a little at least?"

I felt emotion sweep up my throat, and before I could stop myself, I heard my voice rising. "So, you like to fuck guys up the ass, then? You like to suck dick?"

Bodhi looked stunned, clutching his drink, and I thought I saw tears start in Serena's eyes. Elise gave me a pleading "calm down" look, but I couldn't stop.

"You have sex with men, then? Because the last time I checked, that's what being gay means. I mean, if you're a *fag*, after all, as your friend seems to think." I snorted. "Since you write poetry. Apparently that's all it takes."

Bodhi looked around the living room as if he hoped one of the walls would open up to reveal an escape door he could vanish through. My face was hot but my palm was icy from the drink, so I set it on the table. I had been squeezing the glass so tightly that I was surprised it hadn't cracked.

There was a pause, and then Bodhi slowly said, "They all write fiction, those guys. They used to tease me, is all." He shrugged. His voice was indistinct. "I mean, I do like guys, not really in that way, but I'm not necessarily straight, really. I'm open to the human experience."

"Great," I said. Even though Elise was signalling me with desperate eyes, I didn't bother to lower my voice. "Great. Maybe you should have some of those 'human experiences' with another man before you go around letting your meathead friends call you 'fag' as a nickname."

Bodhi stayed silent. I turned to Elise. She was looking at Serena, whose placid smile had slipped away. Her dark-grey eyes were defensive and she held Bodhi's arm as if she was responsible for keeping it attached to his body. In the quiet, I heard the sink dripping. It felt like it was falling into some hollow deep in my throat. Suddenly parched, I took a big sip of my melting drink. But I couldn't drink away the bad feeling, that feeling I got when I lost my temper and raised my voice. I didn't have to look at Elise to know that her face held disappointment. But I also knew that, in this instance, her disappointment wasn't just for me—it included everyone in the room. We sat in tense silence as the sink dripped.

Finally, Elise spoke. Looking closely at Serena's face, she asked, "You don't think it's okay, do you, for him to say that?"

Serena was looking down at her lap, still grasping Bodhi's arm. After a couple of minutes, she looked up, but instead of meeting Elise's gaze she fixed her eyes on one of the paintings hanging on the wall. "I just ..." she started hesitantly. "I just think ... you're overreacting." Her eyes bore into the blue background of the painting. "I mean, why does Bodhi have to be straight, just because he's with me? Why do I have to be straight?" Something flickered in her eyes then. Anger? Self-righteousness? I couldn't tell. She looked at Bodhi as if for reassurance but he just stared blankly ahead.

Elise was trying to keep her face together; it looked like at any moment it might fall to pieces. When she spoke, her voice was low and a bit scratchy. "That's not what I asked. That's not what I said." Was she going to cry?

Serena still wouldn't look at her. "You want to put us in a box," she said. "Wrap it up all neatly. You're gay; we're straight. Okay." She let out a sigh.

I looked at Bodhi for a reaction but he was still staring off into space, a slight smile on his face.

Elise took a sip of her melting drink and shivered. I put my arm around her shoulders. "You cold?" I asked. "I can get a blanket."

She shrugged me off and leaned forward in her chair, reaching her hand out. It hovered over Serena's knee but didn't land on it. "I wish you could understand," she said. "I'm not saying you have to be straight or be anything. But he left that word on *our* answering machine. In *our* home."

"I do understand," Serena said. "I get it." She looked up at Elise then, with a sad little smile. I could see she was trying to appeal to her, that she wanted to make the moment better somehow and believed that if she kept explaining Elise would understand and we could return to the easy camaraderie of the earlier part of the evening. "But Jay didn't mean it the way you're taking it. He just really loves Bodhi." She squeezed Bodhi's arm. "He loves him and he doesn't know how to express it."

A biting rejoinder came to my mind but I swallowed it. There was a long pause. The sink dripped, the slush melted in our glasses.

Surprisingly, Bodhi was the one to break the silence this time. "Maybe we should all just sleep," he said, rubbing his eyes. "It's late. Maybe we can talk more in the morning." He gave a small smile, looking around.

Serena looked relieved and patted his arm, but Elise's face was scrunched up as if she was thinking hard.

I chimed in, "Yes, it's late. And we've been drinking." I attempted a light-hearted laugh.

Serena stood up and held out her hand for Bodhi, who rose unsteadily to his feet.

Elise sat silently, swirling the remaining inch of her drink with her finger and staring at the floor.

"Sweetie?" I asked.

She suddenly sat up straight. "Let's read the cards." Her voice was surprisingly hopeful. "They'll help us." She looked expectantly at Serena. "Don't you think? We can ask why this is happening, what we're supposed to learn from this?"

Serena and Bodhi looked uncertain but before anyone could answer Elise rushed off to the bedroom where she had left her tarot deck. I didn't think it was a good idea but didn't want to yet again be the voice of discouragement.

Serena tugged Bodhi's hand, pulling him closer to whisper in his ear. Then she gave me an apologetic grin as they slipped into the spare room and carefully shut the door.

Elise returned to see me alone, gathering up the drink glasses. "I guess they were really tired," I said.

Elise's face fell and she collapsed onto the couch, clutching her deck. "I guess," she repeated dully. She shuffled the cards slowly, stopping to gaze at some of the bright images. I glimpsed an armoured figure on a charging horse and people leaping from a tall tower in flames. From the spare room I thought I heard a window sliding open. For a brief moment I thought they might be trying to escape and the thought made me want to smile in spite of the situation, but then I realized that it was most likely just Bodhi lighting up one last joint before bed.

"Let's sleep, sweetie," I said.

THE NEXT MORNING, while Elise and I were still curled around each other in the dark of deep sleep, Serena and Bodhi snuck out of the apartment into the bright May day. When we got up to make coffee, we saw their note on the kitchen table, propped under a dirty plate from the night before. Bodhi—I knew it was him, some-how—had drawn a picture of a tree with a bird in it, and the bird was trilling "I hope we can be friends." He'd sketched a few music notes around the words. Serena had forgone any drawings and had simply wrote "Thank you for hosting us."

Elise read the note out loud, slowly, and then read it again silently, her lips moving as if trying to make sense of the words. Then, still clutching the note, she sat down on the couch, put her face in her hands, and cried.

LATER THAT DAY I came back from getting groceries to find her moping at the kitchen table, her tarot cards spread out in front of her in a sheet of sunlight, a squat pot of green tea steeping on the counter behind her.

"I don't know what to do," she said.

"You don't have to do anything." I set the bags down on the living room floor and walked over to wrap my arms around her. "Yet, at least. I mean, give it time. I'm sure it will be fine in time."

"They must have been in a hurry," she said. "They left some things." She held up Bodhi's lighter, which she had found wedged behind one of the couch cushions. "And this was shoved under the futon in the spare room." She showed me a red notebook. "Serena must have stashed it there after writing before bed." Elise flipped through the pages.

"I don't think we should read it," I said, putting out my hand as if to grab the notebook. "Shouldn't we send it back to her?"

"No."

"We shouldn't read it though. If you don't want to send it to her … maybe we could tear it up, put it in the recycle bin?"

"No." Her lips were set in a stubborn line and her tone brokered no argument. "Besides, I already read a lot of it." She opened the notebook to a page in the back. "Look at this."

I felt uncomfortable about invading Serena's privacy in this way but my eyes were drawn to the page, which showed a drawing of four stick figures, a man, a woman, and two children. You could tell who was who because Serena had written names above their heads: "Bodhi," "Serena," "Baby 1," "Baby 2." The Bodhi figure was the first in line and at least a head taller than the Serena figure, although in real life they were the same height. He was wearing pants. The Serena stick figure was in a dress, holding one of the children's hands. They were all smiling.

"What a weird picture," I said, when Elise showed it to me.

"It's her dream," she said.

"Pretty boring dream, if you ask me."

"Don't scoff," said Elise, closing the notebook. "It's not for us to judge. It's her dream." She paused, looking down at the cards for a minute. She started to stack them up, dispiritedly, and then stopped. She blinked away tears. "It's just that I'm not, you know, in it. I'm not a part of it."

I squelched a feeling of annoyance. I wanted to say, "Of course you aren't. Don't be stupid." But what came out was: "Well, they're in love with them, you know."

"What's that supposed to mean?" She wiped the back of her hand across her eyes.

"They're in love with them, we're in love with us. We have different dreams, I guess is what I'm trying to say."

Elise looked miffed. She turned to the window, examining the lilac bush outside as if it was the most fascinating thing she'd ever seen.

"She's probably the same with all of her friends," I said, trying to console her.

"I'm not just another one of her friends," she said angrily.

"I know," I said, in what I hoped was a soothing tone. "You're sisters. I know."

This made her even more furious. She stood up abruptly, slapping Serena's notebook down on the table, scattering the tarot cards. "You don't understand. You really don't understand anything." She ran into the bedroom and slammed the door. I could hear her pull the duvet over her head to muffle her sobbing. I wanted to go to her and wished I knew what to say to make things better. But I was at a loss. I took the bags into the kitchen and started to slowly unload the groceries.

SERENA'S LAST LETTER to Elise arrived nearly three months after her and Bodhi's visit, while Elise was at work. It was in a plain white envelope, which was odd, as Serena's envelopes were usually elaborately decorated with heart and flower stickers, unicorns and rainbows, Elise's name drawn in curlicues of silver or gold. I didn't have a good feeling about the letter and I considered hiding it for a few days while I gauged Elise's mood to see if she could handle whatever the contents revealed, but I quickly realized this was as creepy as it was controlling, and so I placed the letter on the kitchen table before leaving for beers with a friend.

When I got home around midnight the apartment was dark except for a wavering light emanating from the spare room. I knocked on the door, but there was no answer. I knocked again.

"What?" Elise's voice was annoyed, but also sounded snot-filled, as if she had a cold.

"You okay?"

She didn't answer.

I waited to see if she'd say something, straining to hear if she was crying. After a few minutes, I said, "I saw the letter." I thought I heard snuffling on the other side of the door. "Honey, can I come in?"

The door opened suddenly—I hadn't realized she'd been standing so close to it. She folded herself into my arms. The room smelled like honeyed wax and ashes and over her shoulder I saw that she had rearranged her shrine—it looked like some of the pictures had been removed. The light from two fat white candles cast strange shapes on the walls, and our shadows loomed behind us.

"She thinks I'm in love with her," Elise sniffled. "She thinks that's what the problem is."

"But aren't you?" I was surprised to hear myself asking the question out loud.

She burrowed herself deeper into my chest, her tears dampening my shirt. "She was my sister," she said.

I patted her back, not sure what to say.

"I burned the letter," she said, through tears. "I just want to forget about it."

Behind her, I thought I saw a shadow leap, as if one of the pieces of furniture had suddenly come to life—but it was just darting candlelight.

"Honey," I said. "Honey …" I realized I had no words to comfort her. What could I suggest? That she visit her psychic to find out what had happened in a past life to lead to this? That she read the tarot yet again to see if the cards might reveal, this time, that Serena had her back, that Serena still loved her? I looked toward the shrine to see if I could locate her favourite crystal, the big pink one she said was good for healing, the one she often held next to her heart. But in the flickering light I couldn't see where it was.

DISEMBARK

"TIME TO GO," your mother says, glancing at her wrist as if she expects to see a watch there. A few yards behind her there is a churning river where a boat waits in the darkness, smaller than the one you just disembarked from. It looks like a battered aluminum canoe. Lights from the lanterns glance off of it and at its helm is a child in a too-big black robe, hands peeking out of large drooping sleeves. The child shifts impatiently, steadying herself and the boat with a tall oar.

Your mother adjusts her dress, which is actually more of a gown, sewn with elaborate twisting roses in red and black, and takes a drag of her cigarette. Dangling from her other hand is a jean jacket, the one you wore in high school, spangled with buttons. You can make out one with John Lennon's face and the word "Imagine."

She holds it out to you. "Are you cold? You might need this."

You aren't sure if you're cold. You haven't been aware of your body ever since you left the party. The party—it is already a shady recollection. Sharon throwing up in a stainless steel bowl in the kitchen, almost-strangers dancing in the living room, cups and cups of whisky punch. There was chocolate cake—you remember that— the too-sweet icing sticking to your teeth. And someone blew out the candles. But who?

On the other side of the river is a long table at which a woman in a flowing green skirt sits with several other people. Even from a distance, you can tell it's a panel discussion, and even from this far away, you hear her perfectly as she says, "It seems our world wants a lot of poetry. One thinks in poetry." She is lit by blue and rose lights, as if on stage, although the table stands on scrubby dirt surrounded by clumps of tall grass. You hear the suck of breath as another participant prepares to speak. They are going to disagree with the woman in green; you can tell.

"Are we going to the panel?" you ask your mother.

She nods. "Yes. But not this one. There's another panel farther up the river. And we're already late, because your first ferryperson was drunk again." She finishes her cigarette and looks around as if searching for a place to stub it out. Lanterns bob about like untethered balloons, briefly illuminating the faces of people rushing past. Your mother drops the cigarette and grinds it under her heel, then reaches down and pockets it.

You hadn't noticed that the first ferryperson was drunk, but maybe that's because you're still a little tipsy from the party. You suddenly remember something and reach for your back pocket. It's still there, the flask of scotch. Pulling it out, you offer your mother a drink.

She makes a ghastly face. "I hate that crap. Drive you to an early grave, you know." She raises her eyebrows and you see they have been drawn on with a thick blue-black pencil. When you knew her, she never wore gowns or makeup and she drank gin every day, sometimes starting as early as breakfast.

You take a big gulp and shove the flask back in your pocket. Your mother drapes the jean jacket around your shoulders and pats your arm. She is a lot kinder here than she was before. Before you can thank her, the child in the black robe pulls out a large conch and blows it. As the trumpeting fills the air, several people scurry toward the boat, some holding manila folders or laptops. One is talking rapidly into a phone, trying to make travel plans to France, it sounds like. Your mother pulls your hand and you find yourself standing in the wobbling canoe, trying to steady your legs. She guides you to one of the low benches where you sit, clasping the side of the boat as the child starts to row you all upriver.

"I gave you the option of sleep," your mother reminds, as if in response to some complaint you haven't voiced. "I gave you that option and you refused."

When you disembarked, she had offered you a comfortable-looking bed covered in a white quilt, but you had refused it because you were afraid it was not a bed, but a grave.

You shrug like a petulant teenager and, trying to be surreptitious, take another small swig of your whisky. You hope she isn't judging you.

"I just thought you might want to sleep," she says. "It's a hard voyage here and sometimes people are tired when they arrive."

In the bottom of the boat near your mother's feet is a collapsible cane that you hadn't noticed before. Your mother catches you looking and explains, "That's for you. I wasn't sure if you'd need it or not."

"Why would I need it?"

"We never know how people are going to arrive, what condition they'll be in." Your mother adjusts the neckline of her dress as if to emphasize her cleavage. "My guide told me you might not walk very well." She looks down at your legs. "But so far you can, it seems."

"Why wouldn't I be able to walk well?" you ask.

"I just wasn't sure how your legs would be. After the way you left." Her face sets into a familiar expression that you haven't seen in years and you know she has decided that the conversation is over. But then she smiles at you and touches your hand. "I have to prepare for our panel, honey." She pulls her legs up and crosses them over one another and closes her eyes, resting her hands on her lap.

You stare at her face for a while. It is less wrinkled than it was when you last saw her. "Honey." She had never used this word before. And her strange peaceful aura … also new.

The boat makes surprisingly swift progress, passing people on the banks sitting at long tables, clutching sheets of paper, or lit in rose light, standing in front of large screens with pointers. In each instance, the small audience seems rapt, sitting calmly in their folding chairs. Lanterns sway about like disembodied beings. There are tufts of tall grasses here and there, but no trees, and no birds or animals that you can see.

A heavy quiet settles over the small boat as it rushes upstream.

You notice that the other passengers are also sitting in meditation pose, their eyes closed, and you take the opportunity to sip a bit more whisky. But as you close your eyes and drink, a curious thing happens—rather than warming you, the liquor turns cold as it falls down your throat, and you feel it go through your body and out your toes, through the bottom of the little boat and into the river. You think you hear a splash. You open your eyes to see your mother staring at you. She motions for you to dump the rest of the whisky overboard, and you watch as your hand extends over the side of the boat and turns the flask upside down. Your mother holds out her hand and you give her the empty flask, which she disappears into one of the pockets of her voluminous gown.

The boat pulls up to the bank and the child in the black robe sounds the conch again. The other passengers slowly alight, steadying each other as they step to shore. Once on land, they move off swiftly in different directions, some chattering on their phones, others with their heads down, looking at papers in their hands.

"We're here." Your mother rises, dusting off her dress. "Are you ready?"

You nod, although you're not sure what you're supposed to be ready for. Your jean jacket lies crumpled in the bottom of the boat and you pick it up and sling it over your shoulders. Your mother grabs the cane and puts it in one of her pockets.

On shore, she pulls a pack of cigarettes out of another pocket, shakes a cigarette free and lights it. A phone appears out of yet another pocket and she starts scrolling while she smokes. Although there is no wind, the smoke rises swiftly up and away. "I have the notes here somewhere," she murmurs, taking a deep drag. "You'll be the one presenting," she adds.

"Me?"

"It's your panel," she says. "You have to present."

"I thought I was just ..." You search for the words. "I thought I was just shadowing you. I don't know anything. I just got here."

"You know enough."

"What do I have to do?"

"Listen, I'm trying to find the notes, okay?" She sucks at her cigarette. "You always were so impatient," she says, almost absent-mindedly. Then she smiles. "Here they are. My guide sent them yesterday." She scrolls quickly through several pages, nodding her head. "It's pretty straightforward."

"What is?"

She reads as she speaks. "You just have to share ... why you left the way you did ... the challenges of this last ..." She pauses and looks up at you. "You look scared. Would you like a drag?" She extends the cigarette in your direction.

"I don't know anything," you repeat. "And you know I don't smoke."

She shrugs. "Sometimes people take it up here. It's something to do."

You are surrounded by patches of tall grass that you now see are a sort of bluish-grey, tips lit up silver by the passing lanterns. The earth itself looks black, and tamped down as if it has been trodden on by hundreds of elephants. People flit by, in conversation or silently, carrying briefcases and tablets, punching on their phones.

Everyone seems to have a destination, to know where they are going.

"It's over here." Your mother grabs your arm and leads you toward a table wedged into a small clearing circled by clumps of the tall grass. The table isn't as big as the tables that you saw on the journey upstream, and it is round. There are already two people sitting there, each reading something on a laptop.

Your mother hands you the phone. "Here are a few pointers."

You glance at the screen. The print is small and it's difficult to read the words. "Act natural," you manage to make out. "Talk slowly. Don't overexplain." It is a bulleted list. "Be clear. Don't forget they are on your side. They are here to help you."

You walk over to the table and set down the phone. Your mother trails behind you as if suddenly uncertain of her role.

One of the people at the table stands up. He is a tall man with red circles high up on his thin white cheeks, enveloped in a rather baggy navy three-piece suit. Extending his hand, he says, "I'm Bob Stanton from the Hospitality and Graciousness Department at Free State. Pleased to meet you."

The other person, a woman with straight black hair falling to her shoulders and an unlined brown face, is dazzling in a red two-piece suit and a polka dot tie. She also stands up. She wraps both of her hands around yours and smiles broadly. "Tanvir Singh, Dean of Energetic Arts at New Harvard. Welcome."

They both sit back down, closing their laptops. You look for your mother, but she has disappeared into the shadows. "Where is she?"

"She'll be back," says Tanvir. "Don't worry. But for now you can just present to us. You have a paper?"

You look at the phone on the table as if it is a dead thing. "Not really," you say, placing one hand over the other and trying to look confident. There is no audience for your panel, no other folding chairs set up, which is a relief.

They lean forward attentively.

You wrack your brain, trying to remember what you are supposed to say ... something about your journey? "The first ferryperson was drunk," you blurt out.

Tanvir and Bob exchange glances, not unkindly.

"And then the second one was a child ..." You taper off, uncertain how to continue.

Tanvir smiles encouragingly. "Jolene, we were hoping to hear about your last incarnation. You left a little ... suddenly."

It is strange to hear a stranger use your name so familiarly. "It's Jo, actually," you say. "And I ..."

Before you can continue, an overwhelming feeling surges behind your eyes and you're swept out of yourself, flying down a dark tunnel. You're dizzy, but you can't slow down, and there's a sound like rushing water. The dizziness gives way to a floaty feeling, as if you are hovering somewhere. You try to open your eyes but you can't, and then you realize they aren't closed. You are adrift in a pure darkness. Blinking a few times, you try to locate yourself, and from a long way off, you hear someone screaming, "Goddamn it! Goddamn it! Goddamn it!" Then "Fuck! Fuck! Fuck it all!" Is that your mother's voice?

Your vision returns. You're standing next to a bed, holding your mother's hand. It is like holding the skeleton of some small animal;

you can feel each fragile bone, brittle under your fingers. Her face is grey and she is so thin that you can see each muscle, each vein. The tubes running up her nose look like small translucent snakes. She always hated snakes. And spiders. She made you kill any bug she ever found in the apartment. The room smells like dusty medicine and unwashed bedsheets, and underneath this you can smell yourself—greasy hair, old sweat, and whisky. A machine behind you beeps. You gently squeeze her hand, but there is no response.

The rushing water sound again, the dark tunnel. Your mother's voice screeching, "God-fucking-damn it!" Blinking out of darkness, you see an indistinct shape floating above water. You have the sense of stained clothes, a gin bottle clasped to her chest. The dark water undulates. Where are you? Her voice is a lament: "I told you, I told you." Is she crying? Something tightens inside your chest like a thick rubber band; it's difficult to breathe. There's an oil slick on the surface, but you're plunging through it so fast, down into the inky depths. There are no fish, there is no moon, and the arms of the frigid water pull you deeper and you can't speak, you can't breathe.

And then you're back. The lanterns bob cheerily, illuminating the darkness, the tall grasses wave. You see a few shadowy people hurrying by, off to their panels. Tanvir and Bob are looking at you, concerned.

"We lost you there for a minute, Jo," Bob says. "Are you okay?"

"I don't know what happened," you say. "My mom—"

"She's not far off," Tanvir interjects. "She's never very far from you."

"She was so angry. I mean, sad."

"She often showed her sorrow that way, didn't she?" Bob has opened his laptop and is consulting a document of some kind. "I see here that she left just a few years before you did … she hasn't been here very long, actually."

Tanvir pulls a piece of paper out of a manila folder on the table in front of her and examines it. "It says here that you left the party and walked to the bridge. Do you remember that?"

"I don't remember anything," you intone dully, but as you're speaking, you see a person who looks like you walking down a deserted city street late at night, pulling their peacoat close around them to fend off the cold. The storefronts are shuttered, the sidewalks patched with ice, the moon a mere splinter obscured by clouds. You weave as you walk, and you can't see very well. An intense desperation fills your chest. You reach for the flask in your back pocket.

"You don't have to recount all the details if you don't want to," Tanvir says.

"I think I might have drowned," you say.

Bob shuffles some papers in a folder. Tanvir nods, then asks gently, "Do you remember how you got in the water?"

You shake your head.

"Don't worry," Tanvir says. "You'll have time to process it all later with your guide."

"Aren't you my guides?" you ask, fiddling with your mother's phone on the table in front of you.

Tanvir laughs kindly. "Oh no, no. We're not that advanced." Behind her a figure hurries toward a small crowd gathered around a conference table, their face lit up from below by their phone's light. You see their lips moving as if they're trying to memorize what they're reading.

"I'm confused," you say. A dull ache has started at the top of your spine. It travels up your neck to your crown, pounding like the start of a particularly gruesome hangover. "This whole place is very confusing."

She laughs again. "I know. It is, isn't it?" She looks over at Bob. "Remember when we first got here?"

Bob guffaws. "Chaos!"

"Utter chaos," Tanvir confirms.

"On the other side we were just adjuncts," Bob confides. "We didn't even have benefits."

"At the end of my life, I lived in a van and ate one meal a day: tuna fish," Tanvir says.

"I sold my own plasma and waited tables after my classes," Bob shares.

"Adjunct teachers? Like at a college? That's what my mom did."

"We know," Tanvir says.

"We were colleagues," Bob adds. "That's why we volunteered to be on your committee."

"We thought we'd help your mother out," Tanvir says.

"She was really broke when she died too," you say. "They never gave her any insurance and she had all of these hospital bills …"

"We read about the fundraiser you threw." Bob looks again at the document on his laptop. "Your friend's band? That was a high point."

"It didn't feel like one," you say. A cracking pain shoots up your back and you lean forward in your chair, hoping to lessen it. You wish you had a bit of scotch.

Just then your mother returns, sliding out of the tall grass as if she'd been standing there all along. She puts her hand on your shoulder. "Can I join now?" she asks.

"Of course," Tanvir and Bob say in unison.

"I didn't really present anything," you confess.

"You did wonderfully." Tanvir smiles. "I think you're ready to move on to the next step. What do you think, Bob?"

"A successful intake, by all counts," agrees Bob. He beams at your mother. "Your kid is really something. That fundraiser?"

"I know." Your mother gives you a proud smile as if you're in third grade and you've just brought her home a messy painting from art class. In life, she'd never given you any compliments on the pieces you brought home, and after a while you'd stopped showing them to her, balling them up and stuffing them in the garbage can right outside the school doors. You kept one—a poodle-sized papier mâché tiger with a ferocious grimace and sloppy stripes, because your fourth grade teacher had said it had a lot of personality. That was enough to make you sneak it home and hide it in the village of stuffed animals that populated your bed, hoping that your mother might one day admire it—but she never noticed it, or if she did, she never cared to make a comment.

Your mother taught art at three local colleges and never had much patience for amateurs. She used to love to disappear into her work, holing up in her bedroom for entire weekends, dizzy with oil fumes, painting large smeary abstractions in bronzes and blacks.

You'd knock on her door to see if she wanted something to eat and she'd grunt testily or creak open the door to ask for more gin or just ignore you. But she never had much time to paint once she started shuttling around the city from campus to campus.

"Thanks for helping her arrive." Your mother smiles at Tanvir and Bob.

"It's our pleasure," Tanvir says. She and Bob both stand up to shake your hand, then they turn toward your mother.

"Off to the next panel," says Bob.

"They sure keep us busy, don't they?" your mother jokes.

"Yes, but at least we have benefits," Tanvir quips.

They all break into peals of laughter. Tanvir wipes her eyes and pats your mother on the back. "Ah, the sweetest benefit of all—time," she says.

"Endless time," Bob echoes, still grinning.

"Time unlimited," your mother cackles.

You feel left out watching them. They pat each other on the back a few more times, and then Tanvir and Bob gather their papers and computers and give you one last smile before drifting away into the lanterned darkness.

Standing alone with your mother, you are suddenly cold. You pull the jacket off your shoulders and slide your arms into the sleeves.

"See? I knew you'd need that at some point," your mother says. "The temperature really fluctuates here."

It's not just the cold that bothers you. Your head feels like it's being drilled by a jackhammer and your legs are shaky and weak. There's a sloshy feeling in your chest and belly, and so much pain, as if a huge hand has reached inside your torso and twisted up your organs in its powerful fingers. You touch your back pocket, then remember that you no longer have the flask.

Your mother notices. "It's gone, sweetie. No more of that here, for you at least." She takes you by the arm and leads you back over to the round table, motions for you to sit down and then sits beside you. "We don't have a lot of time and I have a few questions for you still."

"Why didn't you stay for the panel?" you ask.

"I wanted to give you some space. I thought it might go better if I wasn't there."

"Why did you think that?"

"Tanvir and Bob are both very good at what they do. Sometimes they ask questions I wouldn't think of. Also, I'm your mother. That can complicate things, make things more emotional." She pulls her cigarettes out of one of her pockets and lights one, blowing the smoke over her shoulder. She smokes quietly for a while before speaking. "Sweetie … I'm sorry. The end of my life was shit, pure shit. We can't deny that."

"The rest of your life wasn't that great either."

She smiles ruefully. "That's probably true."

"It's definitely true. You just don't remember how bad it was because you were always drunk."

Your mother takes another thoughtful drag and holds it, looking at you and then looking around. The grasses shimmer in the light from the lanterns. A few shadows flit by. She blows smoke slowly out of her nostrils. "I wasn't *always* drunk, sweetie. I had three jobs, remember? And I didn't go to them drunk."

"You didn't?"

"No, I didn't." She sounds tired. "Listen, sweetie, this conversation is important but probably not the best use of our time. The ferry will be back soon. I want to settle a few things before your next stop."

You shiver, still cold even in your jean jacket. Your mother leans forward and buttons it up, lifting the collar up so that it shields your neck. You are still surprised by all the motherly gestures, but you let her do it.

"You'll start warming up soon. A lot of people are cold when they arrive here. Listen, honey … you probably don't want to hear this, but when I came here, I changed. I'm not the same person anymore. And you will change too."

You think of the whisky pouring cold through you, dripping out from your toes.

"You have every right to be angry. God knows I was furious when I arrived. But you'll find things work a little differently here." She finishes her cigarette and leans forward to stub it out on the black earth, then pockets it. You watch each of her actions. Even though she didn't smoke in the life before, here she is a confident smoker—it is as if she's always smoked. She looks at you and smiles, then gives a little shrug. "Your guide will explain more later."

The pain in your head keeps building. You think of the comfortable bed, the padded white quilt, and wish you had taken the opportunity to rest when you disembarked. You gingerly place your hands above your ears, touching your crown.

Your mother notices. "Headache?"

You nod.

"Here's something I learned from my guide." She rubs her palms together slowly, then picks up speed, as if she's rubbing two sticks together to make a fire. "Rub them together really fast for a few minutes. Then …" She stops and places her hands over your eyes, and after a minute moves them down to your cheeks, then to your chin. Her palms are pleasantly warm and they heat up your face. The smell of smoke is strangely comforting. "Doesn't that feel nice?"

"Yes." You keep your eyes closed, not wanting her to take her hands away. But her palms cool and she drops her hands back to her lap. She looks at you. Even though it is hard to read her eyes in the indistinct light you can tell the look is intent. "Honey, why did it get so bad after I left?"

Your breath catches in your throat. "I don't know," you manage to say.

"You promised me in the hospital that you were going to quit."

"I know," you say.

"Were you lonely?"

"I'm not sure." There's a flash of Sharon looking sick, a party hat lopsided on her head. You remember now—it was her birthday and you gave her a bottle of vodka with a silver bow stuck on it. You had spent a lot of time together the last few months, drinking and playing video games. But you never really talked about anything. She was the only person you hung out with, and you didn't even tell her where you were going when you left the party.

"I tried to contact you many times but could never get through. Did you have any dreams about me?"

"A few." You try to remember—something about writing a note on a piece of Bristol board and not being able to fit it into an envelope, being upset by this. Something about a ham sandwich she made, forgetting it in your locker at school.

"Did I tell you anything?"

"You hugged me," you admit.

"I tried. But you were very closed." She lights another cigarette, blowing the smoke upwards.

You feel a sudden surge of anger but when your voice comes out it's flat, emotionless. "Did you ever wonder why I was so closed?"

Your mother pulls at her cigarette. A passing lantern illuminates her face and you see that her eyes are deeply sad. "I know I could have done better, Jo. I know that."

It is weird to be crying in this strange place, to feel tears on a face that hurts so much it must be broken. You swallow the lump in your throat. Pain streaks up your legs and you wonder if you'll be able to stand when it's time to. You remember once telling Sharon that your mother had been a "mean drunk." In high school your mother had written you a letter—using her favourite pen, gold ink—detailing everything she didn't like about you, including your weight, your attitude, the length of your hair, the department store perfume you had saved for weeks to buy and were just learning to wear, and your grunge-loving boyfriend who was two months younger than you. She had left it on the table for you to find when you came home from your after-school job at the bakery. When you told Sharon about it, you had pondered the words "mean drunk" after you said them, had wondered if you were a "nice drunk." You had hoped you were at least a neutral drunk. Here, your mother is not a nice drunk or a mean drunk—she is not a drunk. And she is sorry, that much you can tell.

She smokes patiently, watching your face. Finally she asks, "And the way you went?"

"It wasn't *planned*, okay?" Your voice is angry now. "Sometimes things just happen. I was drunk."

Your head pounds. And suddenly you can feel the air turning to vicious wind, sluicing through you as you race downward toward the stench of rushing water, oil, and garbage. You remember thinking "I must be about to hit" three times before you actually did. You remember thinking that maybe you could have fixed things some other way. The last thing you thought was that you were glad your mother was already gone so she wouldn't have to know about it.

"I just wanted to disappear," you say.

Your mother shakes her head regretfully, her cigarette burning down between her fingers. "I know." She looks like she is about to say more but is interrupted by her phone ringing. She pauses a moment, then reaches across the table for it and answers, "Hello?" You hear a muffled voice on the other end. "Hmm ... okay," your mother says, looking at you. "I'm just here with Jo, welcoming them. I was going to head up that way shortly. Yes. I don't know ... soon?" She looks at her wrist where a watch would be. "Okay. Yes. I'll see you then." She hangs up.

"Who was that?"

"My guide. We have an appointment today. She's just checking in."

"When will I meet my guide?" you ask.

"That's where you're off to next," your mother says, bending down to stub out her cigarette.

In the near distance you hear the bugling of the conch, the sound of a large oar churning water. You shiver, this time not from cold, and touch your head, noticing it is less tender. You press your feet into the ground, testing your legs. A dull pain radiates from your soles up to your thighs as you stand up, but you know you'll be able to walk.

"Will you wait for me?" you ask.

She rises out of her chair and shakes out her dress. "I'm sorry, honey. I can't. But I'll visit you soon. And you'll be in good hands upriver."

Your mother opens her arms. For the first time in years, you let her hug you, and you even hug her a little back. She smells like smoke and soap, the inside of a closet that stores pressed dresses. As she squeezes you into her chest, you feel the buttons on your jacket crunch against her dress's embroidery. Pulling back, you look down, and unhook one. It's just a picture of Earth, swirls of blue, green, and white, no words. You don't know why you choose this particular one. "Here," you say, offering it to her.

Your mother holds it up and laughs. "Remember that slogan?"

A few lanterns drift by, lighting up the button like a little moon. "What do you mean?"

"It was so popular in the nineties. '*Earth: Love Your Mother*.'"

"Oh God. Yeah. So cheesy." You laugh.

She waggles the button at you. "I thought you had a pin that said that."

You shake your head. "No way."

"Are you sure? I remember being jealous of that goddamned pin."

"Really?"

She shrugs a bit sheepishly. "Yes."

Then your mother carefully fastens the button to her dress like a rare and delicate flower. She puffs up her chest to show you how good it looks.

Behind you, you hear the boat bumping the bank, people talking quietly, shuffling to get off.

"Time to go," your mother says, squeezing your hand.

NOTES AND ACKNOWLEDGEMENTS

THESE STORIES WERE written on the traditional, ancestral, and unceded territories of the Qayqayt, Musqueam, Kwikwetlem, and Kwantlen Nations.

The Martín Espada quote in "The Charismacist" is from the poem "Revolutionary Spanish Lesson" in the collection *Rebellion Is the Circle of a Lover's Hands*.

Deep gratitude to Karen Smith and Cathy Stonehouse, whose careful reading and insightful suggestions made these stories so much better. A special thank you to my other readers who read one or more of these stories and gave helpful feedback: Junie Désil, Shazia Hafiz Ramji, Christine Leclerc, Virginia Currin, and Dan Currin. Thank you also to my editor at Anansi, Leslie Joy Ahenda, for her thoughtful suggestions, and acquiring editor Douglas Richmond, for taking a chance on these weird stories. Thank you to Christine Leclerc for coming up with the title "The Charismacist."

Notes and Acknowledgements

So much gratitude to Lindsay Wong and Carleigh Baker for their thoughtful blurbs.

Thank you to the editors and readers of the following publications, in which these stories first appeared: "Banshee" in *Plenitude*, "The Brotherhood" in *Superstition Review*, "Joey, When She Knew Him" in *Foglifter*, "The Knife" in *Isele*, and "New Beds" in *Room*.

Many thanks to the Canada Council for the Arts, the BC Arts Council, and KPU's .06% Faculty PD fund for funding that allowed me much-needed time to work on this book.

A special thank you to my dearest one, Karen, for her love, patience, and support.

Without the communities I am so fortunate to be a part of I would not be able to live, let alone write. To my beloved friends and family: thank you, thank you, thank you.

SARAH RACE PHOTOGRAPHY

JEN CURRIN's *Hider/Seeker: Stories* won a Canadian Independent Book Award, was a finalist for a ReLit Award, and was named a 2018 *Globe and Mail* Best Book. They have also published five collections of poetry, most recently *Trinity Street* (Anansi, 2023); *The Inquisition Yours* (Coach House, 2010), which won the 2011 Audre Lorde Award for Lesbian Poetry and was a finalist for a LAMBDA, the Dorothy Livesay Prize, and a ReLit Award; and *School* (Coach House, 2014), which was a finalist for the Pat Lowther Award, the Dorothy Livesay Prize, and a ReLit Award. A white settler of mixed, mostly western European ancestry, Currin lives on unceded Qayqayt, Musqueam, Kwikwetlem, and Kwantlen Nation territories in New Westminster, BC, and teaches creative writing and English at Kwantlen Polytechnic University.

jencurrin.com
Instagram: thebookishpicnic